BRAINS, BATS, AND A BADDASS

I survived the apocalypse. Then I got bit. Now? I have a zombie army, a smart mouth, and exactly zero patience for your sht.*

Written by Jeanette Clarke

Copyright © 2025 Jeanette Clarke
All rights reserved.

No part of this publication may be reproduced, transmitted, downloaded, decompiled, reverse engineered, or stored in any form or by any means—electronic, mechanical, photocopying, recording, or otherwise—without the express written permission of the publisher and author, except for brief quotations in reviews or articles.

This is a work of fiction. Names, characters, places, and incidents are either products of the author's imagination or used fictitiously. Any resemblance to actual persons, living or dead, events, or locales is purely coincidental.

For information, inquiries, or permissions, please contact the author at: info@authorjeanetteclarke.com

First Edition: Feb. 2025
Corpus Christi, Texas

Printed in the United States of America

Dedication

To my husband—thank you for humoring every crazy scheme, every midnight ramble about fictional people making dubious life choices, and every impossible plot twist that nobody else believed could work. Your unwavering support and belief in my chaos mean more than words can say. This one's for you.

TABLE OF CONTENTS

CHAPTER ONE
9

CHAPTER TWO
39

CHAPTER THREE
72

CHAPTER FOUR
100

CHAPTER FIVE
120

CHAPTER SIX
142

CHAPTER SEVEN
171

CHAPTER EIGHT
197

CHAPTER NINE
223

CHAPTER TEN
245

CHAPTER ELEVEN
264

CHAPTER TWELVE
283

CHAPTER THIRTEEN
301

CHAPTER FOURTEEN
318

CHAPTER FIFTEEN
335

CHAPTER SIXTEEN
355

SNEAK PEEK
372

"Look, I never asked for a horde of undead butlers, a love quadrangle, *and* daily orchard makeouts—but if the apocalypse insists, who am I to argue?" - Becca

CHAPTER ONE

Becca Montgomery stood on her tiptoes as she reached for the top shelf, balancing a box of Doritos that definitely weighed more than she wanted to admit. Her little step stool—provided by the store for "vertically challenged" employees—was wobbling under her feet. She silently cursed whoever decided to shelve snack inventory so high off the ground.

The overhead fluorescent lights flickered for about the tenth time that hour, giving the entire store the ambiance of a slowly dying spaceship. Perfect for her mood.

"Next time, I'm telling Lisa to get her butt on this stool," Becca grumbled to herself. Lisa, her supervisor, was probably hiding in the office, sipping decaf coffee and scrolling social media. Typical.

Her headphones were plugged in, and some old '90s hits were pumping directly into her eardrums. If she was going to endure stocking shelves in a near-empty store at eleven in the morning, at least she'd do it with style. She was bopping her head along to Ace of Base's *"The Sign"*—lip-syncing the chorus with dramatic flair—when she heard the doors slide open behind her.

She glanced at her watch. It was only 11:15 a.m., but it felt like an eternity since her shift started. The store was at the far edge of town, which meant they rarely had a ton of foot traffic. Usually, the busiest they got was around 5 p.m., when people stopped by to buy last-minute dinner items. The only folks who rolled in before noon were either retired, bored, or possibly lost.

"Welcome to GoodMax, where prices are so low you'll feel guilty!" she called out half-heartedly, repeating the store's stupid tagline. She pulled out one earbud to hear if the newcomer said anything. When all she heard was a low, wet gurgling sound, she frowned. That was definitely not the typical morning-greeter reaction. Usually, she'd get a nod or a "Thanks" or a "Where's the bathroom?"

Nope. Today, she got a *gurgle*.

She blinked and turned around, Doritos box still perched precariously in her arms. *Maybe they're sick?* A cold or something. But that gurgle didn't sound like a regular cough. It sounded like a cat hocking up a hairball wrapped in bubble wrap. Slowly, carefully, Becca hopped off the step stool, letting the box of Doritos slip to the floor. Corn chips spilled out in a crunchy cascade as the flaps burst open. She didn't care. She was too busy staring at the figure standing a few feet away.

He was a tall man—probably mid-fifties—wearing a gray polo shirt and khakis. Only the left half of his face was... well, it was *there*, technically, but it looked like the flesh had been half-peeled away. His left eye was murky, almost milky white, and the skin around it was torn. Becca instantly felt her stomach do a somersault.

"What the—" she started, stepping back so fast she nearly slipped on a neon-orange Dorito underfoot. "Sir, are you okay?" she asked, forcing her tone to be calm. Calm was good. Calm was how you handled bizarre things, right?

He responded with another gurgle. A bit of spittle—or something worse—dribbled down his chin.

Nope, she thought. *That's not normal. That's definitely the opposite of normal.*

Becca pulled out her other earbud so she could hear better. Her heart pounded in her chest, and she felt a bead of sweat trickle down the back of her neck. She glanced around for someone—anyone—who might confirm she wasn't hallucinating. Unfortunately, the snack aisle was empty aside from her and this... guy. But she could hear faint voices somewhere in the store; presumably, other customers or employees.

She took another step back, not sure what she was planning. "Sir, I—maybe you should see a doctor," she said lamely. She was no medical expert, but a half-missing face was definitely outside her skill set. And Lisa always bitched about worker's comp or liability. But this? This was well beyond typical store liability.

The man took a lurching step forward. His foot dragged across the tiles, leaving a dark trail that Becca prayed was spilled coffee. But deep down, she knew it wasn't. She considered grabbing her phone to call 911. Except the only phone she had on her was locked in her locker in the breakroom, because Lisa insisted on a "No phones on the sales floor" policy. *Stupid rule.* She hated Lisa so much right now.

As the man came closer, she caught the smell. It was like rotten meat left in a dumpster under the summer sun. Her stomach lurched again. She lifted a hand to cover her nose and mouth, and for a split second, she considered running. But the practical side of her brain screamed: *He might need help.* Another part of her brain answered: *That's not a man, it's a monster.*

Before she could make any real decision, he lunged. It wasn't graceful—it was more of a half-stumble, half-flop in her direction—but it was enough to send her survival instincts into overdrive. She yelped, nearly twisting her ankle as she hopped backward. Her foot kicked the empty Dorito box, but her gaze remained locked on the shambling horror.

He was gnashing his teeth. Where the side of his cheek was peeled, she could actually see them. It looked like someone had taken a chunk out of him, and he was in dire need of a hospital. Or a morgue.

"This is not how I planned to spend my Thursday," Becca muttered. Fear was clawing at her insides, but the absurdity of the situation triggered her usual defense mechanism: sass. She was the queen of snark when she felt threatened, and right now, she was definitely threatened.

Just then, an automated voice droned over the store's intercom: "Welcome to GoodMax. Please enjoy our weekly specials in aisle two."

Becca let out a strangled laugh. *Yeah, that helps.*

She took another measured step back, heart thumping like a drum solo. Then she spotted the store promotion baseball bat leaning against an endcap display. It was bright orange with the GoodMax logo printed across it—part of a summertime sports promo from a few weeks back. People used to take selfies with it, ironically. Right now, it looked like her only potential weapon.

Without hesitating, she darted sideways and grabbed it. Her hands shook, but she gripped the handle tight. The man came closer, arms reaching out for her. Up close, his eyes were empty, almost hollow. His lips peeled back, revealing cracked, bloody gums.

"Okay, buddy, you asked for it," she said through gritted teeth. She wasn't exactly a martial arts expert, but she'd watched a few YouTube self-defense videos. Plus, her older brother used to pitch for his high school baseball team, and he'd taught her a thing or two about swinging a bat.

She pivoted her feet. The man snarled, a low, animalistic sound that made her skin crawl. Then she swung.

The bat connected with his shoulder with a dull *thud*, sending shockwaves up her arms. He staggered but didn't go down. *Holy crap.* That would've dropped a normal person. She swallowed hard, adrenaline zinging through her veins.

"Dude, stay down!" she hissed, taking another swing. This time she aimed higher, catching him in the side of the head. *Crack.* It was a horrible sound—like a rotted pumpkin being smashed on concrete. And just like that, the man's knees buckled. His body slumped to the floor in a heap, half his face caved in from her bat.

Becca stood there, trembling, her breath ragged, the bat still raised. She expected him to get back up, but he lay there, motionless. Gradually, her terror gave way to something else—faint relief, maybe? And then a dawning horror. She'd just… well, she'd killed a man. Right? Or at least brained him so hard that he definitely wasn't breathing. She was pretty sure that was a line you couldn't uncross.

A sob threatened to bubble up in her throat, but her body was too busy pumping out adrenaline to let it break free. She took a few shaky steps backward, until she bumped into the Doritos display. Yellow, triangular chips crunched under her shoes.

In the distance, she heard screaming. It sounded like a woman—maybe multiple women. *What is going on?* she wondered. She looked down at the bat in her hands. It was slick with something dark. She couldn't see very well under the flickering fluorescent lights, but it sure as hell wasn't just dust.

I need to find other people. I need to call 911.

Before she could move, a loud, shrill voice pierced the air. "Hello? Is anyone here? I need a refund! This coupon is expired, and you guys need to honor the price anyway! It's the law!"

Becca actually rolled her eyes. *Seriously? A Karen? Right now?* This was possibly the worst timing in the history of the universe.

She pressed the baseball bat to her side, wiping her free hand on the front of her GoodMax polo, ignoring the fact that she'd probably just smeared questionable bodily fluids on herself. "I'm here!" she called out, her voice trembling. "Ma'am, you need to get out of the store. It's not safe!"

There was a pause, then the voice got closer. "What do you mean, not safe? I just want my deal on these paper towels!"

Becca exhaled sharply, trying to quell the rising panic. She moved down the aisle, stepping around the body on the floor as if it might spring back to life. Maybe she was being paranoid, but after seeing that… *thing*, she wasn't taking any chances.

When she rounded the corner, she found the source of the shrill voice: a woman in her late forties, hair teased to within an inch of its life, wearing a hot pink tracksuit and white sneakers that had definitely seen better days. She had a wad of coupons in one hand and a stuffed GoodMax bag in the other. Her expression said *I'd like to speak to your manager* but her eyes said *I will also commit murder if my deal is not honored.*

Behind the woman, about ten feet away, was another figure. At first, Becca thought it was another zombie, but as her vision adjusted, she realized it was a teenage boy who also seemed freaked out. The boy was scanning the shelves with wide eyes, probably searching for a place to hide.

Becca forced a smile that definitely did not reach her eyes. "Ma'am, please listen to me. Something is going on. People are… sick. We need to leave."

The woman, who absolutely oozed impatience, waved a dismissive hand. "Oh, I know. Some weirdos were fighting near the bakery. That's why I'm trying to check out before things get worse. If your registers are closed, that's unacceptable. I have to be at my salon appointment in twenty minutes."

Becca's jaw dropped. She had so many retorts swirling in her brain. But then more screams echoed through the aisles, followed by a series of crashing sounds. The woman flinched for the first time, actually looking concerned. The teenage boy's eyes went even rounder.

"All right," the woman said, her voice finally showing some uncertainty. "Maybe we should call the cops?"

Becca snorted. "I'd love to, but store policy says employees can't have phones on the floor. My phone's in my locker in the breakroom, and I'm not sure if the landline still works. This place is basically an off-brand ghost town half the time."

The teenage boy licked his lips. "I-I can check my phone," he murmured, his voice cracking. "But the signal's really bad around here."

"Give it a try," Becca said, nodding. Then she took a shaky breath and turned to the woman. "What's your name, ma'am?"

She pursed her lips. "It's Leslie. And I don't appreciate being talked down to."

Becca managed not to roll her eyes again. *Just a little longer. Keep it together, Bec.* "All right, Leslie, I'm Becca. We really need to gather up any other survivors in the store and get somewhere safe. The breakroom is probably our best bet; it locks from the inside, and it has some supplies."

"What's going on?" asked the teenage boy. He was fiddling with his phone, obviously not getting any bars. "Are people... attacking each other?"

Becca swallowed, a wave of nausea rising in her gut as she remembered the half-faced man. She nodded slowly. "Yeah, they look... infected." She wasn't ready to drop the Z-word yet. That was next-level horror movie territory, and she was still holding onto the faint hope that there was some rational explanation. *A gas leak? Some bizarre LSD outbreak? Bath salts?*

Another crash reverberated, and an older man ran into view, face pale, eyes wild. He was wearing a postal uniform. He caught sight of them and gasped. "They're biting people!" he shouted. "One of 'em tried to chew on me like a steak!"

Leslie's face finally lost its haughty edge. "Oh, dear God."

"All right," Becca said, forcing her voice to stay steady. "Everyone, follow me. We'll head to the breakroom. If there's anyone else on the way, we'll grab them. Let's move quickly and quietly."

They all nodded, even Leslie, though she clutched her bag of coupons like a lifeline.

Becca led the small group through the labyrinth of aisles, hugging the walls as best as they could. Her senses were on high alert, her knuckles white around the bat. Her ears strained for any shuffling footsteps or guttural moans. Occasionally, they'd hear a scream in the distance, but it felt too risky to investigate. They were outmatched, unprepared, and definitely under-armed.

Of all the days to leave my phone in the locker, she thought bitterly. Lisa had caught her texting once—just once—during a slow shift last week, and the lecture that followed had been the stuff of legends. Now, that same phone was out of reach when she needed it most.

As they crept past the produce section, the overhead lights flickered again, sending sharp shadows skittering across the floor. It was eerily quiet except for the occasional beep from the store's automated announcements. Then a strangled cry came from the deli counter. Becca froze mid-step, turning to see if she could spot the source. Her heart hammered in her chest, an anxious drumbeat that seemed to vibrate in her skull.

"Should we…?" the postal worker whispered, pointing toward the sound. His eyes were wide, brimming with concern. He was probably in his early sixties, with a slight stoop and thinning gray hair. *Poor guy probably thought his biggest concern today was delivering junk mail,* Becca thought, a pang of sympathy washing over her.

She considered ignoring the noise, but her conscience refused to let her. "I'll check," she whispered back. "You guys wait here." Then she paused. "Actually, no —if anything jumps out at me, I don't want to be alone. All of you, come with me, but… quietly."

They moved slowly toward the deli, the smell of cold cuts mingling with a strange coppery tang. Rounding the corner, they found a middle-aged woman cowering under the glass counter that once displayed an array of cheeses and sliced meats. Now it was splattered with something dark and sticky. Next to her, a man in a GoodMax apron lay facedown, not moving.

Becca's stomach clenched. "Ma'am," she called gently. "Are you hurt?"

The woman looked up, her eyes rimmed with tears. "H-he attacked me," she stammered. "He tried to bite me. I think I scratched him with the deli slicer. I think I killed him!" Her voice spiraled into a panicked wail.

Becca scanned the area for any more threats. Seeing none, she hurried forward. "You did what you had to," she said, voice low and soothing. She was no therapist, but she knew firsthand how jarring it was to defend yourself so violently. "Come on. We're heading to the breakroom."

The woman seemed hesitant, glancing at the unmoving body of her coworker, whose name tag read *Felix*. Then, nodding slowly, she reached out, and Becca helped her to her feet. "Th-thank you," the woman murmured. Her nametag said *Marsha*.

"Let's go," Becca said, gesturing for everyone to follow. A memory flickered in her mind of the half-faced man in aisle seven. "And watch your step."

They inched their way through the store, past toppled displays of cereal boxes and scattered bottles of soda. The teenage boy, who introduced himself as Carlos, clung to Leslie's side, as though the older woman's sharp attitude might ward off more attackers. Leslie, for her part, kept complaining under her breath about losing her discount, but the edge in her voice had softened. The postal worker's name turned out to be Edgar, and he carried an umbrella he'd found lying around, clutching it like a makeshift weapon.

Finally, they reached the employee-only hallway that led to the breakroom. Becca quickly punched in the four-digit code on the keypad, her hands shaking so badly that she had to re-enter the numbers. Once the door beeped, she pushed it open and ushered everyone inside.

The breakroom was about as depressing as one would imagine: dull white walls, a few mismatched chairs around a beat-up metal table, and a vending machine that had only half its coils stocked. But it was a safe space that locked from the inside, and right now, that was better than any five-star restaurant.

Lisa, her supervisor, was inside, along with one of the cashiers named Tasha. They both looked shell-shocked. Tasha was hunched over, clutching her phone and shaking. Lisa was pacing back and forth, holding a mop handle like a spear.

When Lisa saw Becca come in with the group, her eyes widened. "Montgomery! Where have you been?"

Everything's gone insane out there!" Lisa's voice wavered, somewhere between fear and anger.

Becca closed the door behind them and locked it. Then she leaned the baseball bat against the wall. "I was out on the floor, you know, *working*. At least until I got attacked by some... infected psycho." She let out a shaky breath and turned the lock. "We need to barricade the door."

Lisa nodded, swallowing hard. "O-okay. Good idea." She glanced at Edgar's postal uniform. "Are you an officer of some sort? A policeman?"

Edgar let out a mirthless laugh, the lines around his eyes crinkling. "No, ma'am. Just your average mailman, delivering your spam flyers. Now I guess I'm stuck in the apocalypse with the rest of you."

Lisa's lip trembled. "Great. Just... great."

Tasha, the cashier, looked up, her cheeks stained with tears. "I tried calling 911," she said, her voice hollow. "I got through once, and all I heard was screaming on the other end. Then the line went dead. After that, I couldn't get a signal. Everything's jammed."

A heavy silence fell over the group. Becca could practically taste the fear in the room. But fear was an emotion that spurred her to talk, to fill the silence with snarky banter. She let out a shaky laugh. "Well, that's not creepy at all. It's like the phone lines decided to have a meltdown the same day the world did."

Lisa shot her a look that said *not now*. But Becca was past caring about Lisa's disapproval. She'd just brained a zombie with a neon-orange baseball bat. She was beyond worrying about her boss's micro-expressions.

"All right," Becca said, grabbing the nearest chair and sliding it under the doorknob. Then she glanced around, spotting the heavy vending machine in the corner. "We should push that in front of the door too, just in case. Edgar, Jell-O arms, you wanna help me?" She nodded at Jell-O arms—aka Carlos—who seemed scrawny but hopefully capable enough to push a machine.

Carlos blinked. "M-me?"

"Unless you're volunteering Leslie," Becca said with a shrug, eyeing the woman's fancy pink tracksuit.

Leslie, huffing, set down her GoodMax bag. "I'll help. I'm stronger than I look." She flexed an arm that didn't appear to have much muscle definition, but hey, desperation was the mother of adrenaline or something like that.

Together, they pushed the vending machine until it scraped against the linoleum floor and butted up against the door. The relief that followed was fleeting but tangible. At least now they had a physical barrier between themselves and the creatures roaming the store.

Becca took a moment to collect herself, leaning against the wall and letting out a long breath. Her heart was still hammering away, and her hands had a slight tremor.

Stay calm, stay centered, she told herself. *You have people depending on you.*

She scanned the group:

- Lisa, mid-40s, black hair pulled tight in a bun, store manager who thrived on calling out tardiness.
- Tasha, early 20s, a sweet cashier with pastel-dyed hair who looked like she might start sobbing again at any moment.
- Marsha, the deli worker, shell-shocked and trembling, a faint line of dried blood on her forearm.
- Edgar, the mailman, who'd probably had the worst day at work ever.
- Carlos, the teenage boy, phone in hand, expression oscillating between fear and curiosity.
- Leslie, the coupon queen in a neon pink tracksuit, whose bravado was overshadowed by genuine confusion over *why* exactly the world was ending when she had errands to run.

It was an odd bunch, but it was all they had. "So," Becca said, swallowing hard. "I guess we should figure out a plan." She flopped into one of the plastic breakroom chairs, letting the adrenaline drain from her limbs. "'Cause I don't think the cops are coming anytime soon."

Lisa nodded. "Right. We need to… maybe see if we can contact someone outside. Or wait for help?" She turned to Tasha. "Any luck on data coverage?"

Tasha sniffled, brushing away a tear. "It's still jammed. My texts won't go through. There's no Wi-Fi in here either—unless I use the store's system, but that needs my manager credentials."

Lisa perked up. "I can log you in. Let me try that." She grabbed Tasha's phone, typed a few things, and handed it back. Tasha tapped at the screen, her eyes lighting with momentary hope, but then her face fell again.

"Still nothing," she muttered. "It's like the Internet's just... gone."

"So we're on our own," Becca concluded. Then she forced a shaky smile. "Could be worse, right? At least we have a whole store of supplies?"

Marsha, the deli worker, let out a rueful laugh. "Supplies we can't get to unless we want to face those things." She hugged herself. "Felix wasn't a violent man. He wouldn't have attacked me unless... unless he wasn't Felix anymore."

A chill rippled over Becca's skin. She wanted to say something comforting, but she wasn't sure what. She'd had the same realization with the man in the polo shirt. *That wasn't a normal person anymore.*

The group fell silent. Edgar cleared his throat. "So, do we think it's some sort of virus? A plague? Could it be, uh, *zombies*?"

That word hung in the air like a bad smell. No one wanted to say it out loud, but they were all thinking it. Zombies. The reanimated dead, like in the movies. It felt ridiculous. It felt insane. But there was no denying what they'd seen.

"I just…" Lisa trailed off, wringing her hands. "I can't believe this is happening."

Becca exhaled. She needed to maintain a shred of hope, or at least the appearance of it. "Look, maybe it's contained to just this area," she said, trying to keep her tone bright. "Maybe the national guard will show up any minute and block everything off. We just have to hold out until then."

Carlos, who'd been unusually quiet, spoke up. "What if… what if it's everywhere?" His voice trembled. "My mom works across town. I'm supposed to meet her after school. What if she's—"

Leslie put a hand on the boy's shoulder. "Hey, it's okay. Don't jump to conclusions." She caught Becca's gaze, her eyes filled with worry. The harsh lines of her face softened just a bit. "We don't know anything yet."

Becca thought of her own family, her dad and older brother who lived a few states away, and her mom who'd passed away years ago. *If this is happening everywhere, how would I even get to them?* The weight of that question pressed down on her chest, but she tried to push it aside. She had to focus on the here and now.

They needed a plan, indeed. She racked her brain for a strategy. "Okay, let's think about the breakroom," she said, running a hand through her hair. "We have some emergency supplies here—first aid kit, maybe some extra flashlights. Vending machine snacks. The store has more food, of course, but that's out there with *them*." She grimaced.

Lisa pursed her lips. "We need to be systematic," she said, her manager instincts kicking in. "We can't just sit here and starve for days on a bag of chips."

Tasha sniffled. "Actually, there might be some leftover donuts from this morning's staff meeting, if no one else ate them." She motioned to a corner table with a plain cardboard box.

Leslie immediately brightened. "Thank God, I'm starving. This fiasco is messing with my blood sugar."

Edgar raised an eyebrow. "We can ration them. We don't know how long we'll be in here."

Becca stood up, dusting off her pants. "I'll check the supply closet too," she offered, figuring it was a good excuse to move and do something. Anything to keep her mind from spiraling. "We might have some bottled water or random stuff that could be useful."

She snagged Tasha's phone to use as a flashlight, since the overhead lights kept flickering ominously, and stepped into the dimly lit hallway that housed a row of lockers, the supply closet, and a door leading to the manager's office. Each step echoed, and she felt a chill creep along her skin. Every time a scream or crash from the main store rattled through the walls, she tensed, expecting a horde of zombies to burst through the ceiling.

When she reached her locker, she punched in the combination with shaking fingers. *Please let my phone have some signal,* she silently prayed. She yanked the door open, rummaging through a tangle of personal junk until her hand closed around the familiar rectangle of her phone. She tapped the screen. No missed calls, no messages, no bars. Great.

With a grimace, she slid the phone into her back pocket. Then she turned her attention to the supply closet. Inside were shelves lined with cleaning products, plastic cups, some cheap instant coffee packets, paper towels, and a box labeled "seasonal promotional items." She kicked that aside, rummaging further until she found a small plastic bin labeled "Emergency Supplies." Her pulse quickened. *Yes, something practical.*

She opened it to find a dusty first aid kit, a couple of flashlights that probably needed batteries, and an emergency blanket that looked more like tinfoil than anything else. She also spied a couple of water bottles, but not many—maybe four or five.

Better than nothing. She stacked the supplies in her arms, then heard a faint *thump* from behind the manager's office door, which was slightly ajar. Her heart jumped into her throat. She froze, breath catching. *Was that Lisa's voice? Or something else?*

"Hello?" she whispered, but no one answered. Another *thump*, then silence.

Her instincts screamed at her to leave it alone, but curiosity (and a sense of responsibility) won out. If someone was in trouble, she couldn't just ignore them. Carefully, she approached the office door, nudging it open with her foot. The office was dark except for the glow of a computer monitor. Papers were strewn everywhere, and a tall filing cabinet stood half-open.

Nothing jumped out at her. She flicked on the phone's flashlight to sweep the room. Then she heard a scraping sound from behind the desk.

"Is anyone here?" she whispered, inching closer. Goosebumps prickled along her arms. She set the bin of supplies on top of the filing cabinet, raising the phone higher to cast more light.

A shape moved, hunched over, behind the desk. It was a person, or at least it looked like one. The figure's clothes were disheveled, and as they turned, the beam of the flashlight revealed a face twisted in agony, streaked with fresh blood. It was a man with a GoodMax name tag: *Dwight.* He was one of the assistant managers. Becca barely knew him, but she recognized the mustache. Or the partial remains of it. Because half of it was missing, as if it had been torn off.

She suppressed a scream as she realized he was clutching at a chunk of flesh on his neck. Blood trickled through his fingers. His eyes were wide with pain and fear. He hissed, "Help… me…," voice ragged.

Becca moved forward, instincts warring inside her. This was the second time she'd encountered an injured person. But Dwight still seemed human, albeit badly hurt. She crouched beside him, mouth dry, scanning his wound. "Oh my God. Dwight, what happened?"

He coughed, a wet, rattling sound. "Some crazy bastard… bit me." His voice sounded thick, as if speaking took enormous effort. "I locked myself in here. But I'm… not feeling so hot."

Becca fumbled for the first aid kit, cracking it open. She wasn't sure it could handle a zombie bite, but maybe she could at least slow the bleeding. Her mind went to old horror movies—did bites automatically turn you into a zombie? Or did it differ by franchise?

"This might sting," she said softly, ripping open an alcohol pad. She pressed it to his wound, and he let out a tortured groan. "Sorry," she said, wincing. Dwight's eyes were rolling back. She could practically feel the heat radiating off him. A wave of dread settled over her. *This is bad. Really bad.*

"We'll… get you help," she lied, glancing at the door. "We'll find—"

"Don't… bother," Dwight gasped, a strange, rattling laugh escaping him. "We're all… screwed. I can…

feel it." He coughed again, flecks of blood spattering his chin.

A wave of guilt and pity washed over Becca. She was in way over her head. She pressed gauze to his wound, but it was obvious he was fading fast. Then, in a moment of clarity, she realized she shouldn't be this close to him, not if that bite meant… infection. *But he's still alive,* she argued with herself. *He's not one of them yet.*

Dwight's breathing quickened. His eyes fluttered shut, then opened again, the pupils dilated. "It hurts," he moaned. "Just… kill me. Please."

Becca's stomach churned. "No. No, I'm not— I can't—" She wasn't about to bludgeon a coworker to death with a baseball bat just because he asked her to. She was no killer— well, *technically* she'd just ended that monster in aisle seven, but that had been self-defense! This was different. Dwight was still alive. This was… *mercy?*

Dwight seized up, eyes rolling back again, body going rigid. He made a choking noise. Becca reeled away, fear and revulsion mingling in her gut. She grabbed the bin of supplies and stumbled backwards out of the office, heart pounding in her ears. She couldn't do this. She wasn't equipped to handle the question of *Do I kill my dying coworker to spare him from becoming a zombie?*

As if on cue, Dwight let out a feral snarl. Becca's head snapped up. His eyes, previously dull with pain, were now glazed and wild. He scrambled to his feet with a sudden burst of inhuman energy, toppling the desk chair in the process. Blood dribbled from the wound on his neck, but he moved like it didn't matter.

"Dwight?" Becca croaked, but she saw no recognition in his expression. Just hunger. *Oh, God.*

He charged at her, hands grasping. She yelped, turning to flee. The bin of supplies crashed to the floor, water bottles rolling across the tile. Dwight slammed into her back before she could reach the door, sending her sprawling. Her chin hit the floor, dazing her. Pain exploded through her jaw, and her vision swam.

Dwight hissed and tried to claw at her hair, his fingers tangling in the strands. She kicked out blindly, connecting with something soft, hearing a grunt. His grip loosened, just enough for her to scramble forward. *The baseball bat's in the breakroom.* She cursed her stupidity for not keeping it with her.

Dwight lunged again, hands snapping at her shoulders. She ducked, twisting away, searching the office for anything that could serve as a weapon. Her eyes darted to the heavy metal stapler on the desk. It wasn't ideal, but it'd have to do.

She grabbed it, swung around, and hammered it against Dwight's temple. The first blow made him stagger. The second blow knocked him back onto the desk, scattering papers. He snarled, but his limbs flailed weakly. With a jolt of adrenaline, Becca slammed the stapler down on his head repeatedly, tears stinging her eyes. *I'm sorry,*

I'm sorry, I'm sorry, she chanted in her head, each strike ripping another piece of her soul away.

Finally, Dwight went limp, half-sprawled across the desk. Becca stumbled back, chest heaving, the stapler clutched so tightly her knuckles were white. She stared at the grisly scene in disbelief, her breath coming in ragged gasps. This was... insane. Absolutely insane.

Suddenly, footsteps pounded in the hallway. The door flew open. Lisa burst in, with Edgar right behind her, both wielding improvised weapons—a mop handle and an umbrella, respectively. They took one look at Dwight's lifeless form and Becca's trembling, blood-streaked figure, and their faces filled with shock.

"Montgomery...?" Lisa whispered, voice trembling.

Becca let the stapler fall to the floor with a dull *thud*. "He was bitten," she said, her own voice barely above a whisper. "He turned. I... I didn't have a choice."

Lisa's lips parted, but no sound came out. Edgar took a cautious step forward, placing a hand on Becca's shoulder. "You did what you had to do," he murmured, echoing the words Becca had told Marsha earlier. The irony cut deep.

Becca nodded numbly, tears threatening to spill from her eyes. Then Lisa rallied, stepping back into her role as manager, or at least trying to. "We need to regroup," she said, clearing her throat. "Let's… let's get out of here. Are you okay to walk?"

Becca nodded again. Her jaw throbbed where it had met the floor, and her hands were shaking, but she could move. Edgar kept a firm, steadying grip on her elbow as they walked out of the office and back to the breakroom. She could feel Lisa's eyes on her, uncertain and wary. *Is she afraid of me?* The thought sent a bitter pang through Becca's chest.

When they re-entered the breakroom, the others fell silent at the sight of her. She was sure she looked like a horror show, hair disheveled, blood smears on her clothes and hands. Tasha let out a small gasp, and Carlos stared wide-eyed, stepping back. Leslie pressed her lips together, eyes flicking between Becca and Lisa, as if wanting an explanation.

Lisa cleared her throat. "Dwight was bitten," she said quietly. "He attacked her."

Murmurs of shock and dismay rippled through the group. Becca sank into a chair, her legs threatening to give out. She closed her eyes for a moment, focusing on the sound of her breathing. She felt someone press a wad of napkins into her hand, and she opened her eyes to see Tasha offering a kind, if tearful, smile.

"Thanks," Becca mumbled, taking the napkins and trying to wipe off the worst of the blood.

Marsha approached, her gaze filled with sympathy. "I know how it feels," she said softly. "It… it stays with you. But you saved yourself."

Becca gave a hollow nod. She glanced around, noticing that they'd slid the table and some chairs against the vending machine barricade, reinforcing it further. Good. The nightmarish creatures might break through eventually, but hopefully not anytime soon.

Lisa ran a hand over her face, her own eyes red-rimmed. "Okay," she said, voice strained. "We need a plan. A real plan. We can't just wait for rescue that might never come." She paused, as if searching for the right words. "We might need to fight our way out and find somewhere safer."

Becca opened her mouth, a surge of anger rising in her chest. "You think we should *leave*? This place is as safe as anywhere, if we fortify it. We have water, food, supplies—"

Leslie let out a short laugh. "Yeah, *some* supplies, but not unlimited. And from what I saw in the aisles, a lot of it's getting destroyed. Or eaten."

A heavy silence fell. Edgar coughed. "We could try to get to our cars. Drive as far as we can, maybe find a shelter or a police station."

Carlos looked up from his phone, which he'd been compulsively checking for service. "What if the roads are blocked? Or if it's happening everywhere?"

Tasha's voice trembled. "My house is just a mile away. My mom keeps an emergency kit in the basement with enough supplies to last a while. We even have a generator. If we could get there…"

Lisa shook her head. "We don't know how widespread this is. The moment we go outside, we're exposed. Here, at least we have walls."

The discussion escalated, overlapping voices weighing the pros and cons. Should they stay or go? Could they wait for rescue? Or was rescue not coming? The tension in the breakroom was thick enough to taste, and it was laced with fear, anger, and desperation.

Becca pulled her headphones from her pocket. Oddly enough, they were still playing faint strains of '90s music, the battery in her ancient MP3 player apparently unaffected by the chaos around them. She took one bud and stuck it in her ear, letting the familiar beat of *"Wannabe"* by the Spice Girls wash over her for just a moment. It was absurd and incongruous—zombies taking over the store while she listened to a cheery pop tune from her childhood. But it provided a strange comfort, a reminder of a world that had once been normal, safe, and thoroughly less horrifying.

She looked around at her makeshift group. They were haggard, frightened, and some were injured. But they were still alive. If they worked together—maybe they had a chance.

"All right," Becca said softly, pulling out the earbud. The others fell silent, turning to her. For a moment, she felt a swell of something like courage. She might not be the manager or the adultiest adult in the room, but after surviving two zombie encounters, she was feeling oddly… determined. "We do need a plan, and we need it *now*," she said, speaking evenly. "Let's pool our resources, check any weapons we can find, and decide if we're safer staying put or making a run for it. But first, maybe we can find some real food? I don't think a box of donuts and stale vending-machine pretzels are gonna cut it."

A brief ripple of tense laughter broke out, which was something, at least. Becca managed a small smirk. "And let's, uh, not forget to use the store's loudspeakers. We might be able to direct any other survivors to the breakroom if they're holed up somewhere else." She glanced at Lisa. "You have the manager override code, right?"

Lisa nodded, a hint of relief in her eyes that someone else was stepping up. "Yes. We can try to make an announcement."

Becca looked at the door, hearing the muffled sounds of chaos on the other side. "We stay strong, we stay calm, and we help whoever we can," she said firmly. "And if any more of those things come knocking—" she lifted the baseball bat she'd propped against the wall, her expression grim— "we show them exactly why *this* badass likes to knock heads."

She waggled her eyebrows, trying to lighten the mood. It was a meager attempt, but it earned a weak smile from Carlos and a half-snort from Leslie. Good. A little humor might keep them from descending into blind panic.

Because as terrifying as the situation was, one thing was clear: Becca Montgomery was done being the quiet grocery store employee who politely stacked Doritos and swallowed her snark around customers.

She was, in her own weird way, ready to fight back—headphones blasting pop anthems and heart pounding with fear, yes, but also with a streak of stubborn courage that refused to die.

If the world was ending, she was going down swinging… and probably with a sarcastic comment on her lips.

CHAPTER TWO

Becca's leg bounced anxiously under the breakroom table as she surveyed the ragtag group around her. The adrenaline crash from earlier left her jittery and exhausted all at once. In the overhead fluorescent glare, everyone looked half-dead with stress, which was definitely *not* how one wants to look during a zombie apocalypse. But at least they were mostly alive—unlike the corpses now littering the aisles.

Their makeshift barricade remained in place: the breakroom door was blocked by a combination of chairs, a vending machine, and Lisa's precariously placed mop. The muffled chaos beyond the locked door had quieted somewhat, which, in Becca's experience, either meant the zombies had given up or they were regrouping. She wasn't sure which possibility was worse.

Lisa, the store manager—still clutching that mop like a medieval pike—was trying to stay calm, though her red-rimmed eyes betrayed just how freaked out she really was. Tasha, the young cashier with pastel hair, perched on the edge of a plastic chair, absently twisting a rainbow scrunchie around her wrist. Leslie, the hot-pink tracksuit coupon warrior, paced back and forth with an air of impatience, occasionally shooting death glares at the locked door like *open up, I've got deals to snag*. Edgar, the elderly mailman, sat quietly, tapping a foot to some internal rhythm. Carlos, the teen, hovered near the corner, eyes flicking nervously between everyone.

And then there was Marsha, the deli worker, slumped against the wall in shock after her earlier, near-death scuffle. She stared at the floor, occasionally mumbling something under her breath.

Becca exhaled and mentally patted herself on the back for not completely losing her mind. She wasn't an official leader; no one had *elected* her to be queen of the breakroom. But after everything that had happened—killing not one but two zombified ex-humans—everyone was looking at her like she had an ounce of authority. Or maybe an ounce of sheer gall.

"Okay," she announced, sitting up straighter. Her voice still shook, but she tried injecting a healthy dose of confidence into it. "We know there's a *lot* of infected people in the store. But if we're going to survive here, we need to do something about the entrances. We can't have more of those freaks waltzing in through the automatic doors."

Lisa nodded, pressing her lips together. "They're on a timer to open at seven in the morning and close at midnight. Even if we kill the power, the doors can be forced open from the outside if someone's strong enough."

"And from what I've seen, they're *definitely* strong enough," Edgar added grimly. "Or at least determined enough."

Leslie, crossing her arms, raised an eyebrow. "So you want to just waltz out there and lock them? That's borderline suicidal, honey."

Becca gave a lopsided grin. "Well, I never claimed to be the pinnacle of mental health. But yeah, that's the gist. If we can physically secure the front doors—bolt them, chain them, *whatever*—we'll at least keep the number of zombies inside from growing."

Carlos gulped. "How do we do that with a bunch of them already in the store?"

"I have an idea," Becca said. Then she pointed a thumb at Lisa. "We also have a tool that might make it a little easier. *Music.*"

Lisa blinked, baffled. "Music?"

"Yep," Becca replied. She tapped her phone, which still showed *no bars*. "Earlier, you mentioned you have a manager code for the store's overhead system, right? We can pipe in a playlist over the PA."

Leslie made a face, clearly unimpressed. "I fail to see how *muzak* is going to help. I don't think the zombies care if we're playing top 40 or elevator hits."

"Oh, we're *not* playing elevator hits," Becca said, wiggling her eyebrows. "We're playing my playlist—just gotta rig my MP3 player or phone to the system. If we can crank it up, we might create enough noise in a different part of the store to lure them away from the doors."

Edgar let out a slow whistle. "That's… actually not a bad plan. Zombies seem to be attracted to noise, from what I can tell."

Becca flashed a self-deprecating grin. "Exactly. If we give them a loud distraction—like, say, *back-to-back '90s pop anthems at full blast*—they might shuffle toward the speakers instead of me. Meanwhile, I sneak around and lock down the doors."

Lisa frowned in concern. "We'd have to manually override the system from the manager's kiosk near the front entrance, though. That's… ironically close to the doors you're trying to secure."

"Maybe so," Becca said with a shrug, "but we can find a workaround. If I can get to the kiosk without drawing too much attention, I can patch my MP3 player right in." She tapped the side of her battered music device. "I'll set it to a random playlist. Then I'll sprint to the doors and lock them. Quick in, quick out."

She paused, scanning the faces around her. "So, who's with me? I'm not about to get gnawed on by a half-dead freak *alone*."

Silence thickened the air for a beat. Tasha sank deeper into her chair, looking mildly mortified at the idea of going out there. Marsha hugged herself tighter. Leslie's eyes slid away, as if hoping someone else would volunteer first. Even Edgar and Carlos hesitated, though they both looked torn between bravery and abject terror.

Finally, Lisa cleared her throat. "I—I should probably stay back," she said, her voice shaky. "If something happens… I'm the store manager. I can keep the rest of us calm, coordinate from here. You'll need me to manage the overhead system anyway." She lifted her chin, trying to sound official, but Becca wasn't entirely fooled. Lisa was *terrified*—understandably so.

Becca gave her a small nod, then turned to face the group at large. "All right, I need two volunteers. We can't have a giant party out there, or we'll just draw more attention. But three people is safer than one."

A heavy pause. Edgar started to open his mouth, but was interrupted by an unexpected *thump* from the other side of the breakroom door. The chairs and vending machine rattled ominously.   called out:

"Hey! Anyone alive in there?"

Becca locked eyes with Lisa, who looked just as startled. Then Lisa signaled everyone to stay quiet while she approached the door. She hesitated, listening intently. Another voice—a bit rougher, more sarcastic—joined in:

"Dude, they're either zombies or they're not. Standing here won't help."

The first voice shot back, "Shut it, Carter."

Becca's brows lifted. *Carter?* That definitely wasn't someone from the store staff, as far as she knew. She nodded at Lisa, who carefully peeled away a single chair so she could open the door just an inch. She kept the safety chain—installed for "employee security," ironically—latched, so the door could only crack open.

"Who—who's there?" Lisa demanded, sounding more confident than she felt.

"I'm Declan Graves. Ex-cop. This is Jace Carter," the first man answered. "We're survivors—like you. Mind letting us in?"

Becca and the others exchanged wary looks. *Ex-cop? Ex-con?* This was shaping up to be a bad joke. But they needed all the help they could get—if these guys weren't lying, that is. And from the sound of it, they weren't trying to chew through the door, so that was a good sign.

Lisa unlatched the chain. Edgar readied his umbrella weapon, and Becca snatched up her neon-orange baseball bat, just in case. Slowly, Lisa pulled the door open just wide enough for two figures to slip through. They entered in a rush, then slammed the door behind them, pressing their weight against the barricade as if expecting a horde to follow.

For a moment, the breakroom was a chaotic shuffle of bodies as these two new men stumbled to catch their breath. Then Becca finally got a good look at them:

- Declan Graves: Tall, broad-shouldered, with short-cropped dark hair and a perpetual scowl etched into his features. He radiated ex-cop vibes—muscles tense, scanning every corner with piercing eyes. His shirt was torn at the sleeve, revealing an old tattoo on his forearm (some law enforcement emblem, maybe?), and he held a crowbar in one hand.
- Jace Carter: Leaner, slightly younger, with a wicked smirk playing on his lips. His hair was a bit too long, and his left arm sported a swirling tattoo that disappeared beneath a rolled-up shirt sleeve. The black T-shirt he wore was spattered with blood. He held a large knife that definitely looked like it had seen action. Possibly *too much* action.

Declan's gaze swept across the room, taking in the battered group, the makeshift barricade, and the remains of a conversation in progress. He narrowed his eyes at Becca, as though noticing she was the one with the big bat (and presumably the biggest attitude). "You all right?" he asked, his voice clipped.

Becca noticed he wasn't exactly *concerned* so much as *suspicious*. His tone implied, *Why aren't you more freaked out?*

She lifted a brow, crossing her arms over her chest. "I've been better. Zombie apocalypses rank pretty low on my list of ideal ways to spend a day."

Jace let out a short, amused laugh, flipping the knife in his hand with alarming ease. "Zombie apocalypse. That's one way to put it." He took in the group. "We saw your sign." He jerked his thumb at the side window near the store entrance, presumably referencing some kind of taped-up notice. "Said there were survivors in the breakroom. Then we saw a bunch of undead freaks milling around. We cut through a side corridor." He shrugged. "Figured we'd say hi."

Lisa cleared her throat, stepping forward in manager mode. "I'm Lisa. That's Becca, Tasha, Leslie, Edgar, Carlos, Marsha... basically, half my staff and some customers. We're trying to figure out how to secure the store."

"Yeah, good luck," Declan muttered. "Those things are pouring in through the front like kids at a candy store. We barricaded a few aisles, but more keep coming."

Becca took a step forward, ignoring the flutter of nerves in her stomach. She had zero experience dealing with ex-cops or ex-cons, but hey, new experiences were the theme of the day. "I have a plan," she said matter-of-factly. "We blast my 90s playlist over the store's PA system to distract them, then physically lock down the doors. We keep them out—hopefully for good."

Jace quirked an eyebrow, a smirk tugging at the corner of his mouth. "Your 90s playlist?"

Becca gave a defiant shrug. "Yes, *my* playlist. Spice Girls, Ace of Base, maybe a dash of No Doubt. Don't judge me. If you have a better idea, I'm all ears." She tapped her foot, posture screaming *Try me*.

Jace grinned, apparently entertained by her attitude. "Didn't say I had a better idea. Hell, that might even be genius, in a weird, messed-up way."

Declan let out a terse exhale. "It's risky," he said. "What if we get caught between the music-lured zombies and the doors? There's no guarantee we can sneak around them."

Becca leveled him with a look. "We can't stay holed up in this breakroom forever. If more keep coming, we'll eventually be overrun—and starve in the meantime. We need to secure the entrance. Period."

Their eyes locked, tension sparking. Declan's mouth pressed into a thin line, but he gave a curt nod. "Fine. It's your plan. Just don't get us killed."

Becca was pretty sure that was his version of a *yes ma'am*. She exhaled, turning back to the group. "All right. I'm going, that's not up for debate. But I still need two people to come with."

Jace lifted his knife, spinning it in a small flourish. "I'm down. I already swiped this from a dead guy—might as well put it to use." He winked at Becca, who tried not to roll her eyes. The man exuded an air of *dangerously relaxed* that bordered on psychotic, yet somehow it was reassuring to have someone along who wouldn't hesitate to stab a zombie in the face.

Becca's gaze shifted to Declan. He was obviously itching to help, or at least to keep an eye on her. She had a hunch he'd volunteer, but she decided to push the point. "And you, Mr. Ex-Cop? You in or out?"

He frowned. "I still think it's a half-baked plan, but..." He spared a glance at Lisa and the others, who were clearly not eager to volunteer. "I can't let you run around out there with *him*." He jerked his chin at Jace, who rolled his eyes in mock offense. "We'll do it quickly. Grab anything we find that's useful. Then we get back here, regroup, and figure out what's next."

Becca clapped her hands together, ignoring the tension simmering between them. "Perfect. That's two. Let's do this before we lose our nerve."

The group moved the makeshift barricade aside, only enough to slip out into the employee hallway. Lisa—still trembling from earlier events—led them to the manager's computer kiosk so they could wire in Becca's MP3 player. It was behind a locked office door not far from the breakroom, near the staff lockers.

Once inside the cramped, stale-smelling office, Lisa booted up the system. "Okay," she said softly, rummaging through a tangle of cords on the desk. "We can override the store's usual announcements with an auxiliary input." She fiddled with a cable that had a small headphone jack. "Here."

Becca gave a victorious grin. She handed Lisa the MP3 player. "Set the volume as high as you can. Then, as soon as it's running, hide. I'm serious. Those speakers are going to attract *all* the freaks."

Lisa swallowed and nodded, hooking up the device. The store's ancient software flickered across the screen. "Just… promise you'll come back," she said quietly, glancing at Becca with a mixture of guilt and worry.

"Promise," Becca answered, and for once, she kept the snark to a minimum. Because deep down, she wasn't sure if she was lying or not.

Declan hovered by the door, his crowbar resting on his shoulder. Jace stood beside him, idly picking at the dried blood on his knife. It was the strangest standoff of personalities: a stoic ex-cop and a smirking ex-con, both bristling with tension, yet forced to team up. Becca wondered how that dynamic was going to play out when push came to shove.

Lisa tapped a few keys. "All right, your playlist is ready to go. We can't hear it in this office, but it should be blasting in the main store. Are you sure about the tracklist?"

Becca shrugged. "It starts with *'Wannabe'* by the Spice Girls. Seemed appropriate."

She caught Jace's grin out of the corner of her eye. The man either found it hilarious or was simply thrilled by the chaos. *Possibly both.*

With a final click, Lisa nodded. "All set. Good luck."

Becca took a breath, adjusting her grip on the baseball bat. "Let's do this." And with that, she, Declan, and Jace slipped out of the office, leaving Lisa to cower behind a locked door, presumably preparing for the onslaught of 90s pop.

The hallway leading to the main floor was eerily quiet at first. But as they crept closer, a faint tinny sound reached them—like an echo from a distant party. Then the music volume escalated, filling the air with an unapologetically peppy beat.

"Yo, I'll tell you what I want, what I really, really want…"

Becca bit her lip, fighting a bubble of laughter that was half-hysteria, half-incredulity. They were literally about to wage war on zombies with the Spice Girls as their soundtrack. What a time to be alive.

Declan looked like he'd swallowed a lemon, and Jace was trying to hide a chuckle. "I don't know if I should dance or kill," Jace mused softly.

Becca shot him a look. "Both, obviously. But *quietly*, if possible."

They inched along the periphery of the store, crouching behind shelves of promotional items. The aisles around them were a mess—scattered goods, pools of something that looked suspiciously like old coffee or blood (or both). Broken glass crunched underfoot. The overhead lights flickered, casting everything in a disorienting strobe.

In the distance, near the center of the store, shadowy shapes lumbered toward the electronic department (which had the biggest overhead speakers). The Spice Girls' cheerful voices beckoned them like a siren's call. A handful of the undead shuffled in that direction, arms twitching. Occasionally, one let out a wet growl.

Becca exhaled. "It's working. They're moving away from the front."

Declan nodded, scanning the area. "Let's circle around the produce section, then head for the entrance. Once the doors are locked, we—"

A wet snarl interrupted him. From behind a toppled display of paper towels, a zombie in a tattered GoodMax uniform lurched forward. Its jaw hung at an odd angle, like someone had tried to yank the lower half of its face off. Becca flinched, raising her bat automatically.

Jace stepped forward with surprising speed. He slammed his boot into the zombie's kneecap, sending it sprawling to the floor, then brought the knife down in a vicious arc. The blade sank into its skull with a sickening crunch. Dark fluid oozed out, staining the linoleum.

Becca swallowed hard. She'd seen her share of gore by now, but it never got easier. Jace simply yanked his knife free, a grim smile on his lips. "Told you. I'm not squeamish."

Declan shot him a disapproving look, though he didn't protest. "Let's keep moving," he muttered.

As they crept through the aisles, *"Wannabe"* segued into *"The Sign"* by Ace of Base, the chord progression echoing through half-broken speakers. More zombies drifted in the distance, drawn like moths to a neon-lights concert. One or two stragglers shambled nearby, but the group managed to sidestep them, thanks to the distraction.

Becca did her best to keep her breathing even and her footsteps light. The smell of decay clogged her nostrils, and each time she passed a fallen body—some store employee she'd possibly seen around once or twice—her stomach twisted. She forced the guilt aside. *Survive now, freak out later.* That was her motto.

Finally, they reached the front of the store. The large glass doors were parted about a foot, wedged open by a display cart that had been knocked over. Beyond the glass, the parking lot sprawled out under the midday sun, littered with abandoned cars. A few undead figures lurched aimlessly among the vehicles, but none seemed to notice them yet.

"First step," Declan whispered, "we move that display cart and see if we can get the doors shut. Then we see if there's a manual lock or metal security grate."

Becca nodded, noticing the store's roll-down security shutters overhead. Typically, those were used at night, but apparently, no one had activated them before the apocalypse. She frowned. "I've got an idea. My dad was in retail for a while—these metal grates sometimes have an emergency latch near the base. If we can find the release mechanism—"

A sudden movement behind one of the check-out lanes cut her off. *Damn it.* She tensed, gripping the bat. Jace and Declan immediately pivoted, weapons ready. Another zombie?

But as the figure stepped into view, Becca realized it wasn't a zombie at all. It was a man in dark pants and a heavy jacket, blood smeared across his collar. He clutched a pistol in his hand. The second he saw them, he raised the weapon.

"Whoa, whoa!" Becca hissed, throwing one hand up while still clutching her bat in the other. "We're not zombies!"

The man's eyes darted wildly, sweat beading on his forehead. "Get away!" he barked. "I'm warning you—I'll shoot if I have to!"

Declan immediately assumed a calming stance, hands raised. "Hey, I used to be a cop," he said evenly, voice low. "We're just trying to lock the store down, man."

"Cop?" the stranger repeated, fear flickering across his features. "Bullshit."

"It's the truth," Declan insisted, voice still calm. "Put the gun down. We can help each other."

But the man's gaze jumped between them, panic fueling his every breath. "No... you're infected. Everyone's infected!" His hands shook so badly that the gun wavered. Becca's heart pounded. A trigger-happy paranoid was the last thing they needed.

Jace took a subtle step forward, likely preparing to disarm him if necessary. But the man noticed and screamed, "Stay back!"

Becca, mind racing, tried a different tactic: "Look, we have a plan to keep those *actual* zombies out. You can come with us. You'll be safer." Her voice dripped with sincerity—she was an okay liar on a normal day, but under pressure, she was passable at best. She genuinely *did* want to help him, though. A bullet in the gut wouldn't do wonders for her longevity.

The man shook his head, tears pooling in his eyes. "I—I'm sorry," he stammered. "I just... can't do this." Then, before any of them could react, he turned the pistol on himself, pressed it under his chin, and pulled the trigger.

A deafening crack echoed through the store. Becca's ears rang as she stumbled back, a wave of horror crashing over her. The man crumpled to the floor behind the checkout counter, blood splattering across the dusty register screen.

For a moment, none of them breathed. The overhead speakers kept blaring *"I saw the sign..."* in a cruel, cheery contrast to the violence. Slowly, Jace lowered his knife, shoulders taut. Declan cursed under his breath, face darkening.

Becca swallowed the bitter taste of bile. It was an ugly reminder that the apocalypse wasn't just about zombies—fear could kill just as effectively.

"We should move," Declan said, voice flat. "That shot will have drawn attention."

Sure enough, a guttural moan rose from somewhere beyond the bakery. Shambling figures turned, drawn by the noise.

"On it," Becca whispered, her voice tight. With renewed urgency, she sprinted to the display cart blocking the front doors. Jace joined her, hooking his knife into the metal grate to get a better grip, while Declan kept watch.

Together, Becca and Jace managed to shove the cart aside with a grating screech of metal on tile.

She glanced nervously over her shoulder, spotting two zombies lurching around the corner, eyes fixed on the trio. "Hurry!" she gasped.

The doors slid almost closed automatically, the sensors glitchy from lack of electricity. Jace manually forced the glass panels shut, while Becca crouched to find the manual lock near the bottom. Her fingers fumbled, adrenaline surging. The store's official signage read EMERGENCY LOCK – AUTHORIZED PERSONNEL ONLY.

Sorry, Lisa, Becca thought, jamming her fingers around a lever. She yanked it down, and with a satisfying *clunk*, the door sealed.

"Nice job," Jace muttered. "Now the shutters."

Becca nodded, scanning the door frame for the security shutter mechanism. Meanwhile, Declan swung the crowbar at the nearest zombie—a tall woman with half her hair missing. The crowbar's hook caught her in the jaw, sending her staggering, but not quite dropping her. She lunged again, teeth snapping inches from Declan's shoulder. He gritted his teeth and drove the crowbar's blunt end into her skull with a sickening crunch. Blood spattered the tile, and the zombie collapsed.

Another undead figure, a heavyset man with a gaping wound across his chest, stumbled toward them. Jace darted forward, knife glinting. But before he could strike, Becca hefted the bat, unleashing a swift overhead slam. The top of the zombie's head caved in like an overripe melon. It toppled backward, arms flailing.

Becca let out a shaky breath. "They just keep coming," she muttered, glancing back at the kiosk. The next track started blaring: *"Don't Speak"* by No Doubt. The irony of that title was not lost on her—these zombies sure didn't speak, but they moaned plenty.

Declan rejoined them, wiping crowbar gore on his pant leg. "Shutters, now," he snapped.

Becca spotted a panel near the door. She tugged on the release handle, half-expecting it to be jammed. But with a squeal of old metal, the security shutter began rolling down from above. She yanked again, using her foot for extra leverage, until the grate sealed the entrance entirely.

A rush of relief flooded her system. "We did it," she breathed, though her moment of victory was dampened by the stench of death all around. "Front entrance is locked up tight."

Jace nodded, hooking his knife back into his belt. "Nice work, boss."

Declan grunted in agreement, though he still wore a brooding expression. "We need to check for any other access points—employee entrances, emergency exits. If they're open, these freaks will find their way in."

"True," Becca agreed. But she was also aware that *the plan* had only been to lock the front doors. The others were probably waiting back in the breakroom, counting on them to return. "Let's regroup first. Then we can methodically sweep the store."

As if on cue, a voice crackled over the store's intercom—Lisa's voice, trembling but audible: "Becca? If you can hear this… the cameras show you closed the front. Please come back. We see more… more of those things heading your way."

Becca shared a grim look with Declan and Jace. "Let's do this." She retrieved her bat from the floor, inhaling sharply. "We'll go back the way we came. Try to keep it quiet."

They started weaving through the aisles again, following the perimeter. Along the way, they picked off a few scattered zombies—three or four—most of which were aimlessly drifting toward the center of the store, seduced by the shrill vocals emanating from the broken speaker system. For the most part, the plan had worked; the undead population was at the heart of GoodMax, not the edges.

When they reached the staff hallway door, they found two zombies slumped against it as if waiting for someone to open up. Declan and Jace exchanged a quick glance, then Jace executed a swift double-stab, one for each zombie's skull. The creatures slid to the ground without so much as a whimper.

Becca raised an eyebrow. "You're dangerously proficient at that."

Jace shrugged. "A guy learns a few things behind bars."

Declan shot him a withering look, but said nothing. He pushed the bodies aside with the toe of his boot. "Let's go."

They slipped back into the hallway, hearts pounding. As soon as they were inside, Lisa yanked the door open from the breakroom side, relief evident on her face.

"You're back!" Tasha cried, jumping up from her seat. Carlos let out a breath he'd obviously been holding. Marsha sagged with relief, and even Leslie offered a tiny smile, though she kept one hand on her hip like *I have questions*.

"Mission accomplished," Becca announced, forcing a grin. Her blood-splattered bat told the real story. "Front entrance is sealed, security shutter's down."

Lisa nodded, shoulders sagging. "Thank God."

Becca set her bat aside, exhaling shakily as her adrenaline began to fade. She was exhausted, hungry, and covered in gore. *The triple threat of apocalypse glam,* she thought wryly. Her stomach rumbled loudly enough to echo in the breakroom. She pressed a hand to her belly. "Anyone else starving?"

In the relative safety of the breakroom, the tension softened just a bit. People realized they'd gone hours without real sustenance, and there was still a grocery store's worth of food out there—albeit with zombies milling around. But they had *some* supplies, and if they were careful, they could fetch more.

Becca marched over to the corner where a box of random breakroom snacks sat on a table. She rummaged through it. "Okay, folks, we've got... stale donuts, an unmarked Tupperware container with questionable fruit salad, and a half-eaten bag of chips." She made a face. "We can do better. This is a grocery store, for crying out loud."

Leslie raised a hand, her expression fierce. "I am *not* living off canned beans. The last time I ate beans, it—" She hesitated, glancing at Carlos. "Never mind."

Becca smirked, turning to Tasha. "Weren't you the one who said there were donuts leftover? Where'd they go?"

Tasha giggled nervously. "Edgar might have eaten the last two."

The mailman offered a sheepish shrug. "I'm old. Let me have my donuts in peace."

Becca sighed dramatically. "Fine. Since we can't rely on donuts, I'll do a snack run from the shelves. Because if I'm going to risk my life, I want *Doritos,* not beans." She pointed at Declan, who looked like he was about to object. "Yes, Officer Grouchy, you can come too. But we'll keep it short."

Declan frowned, crossing his arms. "We need a real plan for survival. Not just *snacks*."

Becca rolled her eyes. "Yeah, yeah. Step one: survive the next hour. Step two: maybe survive tomorrow. Let's start small, hmm?"

Jace snickered, apparently amused by their dynamic. "She's got a point. If we die hungry, that's just salt in the wound."

Declan massaged the bridge of his nose. "You people... All right. Let's do this systematically. We can block off one aisle at a time, gather supplies, and—"

"Can it, doomsday planner," Becca interrupted with a sassy grin. "It's simple: we sneak out, grab the good stuff—chips, soda, maybe some protein bars—and get back without dying. That's the plan. You can handle the *serious survival strategies* after I'm fed."

Lisa raised a cautious hand. "We *should* probably get some non-perishables, like bread, crackers, or even canned goods if that's all we have." She gave Becca a pointed look. "I mean, not *just* Doritos."

Becca made a grand, sweeping gesture. "Fine, I'll stoop to normal food as well. But if there are any chocolate bars left, I'm claiming them. *Don't test me.*"

Carlos let out a nervous laugh, which lifted the room's spirits a smidge. Even Marsha managed a tiny smile.

"Okay," Declan said, taking charge in that calm, authoritative voice. "We'll do a quick supply sweep. I'll cover you. Carter"—he nodded at Jace—"stay here, guard the breakroom."

Jace raised his brows. "Guard it? I think they could use some help carrying supplies."

Declan shook his head. "We don't want everyone out there at once. Too risky."

Becca chimed in. "Actually, it's all right. Jace, you're good at… *quiet kills.*" She shot a glance at the glimmering knife. "But let's not travel in a huge pack. How about me, Declan, and… Tasha?"

Tasha's eyes widened in surprise. "M-me? I—I don't know if I can—"

"You can," Becca said gently. "And you know this store's layout better than most people here, right? If you've got a map in your head, that's priceless. Plus, you're not as, uh, squeamish as some might think. Remember that time the meat counter was spewing blood from a broken pipe? You didn't even flinch."

Tasha swallowed, a flicker of resolve in her eyes. "O-okay. I'll try."

Jace shrugged, twirling his knife. "Fine, I'll hang back. Keep the breakroom safe from the big bad undead."

Leslie pursed her lips. "Just come back in one piece. *Preferably* with something edible that isn't expired. Or coffee. God, I'd kill for some coffee."

Marsha mumbled something about *"I'm never touching deli meat again,"* but no one acknowledged it. The conversation was already moving on.

And so, once again, Becca found herself creeping out of the breakroom, but this time with Declan and Tasha in tow. The music from the store's PA was still going strong, though it sounded like it might be skipping or short-circuiting. The next track was *"Barbie Girl"* by Aqua, but it kept cutting in and out, resulting in a bizarre remix of plastic-themed lyrics and static.

If nothing else, it made for an *extremely* weird ambiance.

Tasha clutched a box cutter—her only available weapon—like it was Excalibur. Declan led the way, crowbar in hand, scanning each aisle with practiced vigilance. Becca took the rear, baseball bat resting on her shoulder, trying not to picture just how many zombies might be roaming around the next corner.

Despite the stress, she felt a slight surge of satisfaction at the sight of the sealed front doors and shuttered windows. They were secure, for now.

"Okay," Tasha whispered, voice trembling. "Snacks are mostly on aisle six, but we also have that promotional display near the center for new products."

Declan frowned. "That's close to the electronics section—where the music is loudest, and presumably where most of them are gathered."

Becca shrugged. "We'll start with aisle six, take what we can carry, then see if it's safe to nab anything from the promo display. If not, we bail. Sound good?"

They reached aisle six without encountering any zombies, although the occasional wet groan or scraping sound echoed from elsewhere in the store. The fluorescent lights overhead were flickering like a discount haunted house, intensifying the sense of doom. Shelves were half-raided, boxes ripped open in a hurry—likely from the panic when this all started.

Becca scanned the shelves, grabbing a few large tote bags. "All right. Tasha, you fill one with whatever snacks we can find—chips, crackers, cookies, anything. Declan, can you keep watch?"

Declan nodded, stepping to the aisle's entrance to stand guard. Becca grabbed a second tote and began tossing in assorted goodies: Doritos, Cheetos, a few jars of peanut butter (hey, *protein*), and a large bag of M&Ms. She refused to pass up chocolate in the apocalypse.

Tasha worked quickly, stuffing fruit snacks, granola bars, and even a few random candy bars into her bag. "I feel like I'm shoplifting," she muttered, a nervous giggle escaping her lips. "Is it still illegal if the world's ending?"

Becca snorted. "If it is, who's going to arrest us?" She threw a look at Declan. "Oh, right. Officer McBroody might."

Declan rolled his eyes but kept his attention on the aisle intersection. "Ha-ha. Real funny. Just hurry up."

A sudden crash jolted them. Becca and Tasha froze, hearts hammering. Declan tensed, crowbar raised. Another crash followed, accompanied by a chorus of moans. It sounded like a shelf had toppled somewhere near the electronics section. The garbled notes of *"Barbie Girl"* warped into static, then resumed with a squealing hiss.

"That can't be good," Tasha whispered, hugging her tote bag.

Becca grit her teeth. "Let's get out of here. Now."

They shuffled toward the exit of aisle six. As they emerged into the main thoroughfare, Becca glimpsed a horrifying sight: a group of maybe half a dozen zombies pressed up against a fallen shelving unit, thrashing and grabbing. One of them had a twisted ankle that bent at an impossible angle, but it kept crawling forward, undeterred. The squealing music above them only seemed to rile them up further.

They hadn't noticed *her* yet, but if she moved too loudly, she'd be on their radar. She looked to Declan, who nodded. *Quiet.* They began creeping in the opposite direction, heading for the staff hallway.

But Tasha, trying to remain stealthy with an overstuffed tote of snacks, accidentally bumped against a metal shopping basket on the floor. It clattered, spinning noisily.

Every zombie head swiveled in their direction with terrifying synchronicity.

"Run," Declan hissed.

And run they did, shoes slapping the tile as they sprinted back to the breakroom corridor. The undead horde let out unified growls, lurching after them in a grotesque shuffle-run. The store's flickering lights and static-laden pop music turned the chase into a twisted carnival from hell.

Becca clutched her bat, breath burning in her lungs. She was half-tempted to swing around and start bashing skulls, but there were *six or more* of them, and only three of her group. Sure, Declan was a tough ex-cop, and Tasha had her box cutter, but the odds weren't great.

They nearly careened into a stray zombie in the detergent aisle. Declan rammed it with the crowbar, hooking it by the waist and shoving it aside. It tripped over a toppled laundry basket, screeching in confusion. Tasha shrieked as another zombie lunged at her, trying to grab the snacks from her hands—like it was more interested in Cheetos than flesh, or maybe it just smelled *something*. Either way, Tasha jerked the tote away, and Becca brought her bat down on the zombie's head, caving it in.

"Keep going!" she yelled.

The hallway door was in sight. Jace peeked out, eyes widening. "Come on, move!"

The three barreled inside, and Jace slammed the door shut. Immediately, the group barricaded it with anything not already used on the breakroom door—an empty metal rack, some boxes, a mop, whatever they could find. Moments later, several heavy thuds sounded as the undead slammed against the other side, groaning in frustration.

"Shit, that was close," Tasha panted, dropping her tote bag to the floor. Snacks spilled out in a rainbow of packaging.

Becca doubled over, hands on her knees, gasping for air. "Remind me… never again… we do that… we skip the *beans*."

Jace burst out laughing, wiping sweat from his forehead. "You nearly died for Doritos?"

Becca shot him a glare between gasps. "Don't… judge me, man."

Declan shook his head, but there was a hint of relief in his eyes. "We need a better system for supply runs, or we're going to get ourselves killed. Or infected."

Lisa rushed out of the breakroom, looking frazzled. "You're alive, thank goodness! We heard the commotion. Are you hurt? Did you find any food?"

Becca sank onto a nearby stool, rummaging through Tasha's spilled tote. She picked out a bag of baked chips, hugging it to her chest like a treasured artifact. "Oh, we found food, all right." She tore open the bag, ignoring everyone else's wide-eyed stares. "What? I'm starving."

She shoved a handful of chips into her mouth, savoring the salty crunch, ignoring the fact that she was sweaty, gore-spattered, and shaking with residual fear. Because, for just one moment, she wanted to taste something normal. Something that reminded her that life wasn't always a nightmare.

Lisa eyed the battered group. "Now that you're back, we really do need to come up with a bigger plan. We can't keep doing this in small bursts."

Declan nodded gravely. "Agreed."

Jace slipped his knife into his belt, leaning casually against the wall. "So let's hear your big plan, Officer."

Declan rubbed a hand over his jaw, grimacing. "We should do a store-wide sweep. Methodically clear the aisles. If we kill every zombie inside, we can secure the entire building. It's large enough for us to live in for a while. Plenty of food, at least."

Becca's eyebrows shot up. That sounded... bold. Then again, they'd locked the front entrance. If they truly got rid of *every* zombie inside, this GoodMax could become a fortress of sorts. They could seal the side entrances, set up a perimeter. It was insane—but maybe the only real chance at safety they had.

She crunched another chip thoughtfully. "All right. We'll do it. But not *right now*. Everyone's exhausted. We regroup, rest for a bit, maybe scrounge up something like... weapons, I guess? Then we coordinate a full sweep. No more of these haphazard runs."

A ghost of a smile crossed Declan's face. "I'm surprised. That's almost sensible."

Becca snorted. "Wow, you give compliments like a pro, Graves. Keep that up, and maybe I'll let you have some Doritos."

Jace let out a low chuckle. Tasha collapsed into a chair, relieved to be alive. Leslie, who'd been lurking in the doorway, eyed the snacks with shameless hunger. Edgar and Marsha nodded wearily, as if any plan sounded good as long as it didn't involve more immediate life-threatening stunts.

"Fine," Declan said. "We rest. But tomorrow—maybe even tonight if we can—this store becomes ours. We clear every aisle, top to bottom. No more surprises."

Becca lifted her bag of chips in a mock toast. "Hear, hear. But first, snack time." She rummaged in Tasha's bag and tossed a Snickers to Leslie, a pack of peanut butter crackers to Edgar, and some fruit snacks to Carlos. Then she looked around, adopting a mock-serious expression. "All hail the new snack queen. Canned beans are for peasants."

A ripple of laughter passed through the group—tired, frayed, but genuine. For one fleeting moment, the breakroom felt almost… cozy? The apocalyptic reality loomed outside, but inside these walls, they had each other, a half-decent plan, and enough junk food to last at least a few days.

It was a small victory, but Becca took it. She'd been a grocery store shelf-stocker just yesterday, dreaming of a simple life. Now she was, in some bizarre twist of fate, an unlikely leader—armed with a neon-orange baseball bat, a sassy mouth, and a vow to keep her new "team" (or what was left of it) alive.

If that's not badass, she mused, *then I don't know what is.*

She popped another chip into her mouth and grinned.

Tomorrow, they'd fight. Tonight, they'd rest, eat, and maybe even dare to hope.

CHAPTER THREE

Three weeks into the apocalypse, Becca Montgomery leaned against the cereal aisle's battered shelves—her makeshift throne—surveying her domain like a well-fed queen. The GoodMax grocery store, once brimming with undead horrors, had been painstakingly cleared by her scrappy band of survivors. Now it stood eerily silent, cleaned out, and oddly cozy in a *post-apocalyptic fortress* sort of way.

She lounged in a flimsy lawn chair (one they'd nabbed from the seasonal section), wearing a wrinkled GoodMax polo shirt that might have fit her better in a *pre-apocalypse diet plan* era. At her feet sat a half-eaten bag of Doritos, a battered baseball bat, and a pair of stale doughnuts she was hoarding for no particular reason. Around her, scattered remnants of the once-bustling store:

empty shelves, overturned carts, and hand-painted signs instructing any survivors to "Ring the Bell for Service!"—though nobody ever did.

Yes, Becca was living her best *end-of-the-world* life. Or as best as one could, anyway.

Her group—what remained of it—had set up camp in various corners of the store. A few cots in the pharmacy. A small cooking station by the deli counter. Even some tarps and blankets draped strategically for privacy. They'd done daily sweeps those first two weeks, and after the second day, there wasn't a single zombie left inside. Now the undead only occasionally rattled the metal security shutters outside—like sad, hungry raccoons hoping for table scraps.

Jace Carter—ex-con, chaos magnet, and official knife-wielder—strolled up to her with a grin. "Queen Bee," he teased, flicking at a snag on her chair's mesh arm. His tattooed arms were on full display in a sleeveless shirt, because apparently the apocalypse was no excuse to skip arm day. "You going for a new record in how long you can lounge without showering?"

Becca sniffed dramatically, arching a brow. "You offering me a shower, Carter? Because last I checked, we've only got enough water pressure for baby wipes and half-hearted wet washcloths."

He held up his hands in mock surrender, the glint of mischief in his eyes. "Just saying, we're hitting that borderline territory between *cozy musk* and *dead raccoon*."

She rolled her eyes, hurling a Dorito at him. He dodged expertly. "Gotta conserve water for important stuff—like brushing my teeth so I don't end up with the world's worst apocalypse breath," she said.

From the other side of the store—where a makeshift lookout station was set up behind the checkout counters—Declan Graves, former cop and resident scowler, called out, "If you two are done flirting, you want to help me inventory what's left in the produce coolers? We can't keep ignoring the fact that we're running out of supplies."

Becca made a dramatic show of slumping in her chair. "I swear, Graves, you are the *fun police.* Here I am, enjoying my last few Doritos in peace, and you want to talk about produce. Again."

Declan, arms folded over a broad chest, shot her a withering glare. "When we run out of food, you'll be the first to complain, *Your Highness.*"

She considered hurling another Dorito but decided to eat it instead. "Fine, I'm on my way."

Jace snickered softly, giving Becca a playful nudge as they passed by. "You know, you could always let *him* handle the produce while we go do something more exciting—like searching for Twinkies in the storage room."

Becca grinned. "Tempting. But if I don't humor him, he'll never unclench." Lowering her voice, she added conspiratorially, "And honestly? We are getting low on supplies. Might as well find out how bad it is."

They left the cereal aisle—Becca tossed the empty Doritos bag into a nearby trash bin with surprising dexterity—and headed toward the produce coolers. Along the way, they passed a few of the other survivors who'd become like a dysfunctional family over the past few weeks:

- Lisa, the once overbearing store manager, now an exhausted but steadfast rock who coordinated sleeping schedules and distribution of basic goods.
- Tasha, the pastel-haired cashier who'd found unexpected courage and now had a baseball cap proclaiming *TEAM NO ZOMBIES* perched on her head. She sat cross-legged, fiddling with a half-charged phone she used for music whenever the store's overhead system went on the fritz.
- Edgar, the elderly mailman, dozing lightly in a corner. He'd proven surprisingly adept at rigging small traps and had the unwavering dedication of someone who once braved rabid dogs and harsh weather to deliver postcards.
- Leslie, the coupon queen who, unbelievably, still carried around a small folder of coupons—like the apocalypse might *eventually* accept them. She hovered near a small stash of laundry detergent, scowling at the expiration dates.
- Marsha, the former deli worker, quietly cleaning a row of knives. She'd been through a lot but seemed to find solace in busywork.

Everyone seemed *relatively* at ease, given the circumstances. No immediate shrieks of the undead, no constant threat pounding on the shutters. That sense of precarious calm was exactly why Declan was so irritated—*complacency* in the face of a world overrun by zombies.

"Montgomery," Declan barked as they approached. He insisted on calling her by her last name, as if they were still in some paramilitary group. "We have about three days' worth of fresh produce left, if you can even call this stuff fresh. After that, it's down to the cans and freeze-dried junk."

"Freeze-dried *junk* we mostly used up," Jace pointed out, leaning over to snag a wilted carrot from a crate. "Remember? We raided half the MRE packets when we first got here."

Becca scrunched her nose. "Yeah, those were gross. Tasted like cardboard if cardboard had a vendetta against your taste buds."

Declan ignored the commentary. "Point is, we need a plan for when the food runs out." His gaze fixed on Becca. "We can't stay holed up in here forever."

She put a hand on her hip. "You saying we should move on?"

He gave a curt nod. "Supplies are nearly gone. We've got no real power source except that rickety generator in the back, and it's about out of fuel. Zombies might not be banging on the shutters right now, but they're definitely out there. The city's not getting safer, and we have to think long term."

She exhaled, glancing around at the place that had become their weird little home. *Sure, it smells like stale bread and Clorox in here, but it's ours,* she thought wistfully. But she knew Declan was right. They were scraping the bottom of the barrel. Her beloved Doritos stash had dwindled to near-extinction.

"Fine," she said after a beat. "We'll gather everyone and talk about it."

They convened in the breakroom—still the best place for group discussions. The walls sported pinned-up motivational posters leftover from the pre-apocalypse era, ironically reading things like *"Hang in There!"* and *"Teamwork: The Key to Success."* The battered plastic chairs were arranged in a semi-circle, reminiscent of a therapy group, which was maybe exactly what they all needed at this point.

Becca stood at the front, arms crossed, trying her best to project *confidence* while also feeling the pangs of hunger gnaw at her. "All right, guys," she began, "we're running low on basically everything. If we don't move on soon, we're going to be chewing on cardboard boxes and leftover beans." She paused to let that sink in. The memory of those dreaded beans was still fresh for many. "We need to find a new place with actual resources."

Lisa looked pained. She'd spent so long fortifying the store. "But we've made this a fortress. We have the shutters, the barricades…"

Edgar cleared his throat. "Fortresses don't mean much if we starve inside them."

Tasha nodded, fiddling with the brim of her cap. "Yeah, I'm already sick of beans. And that's saying something—I used to be a vegetarian."

Becca gave a grim half-smile. "Then it's settled. We'll pack up, see if we can find somewhere else. Maybe there's a warehouse or a distribution center we can raid, or—"

Jace raised a hand, as if they were in grade school. "Actually, I heard from some travelers who passed by last week—remember those two guys with the weird machetes? They mentioned a *sporting goods store* on the west side of town. Supposed to be big, has guns and gear. If it's not overrun, might be a jackpot."

Instantly, the energy in the room shifted. Guns. Ammunition. Camping supplies. This was no small-time local shop, but a chain store that (in normal times) sold everything from basketball hoops to hunting rifles. A potential gold mine.

Declan raised an eyebrow. "Better than wandering aimlessly, I suppose." He turned to Becca. "We can try it. But we have to be strategic. The city's crawling with zombies, and half the roads are blocked."

"We'll figure it out," Becca said, lifting her chin. She tried not to show the flicker of doubt. "We always do."

They took a collective breath, gazing around at each other. Leslie sighed, hugging her coupon folder to her chest like a security blanket. "Guess that's that. Everyone, pack your stuff—what little we have. We leave tomorrow morning."

The next day dawned gloomily, the sky choked with smoky clouds. The group huddled at the store's loading dock—far quieter than opening the front shutters—and prepared to slip into the city's corpse-ridden streets. They'd load up a few shopping carts with essential supplies, weapons, and whatever else might be useful.

Becca tugged on a pair of black flats she'd snagged from the shoe aisle weeks ago. They were comfortable at first, but after a few scuffles and an impromptu chase, they'd lost most of their cushioning. The soles were nearly paper-thin.

"You have a death wish wearing those?" Jace teased, adjusting the straps of a backpack bristling with knives. "What if you need to run?"

She scowled at him. "They're the only things that fit decently. Stupid apocalypse and its *lack of shoe stores.*" She eyed his boots enviously. "Where'd you get those, anyway?"

"Found 'em in the back. My size, apparently." He gave a smug grin. "Should've rummaged more thoroughly, snack queen."

She flicked a finger at his chest. "You shut your pie hole, or I'll make you trade."

But the truth was, she was already regretting the flats. *Running from zombies is the worst cardio plan ever,* she thought grimly. She wasn't exactly a marathon runner even before the world ended, and the apocalypse hadn't magically turned her into an Olympic sprinter.

Declan, crowbar resting across his shoulders, approached them with a serious frown (as usual). "If we're all set, let's move out. We go in pairs, watch each other's backs. No heroics."

Becca bristled slightly at the last bit, but she let it slide. She'd definitely performed a few borderline heroic (or foolhardy) stunts over the weeks, and Declan made it clear he didn't trust her *lack of caution.* "Got it, Mom," she said drily, earning a quick glare from him.

They slipped outside into the alley behind the store, carefully lowering the rolling door of the loading dock once everyone was clear. A hush fell as they took in the scene. The city's usual hum was replaced by an eerie quiet, punctuated by distant moans and the rustle of trash in the wind.

Cars blocked intersections, some crashed into light poles, others abandoned mid-lane. Broken glass glittered in the morning light. An overturned city bus jutted from the curb like a fallen titan. And, of course, half-rotted corpses occasionally sprawled across the pavement—some stationary, some *very much* not.

Becca's heart pounded. She tightened her grip on her trusty baseball bat. The group began moving, pushing a few loaded shopping carts with squeaky wheels. Each cart was stacked with water jugs, leftover packaged goods, a precious stash of medical supplies, and a random assortment of personal items that people refused to leave behind.

Along the way, they took care to avoid any large clusters of undead, slipping down side streets or ducking behind wrecked vehicles whenever a small pack stumbled by. The nerve-wracking tension weighed on them, but they'd become more adept at moving quietly. Even Leslie had learned to muzzle her usual complaining when a moaning figure lurched too close.

After about an hour of nerve-wracking travel, they found themselves on a stretch of wide boulevard leading toward the sporting goods store. A giant billboard overhead displayed a weathered ad for something like *"Mega Sale on Treadmills!"*—some cosmic joke about cardio being *so* critical in a zombie apocalypse.

Becca's flats were already killing her feet, making her limp a bit. She tried to hide it, not wanting Declan to get that *I told you so* glint in his eye. Jace, strolling beside her, noticed anyway.

"You okay?" he murmured, keeping his voice low.

She forced a smile. "I'll live. If the zombies don't catch me first."

He nodded, though concern flickered across his expression. "We can stop if you need—"

"No," she cut in. "Let's just get there. The sooner, the better."

Declan motioned for them to halt, scanning the horizon. The sprawling parking lot of the sporting goods store loomed ahead. Rows of abandoned cars, some with shattered windows. A few flickering lampposts. And, ominously, a handful of zombie silhouettes wandering aimlessly near the store's entrance.

"All right," Declan said quietly. "It's not a huge crowd, but definitely some activity. If we move fast, we might avoid a major confrontation."

Becca studied the scene. The building was large —two stories tall, with big glass windows that might or might not be intact. The main doors appeared closed, though she couldn't tell from a distance if they were locked. A weather-beaten sign read "SUN VALLEY SPORTING GOODS" in half-missing letters.

Lisa sidled up to them, brow furrowed. "Are we sure we want to go in there if there are already zombies milling about?"

"We're sure," Becca said, steeling her resolve. "Where else are we going to find actual gear? We can handle a few zombies."

Leslie sighed, rummaging in her coupon folder—a nervous habit. "All right, let's do this. But if I get bit, I'm haunting you."

They advanced as quietly as possible into the parking lot, weaving between parked cars. The slow squeak of the shopping carts threatened to give them away at every turn. Occasionally, a zombie would tilt its head at the sound, and they'd freeze, hearts pounding. Then, more often than not, the creature would continue shambling aimlessly. *Sometimes it pays to smell like you haven't showered in weeks,* Becca thought darkly.

A stray moan drifted from behind a pickup truck. Declan signaled for the group to stop while he crept forward to investigate. The crowbar glinted in the sunlight as he readied himself. One swift motion, a dull *thud*, and the moan cut off. Declan waved them onward.

Soon, they were within fifty feet of the store's entrance. Four zombies stood near the glass doors, occasionally bumping into the walls like they couldn't quite figure out how to get in. The big windows were, miraculously, still intact. That was good—if the zombies hadn't smashed them, maybe the interior was less compromised.

"All right," Jace whispered, eyes flicking to Becca. "How do you want to do this?"

She weighed her options. She could stage a loud distraction, luring them away. But that might attract more undead from the surrounding blocks. Alternatively, a quick, *quiet* takedown might be best. "We do it silent," she decided. "Knives, crowbars, no guns. And no screaming, obviously."

Declan nodded. "I'll take the two on the left. You and Jace handle the others. Everyone else, stay back behind the cars."

Lisa opened her mouth to argue—she was the manager, after all—but one quelling look from Declan had her biting her tongue. The group was used to this arrangement by now: let the more combat-proficient handle the close encounters, while the rest stayed safe.

Becca's pulse thrummed. She and Jace broke off from the group, circling around the zombies from the right. Declan went left. She glanced over at Jace, who offered a quick nod, brandishing his knife. Then they moved in.

Zombie #1, an older woman with matted gray hair, jerked her head up as Jace approached. He drove the knife into the base of her skull before she could moan, letting her slump to the ground. Zombie #2, a lanky man missing half his cheek, swivelled toward Becca, arms outstretched. She swung her bat, connecting with a nauseating *crack*. Its head snapped sideways, but it staggered, refusing to drop. Another swing to the temple finally sent it crashing into the pavement. She had to swallow back a surge of disgust as dark fluid oozed onto her shoes.

On the other side, Declan dealt with his two targets in a methodical flurry of crowbar swings. The muted *thuds* each ended with a sickening crunch that was almost drowned out by the traffic hum—or what remained of it—in the distance.

Within a minute, all four zombies lay still, and no additional undead seemed alerted. Becca mopped sweat from her brow, heart racing. "We good?" she whispered to Jace.

He gave her a quick thumbs-up. "Clear."

Declan motioned for the group to bring up the carts. "Let's get inside before more show up."

They pried open the glass doors, wincing at the squeal of metal. The interior was dim, lit only by a few skylights in the ceiling. Racks of sporting equipment stretched in every direction—kayaks, fishing rods, helmets, golf clubs, basketballs. A faint odor of rubber and stale air hung in the store.

"All right," Declan said, stepping inside with caution. "We do a sweep. Check for zombies, then we gather resources. If the place is clear, we can barricade the entrances and set up camp."

Becca nodded, adjusting her backpack straps. Her feet *ached*, but she pushed that aside. If there were weapons here—actual firearms, bows, crossbows, *anything*—it could radically increase their chances of survival.

As they advanced, it became evident the store had been partially looted. Shelves were ransacked, leaving scattered boxes and packaging on the floor. But it wasn't as heavily stripped as, say, a supermarket would be. Possibly, early survivors or raiders had overlooked it in the chaos. Maybe there were still treasures to be found.

A muffled sound reached them from behind a row of mannequin displays. Becca tensed, raising her bat. She exchanged a look with Jace, who nodded. Cautiously, they edged around the corner, only to find… a single zombie, pinned under a fallen metal rack, its torso caved in. The creature growled weakly, gnashing broken teeth.

"Gross," Tasha muttered from behind them. She'd followed, apparently wanting to prove her mettle. "Should I…?"

Becca shrugged. "Go for it, if you're up to it." Tasha swallowed but stepped forward, brandishing a short machete she'd picked up somewhere along the journey. One swift chop ended the zombie's snarling. She looked pale but resolute.

They continued through the aisles, encountering only a couple more lone zombies, easy enough to dispatch. The group spread out in pairs—Declan with Edgar, Lisa with Leslie, Tasha with Marsha, and Becca with Jace—methodically clearing each section.

The store, as far as they could tell, was big enough to accommodate them all. A second-floor loft area showcased more expensive outdoor gear. A locked "Employees Only" room near the back might contain a breakroom or offices. And, crucially, there was an area designated *"Hunting & Firearms"* behind a sturdy metal gate. The gate was locked, but with a bit of luck and some ex-con ingenuity, they might break in.

They converged near the entrance after the sweep, assembling in the center of the store. "That's all of them," Marsha reported, looking relieved. "No more undead, at least not on this floor."

Lisa nodded, wiping sweat from her brow. "We can barricade the entrance with some display racks. Maybe push a car or two out front if we can find the keys."

Declan seemed more at ease now that they were inside. "It's as good a spot as we'll find. Let's start moving our supplies in."

Becca tried to keep the triumph from her face—she didn't want to jinx it—but relief swelled in her chest. *We did it.* A new base, with potential new weapons. A step up from the grocery store's diminishing resources. Her feet, however, screamed in protest. She silently vowed to find something—*anything*—better than these cursed flats among the store's footwear section.

They spent the next hour dragging in their shopping carts, rummaging around for crates and boxes to use as barricades. The sporting goods store had thick glass doors and side exits, both of which could be secured with a little effort.

Becca and Jace ventured into the footwear section, rummaging for a pair of sturdy boots that fit her.

She practically wept with joy upon finding a pair just one size too big, which was still better than her shredded flats. She stuffed some padding in them for good measure.

As they returned to the main floor, arms loaded with potential gear, they heard a commotion at the front entrance. Declan's voice rang out, low and commanding: "Stop right there! Hands where I can see them!"

Becca shot Jace a questioning look, then hurried forward. She arrived to see Declan, crowbar in hand, facing down a newcomer—a lean, bespectacled man in a rumpled lab coat splattered with suspicious brownish stains. He held his hands in the air, a satchel slung over one shoulder.

"Whoa, whoa, calm down!" the stranger said, voice trembling. "I'm not infected, I swear."

Becca halted a few feet away, gripping her bat. "That's what they all say."

The man gulped. Up close, he looked exhausted, with dark circles under his eyes and a haunted expression. He adjusted his glasses nervously, then lowered his voice. "My name is Dr. Eli Hawthorne. I—uh—I've been studying this virus. I heard noise, saw you come in here, thought maybe… maybe I could join you?"

Lisa and Edgar stood behind Declan, similarly on edge. Leslie hovered near the store's display of bicycles, possibly sizing up an escape route in case things went south.

Declan's jaw tightened. "You're a scientist?"

Hawthorne nodded, still holding his hands up. "Biochemist, to be precise. I—I worked on government research before everything collapsed. I've been… tracking the spread, trying to document it."

A taut silence filled the air. Becca exchanged glances with Jace. A *government researcher*? That sounded either very useful or very dangerous. Or both.

"And how exactly did you find us?" Declan asked.

Hawthorne lowered his hands slightly, tapping the side of his satchel. "I was scavenging the pharmacy next door. I heard sounds of a fight, came to investigate. I saw you kill a few zombies, realized you might be civilized. Believe me, I've had… less pleasant encounters with other survivors." A shudder passed over him.

Becca raised an eyebrow. "You got a gun or something?"

He shook his head. "No, just a small Taser, and it's out of juice. I'm no threat, I promise." He lifted the satchel's flap. "See? Just notebooks, a laptop that barely works, some lab samples."

Lisa narrowed her eyes. "Lab samples of *what*, exactly?"

"A few tissue cultures, infected blood samples," he said quickly, then added, "I keep them sealed. I'm trying to learn how the virus mutates so quickly. If I can find a way to stop it…" He trailed off, looking simultaneously hopeful and resigned.

Declan regarded him for a long moment, crowbar still raised. "We're not a charity. We can't risk letting someone in who might compromise our safety."

Becca huffed. "Says the ex-cop who just recruited an ex-con." She gestured to Jace. "We've got a *ragtag assembly* of survivors here. Adding a scientist might actually help."

Jace gave a mock bow. "I was a *charming* ex-con, for the record."

Hawthorne blinked, clearly unsure how to respond to this dynamic. "I—I can contribute," he stammered. "I'm a decent medic. I know first aid, more advanced procedures. And if you have any interest in actually understanding this plague—"

Marsha, stepping forward with surprising boldness, said, "We lost a few folks early on because we had no one who really knew how to treat serious wounds. A doctor might be a good idea, Declan."

Declan's gaze flicked between them all. He looked like he wanted to argue, but the weight of the group's need was evident. He lowered the crowbar slightly.

"Fine," he said curtly. "But you're staying where I can see you. Any funny business, and you're out."

Hawthorne let out a breath, nodding eagerly. "Understood. Thank you."

They led Dr. Hawthorne deeper into the store, giving him a brief rundown of how they ended up here. He looked both fascinated and horrified, occasionally scribbling notes in a small notepad. Despite his exhaustion, there was a manic brightness in his eyes whenever zombies were mentioned, which put Becca on alert. *Smart guys are always a little weird,* she thought, recalling the stereotype. Then again, weird might be their best shot at survival.

"You said you used to work for the government," Becca prodded, once they settled near the store's customer service desk. "Any chance you can tell us *how* all this started?" She gestured around, as if indicating the entire zombified city.

Hawthorne exhaled, fiddling with his glasses. "Where to begin? The project I was involved in—let's just say it wasn't exactly a mainstream CDC project. We were studying potential viral weaponization for defense. At least, that's how it was sold to us. But there were… moral and ethical red flags. Then the outbreak happened, and any official chain of command fell apart."

Declan frowned, arms crossed. "So, you're saying this is *man-made*?"

Hawthorne shrugged helplessly. "That's the biggest question. The virus itself has a structure that suggests some engineering, but also some natural mutation. It's like someone took a highly virulent rabies strain and spliced it with... well, let's just say it's complicated."

Jace made a face. "So basically, you were playing God, and then everything went to hell."

Hawthorne's cheeks colored. "I was just a cog in the machine. By the time I realized how dangerous the experiments were, it was too late." He cleared his throat, perhaps trying to mask the guilt welling in his eyes. "I've been on the run ever since, trying to gather data. Seeing if there's any *pattern* to who gets infected quickly and who might have partial immunity."

"Immunity?" Becca echoed, intrigued despite herself.

He nodded, tapping his notebook. "I've documented a handful of survivors who survived bites for an unusual amount of time—longer than typical. Some never turned, though I haven't been able to confirm if they were actually immune or if the virus mutated slower in them." He paused, dropping his gaze. "I'm hoping if I can compile enough information, I can figure out a vaccine. Or a cure."

A hush fell. Edgar let out a low whistle. Leslie clutched her coupon folder, eyes wide. Lisa looked torn between horror and hope.

"A *cure*?" Tasha said softly. "Is that even possible?"

Hawthorne ran a shaky hand through his unkempt hair. "I won't lie—odds are stacked against us. The infrastructure for large-scale production is gone. But if I can find the *right* data, maybe a small, workable solution can be made. At least for a handful of people. If civilization can pull itself together, that might be enough of a start."

Becca's mind reeled. *A cure.* She hadn't let herself dream of such a thing. It sounded too good to be true, but also too tempting to ignore. "Well," she said, crossing her arms, "if you need lab space, we definitely don't have that. But we've got, um, some first aid supplies. And a sporting goods store that might have hunting paraphernalia for *dissecting deer*, if that helps?"

A small, weary smile tugged at Hawthorne's lips. "I'll take what I can get."

Declan, ever the killjoy, cut in. "Don't get your hopes up, people. He said it himself—this virus is complicated. We focus on immediate survival first."

A flicker of annoyance crossed Becca's face. "Yes, Dad." She turned back to Hawthorne. "You want to stay? Contribute to the group? Fine by me. Just don't do anything that'll get us all killed."

Hawthorne nodded fervently. "I promise. I'll help however I can."

The rest of the day passed in a flurry of activity. They dragged their supplies further inside, piling boxes of leftover goods along the walls. They discovered a *camping section* that still had a few tents, sleeping bags, and some propane stoves. A small stroke of luck.

Lisa set up a corner as the new "breakroom," while Marsha and Tasha sorted out a cooking area near the store's demonstration kitchen—usually for showing off camping gear. Edgar took on the task of securing the side exits, muttering about how the mail used to arrive "rain or shine, zombies be damned." Leslie rummaged for flashlights, batteries, and anything else they might need for lighting once night fell. Jace tested out different knives he found in the hunting section, grinning like a kid on Christmas.

Meanwhile, Declan kept a wary eye on Hawthorne, who busied himself flipping through inventory logs at the customer service desk. Becca joined the scientist after a while, curiosity piqued.

"Whatcha looking for?" she asked, leaning over the desk.

He glanced up, pushing his glasses back up his nose. "Trying to see if they stored any advanced first aid kits or portable medical equipment. This might have been a large enough store to stock some more professional gear—like minor surgery kits or blood testing kits for outdoorsmen."

Becca gave an appreciative whistle. "Fancy. If we're lucky, maybe we'll find a *chemistry set* to go with your infected samples."

He chuckled softly, though there was a note of sadness in it. "I'd need a lot more than that. But every bit helps."

She studied him. "You're really serious about this cure thing, aren't you?"

He nodded, eyes distant. "I lost people. Good people, who might have had a chance if we'd known more. This virus… it's not just about the reanimation, it's about what it does to the host's brain. If we can interrupt that process—" He stopped, swallowing hard. "Anyway, you didn't sign up for a science lecture. Sorry."

Becca shrugged. "Eh, it's more interesting than counting how many bags of beef jerky we have left." She leaned in conspiratorially. "Just don't let Declan catch you messing around with, like, vials of infected blood in the middle of the store. He'll lose his mind."

A half-smile tugged at Hawthorne's lips. "I'll keep that in mind."

By evening, they'd established enough order to rest for the night. Tasha and Marsha cooked up a makeshift stew from canned goods and some questionable produce they'd hauled over from GoodMax. Not exactly gourmet, but hot food was a luxury in the apocalypse.

Becca finally got to slip on her new boots—thankfully they weren't too big now that she'd padded them—and her feet felt the sweet relief of actual support. "I could cry," she told Jace, who snorted.

"Better than flats?"

"Infinitely," she replied, wiggling her toes. "Now I can *run* from zombies with a bit more dignity."

They all sat in a small circle on the store's second floor, near the edge of the hunting gear section, eating dinner by the light of battery-powered lanterns. The tension from the day ebbed, replaced by a tired camaraderie. Even Declan looked mildly relaxed, though he continued eyeing Hawthorne with caution.

"How do you like your new digs, doc?" Leslie asked between spoonfuls of stew.

Hawthorne set down his tin mug, pushing his glasses up. "Safer than anywhere else I've been recently. Thank you for letting me stay. Truly."

Becca smirked. "We're not monsters. Despite the blood on our clothes." She took a sip of water. "And hey, if you figure out some super-secret cure, just remember your *favorite person* who let you in, yeah?"

He chuckled. "You'll be the first to know."

Declan cleared his throat. "Tomorrow, we need to check the rest of the building. There's that locked back room. If we find a manager's key or something, we can see what's inside—could be offices, a supply room, who knows."

Lisa nodded. "I'll help you search for the key in the morning. The manager's station might be near the registers, or maybe in the upstairs office. We'll have to look carefully."

Jace stretched, arms behind his head. "We should probably also see if there are any vehicles left outside in workable condition. We might want an escape route."

Becca yawned. "Sounds like a plan. For now, can we have five minutes without apocalypse talk? My brain needs a break."

"Seconded," Tasha said, stifling her own yawn.

They agreed, letting the conversation drift to lighter topics—if anything could be considered light these days. Leslie recounted a ridiculous memory of chasing a deal on triple-coupon Tuesday before the outbreak. Edgar talked about a near-miss with a Doberman on his mail route, which somehow felt quaint compared to zombies. The group even shared a few quiet laughs, bonded by tragedy but also by the need to keep living.

Later, they bedded down. The store's second floor had large racks of tents, which they conveniently assembled in an open space near the balconies overlooking the first floor. This created a semblance of privacy as well as a vantage point to hear if anything snuck in below.

Becca claimed a small two-person tent, which she barely fit into without her head pressing against the canvas. She settled onto a sleeping bag, exhaustion weighing on her eyelids. The day's adrenaline rush finally tapered off, leaving her limbs heavy.

Just as she was drifting off, a quiet whisper came from outside the tent flap. "Becca? You awake?"

She frowned. "Yeah," she said softly, sitting up. "Come in." The flap rustled, and Declan poked his head in. She blinked in surprise. "Oh. Didn't expect you to—uh, hi?"

He cleared his throat, not meeting her eyes. "Sorry. Didn't mean to wake you."

She waved that off. "It's fine. What's up?"

He hesitated, gaze flicking around the tent's interior as though searching for words. Finally, he said, "I just wanted to, uh, apologize for earlier. I might have come off harsh with the doc. And... I realize that we're in this together. I shouldn't keep pushing you away."

Becca sat there, stunned. Declan, the ultimate stoic, was apologizing? She rubbed her eyes, making sure she wasn't dreaming. "It's fine," she managed. "I get it. You're trying to protect everyone."

He exhaled, shoulders dropping a fraction. "Yeah. I just... I saw how people can turn on each other in times like this. I want to trust you all, but it's not easy."

She offered a tentative smile. "Well, for what it's worth, you're a good guy to have around. Even if you're a grumpy butt. So thanks for keeping us alive."

He almost smiled—just a faint tug at the corners of his mouth. "Get some rest," he said softly, standing to leave. "Long day tomorrow."

She nodded, adjusting her sleeping bag. "Night, Declan."

He disappeared through the flap, leaving her alone with a swirl of conflicting emotions. She lay back, staring at the faint outlines of the store's ceiling above. She never expected to be leading a group of survivors, nor to be forging… well, whatever this was—a strange, tension-laced camaraderie with a man who seemed cut from granite.

Eventually, she let out a slow breath and closed her eyes. Tomorrow would bring new challenges—a locked room to explore, a suspiciously knowledgeable scientist to keep an eye on, and the daily threat of undead munchies. But for now, at least, they had hope. A new place to call home, better shoes, and maybe even the slimmest chance at a cure—if Dr. Hawthorne's research panned out.

"One day at a time," Becca murmured, drifting into sleep with the distant moans of the dead on the wind.

CHAPTER FOUR

Becca woke up to the rhythmic *thwack… thwack… thwack* of someone taking out their frustrations on a defenseless punching bag in the sporting goods store. She groaned, blinking the sleep from her eyes. Not that she'd had an especially restful night—sleeping in a tent on a store floor was only marginally better than a cardboard box.

Rolling over, she realized the tent flap was already unzipped, letting in the faint morning light. The store's overhead lights were off to conserve power, so it was mostly dim inside. A look at her watch said it was around 6:45 a.m. She grunted and sat up, wishing for the thousandth time that a Starbucks would magically appear.

No baristas in the apocalypse, she reminded herself grimly. *Just stale coffee grounds and leftover bottled water.* Still, they were better off here than at the ransacked grocery store. At least there were no rotting produce sections giving off that special *zombie-apocalypse stench.*

Yawning, she poked her head out of the tent, half-expecting to see Jace up to some mischief. Instead, across the store's open space, she spotted Declan repeatedly slamming his fists into a dusty punching bag that hung from a metal display stand. He was shirtless—naturally, because of course he'd be shirtless—and his upper body gleamed with sweat. The bag rattled with each impact. He must've been at it for a while, because every muscle in his back looked tense and defined in the morning light.

Becca gave a tiny snort, torn between being impressed and wanting to roll her eyes. *Because sure, we all do intense morning workouts while the rest of us are drooling in our sleep.* But she couldn't deny it was a *nice view*—and she was only human. A half-smile curled her lips before she called out:

"Hey, Officer McBroody. Trying to punch the apocalypse away?"

Declan spun at her voice, fists still raised, breath ragged. His dark hair clung to his forehead in damp strands. "Didn't know I had an audience," he muttered, slightly embarrassed.

Becca shrugged, unzipping her sleeping bag further and stepping out into the open. She was wearing a pair of sweatpants she'd scavenged from the store's exercise clothing section, along with a baggy T-shirt that read *"Get Fit or Die Tryin'."* She supposed it was an apt motto for the current world situation.

"Couldn't help it," she said. "You make so much noise hitting that bag, it's like you're trying to alert every zombie within five miles."

Declan rolled his eyes, grabbing a towel from a nearby bench. "I'm not that loud."

Just then, a raspy voice piped up from behind a tent: "I'd say you're at least *somewhat* loud, man." Out emerged Jace Carter, who looked thoroughly amused by the whole scene. "Thought we were trying to keep a low profile."

Declan tossed the towel over his shoulder, ignoring Jace's needling. "I needed to blow off steam."

Becca smirked. "And here I thought I was the only one who got antsy cooped up in here."

A beat of silence lingered, and for a moment, it felt like the trio was *almost* comfortable around each other —like a weird, dysfunctional family that had spent just enough time together to know each other's quirks. But inevitably, the tension reasserted itself: Declan still harbored his trust issues, Jace still delighted in pushing boundaries, and Becca kept them both on edge with her brashness.

"Is everyone else awake yet?" she asked, stretching her arms until her shoulders popped.

"Lisa and Edgar are scouting the store's perimeter," Jace replied, leaning against a nearby rack of baseball bats. "Leslie's rearranging her coupon folder in the camping section. And Dr. Hawthorne's messing with those test tubes in the breakroom—says he wants to check if any of them were compromised by the temperature change."

Becca blew out a breath. "Fun times. So. Another day in zombie paradise." She ran a hand over her face. "We need to figure out our next move. Like, *the* move. I don't want to keep bouncing from building to building until we run out of luck."

Declan nodded, retrieving his T-shirt from the floor. "Yeah, we can't keep living off scraps. We should talk about traveling out of the city." He tugged the shirt over his head, which Becca tried (and mostly failed) not to stare at. "Somewhere rural, away from the highest concentration of undead."

Jace snorted, a playful glint in his eyes. "What, like a *farm*? Gonna start raising zombie cows?"

Becca barked a laugh. "Zombie cows—there's a thought. But actually... a farm's not a bad idea. That was kind of at the back of my mind last night. You know, find some farmland with a house, grow crops if we can, keep the undead away with a big fence. Like one of those doomsday preppers used to build." She paused, a grin spreading. "We can finally have fresh veggies that aren't half-rotted. And hey, maybe we can even get some chickens. Because who doesn't like eggs?"

Declan crossed his arms. "We'd have to get our hands on a vehicle that's tough enough to handle off-road travel, carry supplies, and *not* break down at the worst moment."

Jace tapped his chin thoughtfully. "We saw a few trucks in the parking lot that might be workable. One or two looked like they hadn't been hotwired yet. We could scavenge around for keys… or I can *persuade* them." He wiggled his fingers, referencing his lockpicking/hotwiring skills.

Becca grinned. "So you want in on my farm fantasy, Carter? We can grow potatoes or something. Can't exactly rely on Twinkies forever."

He winked. "I'm game for anything that keeps us from starving. And I've always wanted to see you in overalls, if I'm being honest."

Declan cleared his throat, an eye-roll practically audible. "Let's gather everyone, make a plan. We'll need to do a major supply run—fuel, non-perishable food, ammo, anything we can cram into a vehicle. Then we'll attempt to leave the city. But we have to be careful. We don't know how badly the highways are blocked."

Becca clapped her hands, her inner snark shining through. "All right, fellas, let's do it. Operation Farm Life is a go. I shall hum 'Old MacDonald' while we mow down zombies. *E-I-E-I-O.*"

Jace snorted, and Declan just shook his head, muttering something about "Lord help us."

An hour later, the entire group gathered near the store's main registers, which had become their de facto meeting area. The morning sunlight filtered in through the cracked glass doors, and a few overhead skylights provided enough illumination to see without draining their limited battery lanterns.

Becca took center stage—apparently, she'd become the unofficial spokesperson. She liked to think it was because she was naturally charismatic, but it probably had more to do with her big mouth.

"All right, everyone," she began, clapping her hands for attention. "We've been here for, what, a week now? We've made it cozy, I'll give you that. But we're still stuck in a city full of zombies, and we're burning through supplies. So here's the new plan: we find a farm out in the boonies. We fix it up, grow some food, maybe raise a goat or two, and not get eaten. Sound good?"

Lisa—who looked more stressed than usual—frowned slightly. "And how do we know there's even a suitable farm out there?"

Becca shrugged. "We don't. But we know farmland *exists,* and there are fewer people out there. Fewer people means fewer zombies. Plus, we could theoretically defend a rural property better than a giant building with broken windows."

Leslie chimed in, hugging her coupon folder. "I'm not opposed to it. If it means fresh air and fewer rotting corpses…"

Edgar offered a thoughtful nod. "I used to deliver mail in some of the outskirts. Plenty of farmland. If we travel west, we might find something."

Marsha fiddled with the cuff of her sleeves. "What about, um, you know, the undead that are already out there?"

Declan answered, voice calm. "We'll still have to be on guard, but the density should be lower. All in all, it's safer than staying here indefinitely."

Jace rocked on his heels, arms folded. "So the big question: how do we get out of the city? Roads are blocked, cars are scattered all over. We probably need a *convoy* of sorts."

Becca snapped her fingers. "That's where the supply run comes in. We find a reliable truck, gather enough gas, food, and gear to last us at least a week of searching. We won't try to bulldoze straight out of the city in a day if it's too risky, but we'll have mobility. We can pivot if roads are jammed."

Lisa nodded slowly, biting her lip. "And we can't take too long, or the undead might swarm again. We should do it soon."

"Right," said Becca. "So let's get organized." She pulled out a small notepad. "We'll need a scouting party—three or four people—who are comfortable with being on the move, possibly bashing undead heads if needed. They'll gather gas, food, anything else worth taking. Meanwhile, the rest stay here, fortify this place for another day, and pack up. Once the scouting party returns, we load the truck and go."

Dr. Hawthorne, who'd been oddly quiet, cleared his throat. "What about medical supplies? If I'm going to keep researching, I'll need any diagnostic tools I can find. Maybe a portable generator?"

Declan's gaze flicked to him. "That might be secondary to survival, but if we find anything that helps you, we'll grab it."

Hawthorne nodded, resigned. "Fair enough."

Lisa exhaled. "All right. Let's do it."

Thus, the meeting adjourned, and everyone scattered to prepare. Becca, Declan, and Jace volunteered for the scouting party—no surprises there. They were the most combat-ready, and possibly the most reckless. A lethal combination, but also effective.

Not wanting a replay of her blister fiasco, Becca geared up in her newly acquired boots, which were sturdy and a half-size too big but still a million times better than those cursed flats. She donned a lightweight jacket and slung her trusty baseball bat over her shoulder with a makeshift strap. They had discovered a small trove of arms in the locked firearms section, but Becca found she still preferred melee—less chance of attracting a horde with gunshots.

Jace carried a shotgun strapped to his back (an "in case of emergency" weapon) and a wickedly sharp hunting knife at his hip. Declan, meanwhile, opted for a handgun—one they'd found with limited ammo—and his trusty crowbar. He insisted on using firearms sparingly because once they ran out of bullets, they were out for good.

They exited through a side door, leaving Lisa, Edgar, Hawthorne, Leslie, Tasha, and Marsha to hold down the fort. The day was bright, the sun inching toward its zenith. The street outside the sporting goods store was a patchwork of crashed vehicles and scattered debris. They breathed in that stale air, tinged with decay, and scanned for any nearby threats.

"It's too quiet," Jace muttered, flipping his knife in a small flourish. "I hate when it's quiet."

Declan shot him a look. "You'd rather be overrun?"

"I'd rather not be bored," Jace retorted with a grin.

Becca snickered. "Let's not tempt fate, people." She gestured to the parking lot. "All right, let's check for a truck we can salvage. If we can't find anything here, we might have to head down the street."

Sure enough, they found a hulking pickup in the corner of the lot—a battered old beast that, surprisingly, had no smashed windows. The keys weren't inside, though, so Jace immediately set to his hotwiring routine. "Give me a sec," he mumbled, rummaging under the steering column. Declan stood guard, scanning for movement, while Becca hovered nearby, anxious.

After a few minutes of tinkering, the engine coughed to life. "Bingo," Jace said, looking smug.

Becca let out a relieved breath. "Now we just need to fill up the tank. I doubt it has a full load of gas."

Declan peered at the gauge. "Quarter tank, maybe less. We'll need at least a few gallons to ensure we can get out of the city." He looked at Jace. "You handle that, Carter?"

Jace hopped out of the truck, dusting off his hands. "Sure thing, Dad." Declan scowled at the nickname, but said nothing.

"Let's push forward a few blocks," Becca suggested. "There's that convenience store we passed on the way here—it had a small gas station out front. If there's any left, we can siphon it."

Declan agreed, so the trio set off on foot again, leaving the truck for the moment. They preferred to clear the area on foot first, ensure no major threats were lurking nearby.

They moved quietly through the rubble-strewn roads, stepping over broken glass and abandoned luggage. Occasionally, they spotted a lone zombie staggering in the distance, but a well-timed crouch behind a car or a quick detour kept them out of sight. After weeks in the apocalypse, they'd learned that avoiding confrontation was often safer than picking a fight with every undead.

In the hush of the midday, a faint barking noise suddenly cut through the stillness. Becca froze, pulse jumping. "Was that… a dog?"

Declan tilted his head. "Sounds like it." Another bark echoed, frantic and high-pitched.

Jace frowned. "Must be nearby. Could be cornered by zombies."

A pang of empathy shot through Becca. An actual dog, alive in this mess? She found herself moving before she fully thought it through. "We have to help it."

Declan grabbed her arm. "Hold on. We can't risk our lives for some dog."

She turned, glaring fiercely. "You see how messed up the world is, right? If we don't do *some* decent thing, what's even the point?" She shrugged him off. "It might not be able to protect itself. We can't just leave it."

His jaw tightened. "We have a mission here."

She scowled. "Yeah, well, maybe my mission is to save a dog if I can."

Jace let out a soft chuckle. "I'm with Her Highness. Let's at least check it out. Could be worth it—maybe it's a good guard dog or something."

Declan sighed, rubbing his temples. "Fine. But be careful. If it's swarmed, we don't go charging in like idiots."

Becca grinned, already following the sound. "Oh, come on, living dangerously is my specialty."

They found the source of the barking near a narrow alley blocked by a toppled dumpster. A small, scruffy mutt—somewhere between a terrier and a fuzzball—scrambled on top of the dumpster, snarling at two zombies that were reaching up at it with bony hands. The dog was cornered, nowhere to go but a fire escape ladder that was too high for it to reach.

Becca felt her heart clench at the sight. "Poor thing," she muttered.

"Two zombies," Declan murmured. "We can take them. Quietly, though."

Jace nodded, flipping his knife. "I'll grab the one on the left."

Becca adjusted her bat, eyes burning with determination. "I'll handle the other."

They moved in simultaneously, creeping around the side of the alley to get a better angle. Jace lunged first, plunging his knife into the back of the zombie's skull with a sickening crunch. The creature collapsed, releasing a wet gurgle. The other turned, sensing movement.

Becca swung her bat in a swift arc. The zombie took the blow to the shoulder, spinning it around, but not enough to finish it. It snarled, half of its jaw flapping loose. She grimaced, stepping forward for a finishing strike. *Crack.* The zombie went down, motionless.

The dog, still perched on the dumpster, barked at them furiously, as if uncertain whether they were also threats.

"Hey, buddy," Becca cooed, her voice soft. She set her bat aside, raising her hands placatingly. "It's okay, we got rid of the bad guys."

The dog cocked its head, trembling with leftover adrenaline. Becca inched closer, speaking in soothing tones. She'd always liked animals more than people—less drama, in her opinion. As she extended a hand to let the dog sniff, Jace hung back, shrugging. "You're seriously adopting a dog in the apocalypse?"

"Duh," she shot back, eyes still on the furry creature. "Zombies can't be that much worse than my old landlord." The dog sniffed her hand uncertainly.

But at that very moment, a rasping moan drifted down the alley. Becca snapped her head around. Another zombie, presumably drawn by the commotion, rounded the corner, eyes locked on them. It shuffled forward, faster than she expected. Before Jace or Declan could react, it lunged.

"Becca, watch out!" Declan roared.

Too late. The zombie careened into her, knocking her off-balance. She stumbled, jarring her bad foot (the one still recovering from wearing flats for weeks). As she fell, the dog yelped and jumped away, landing on the dumpster's far edge. Becca tried to twist, to grab her bat, but the zombie's weight pressed her down.

She felt claws—once human hands—dig into her jacket. *No, no, no.* A surge of pure panic flooded her. She wrestled with it, adrenaline pumping. Out of the corner of her eye, she saw Jace rushing forward, knife raised. But the zombie snapped its jaws, and in that split second, *teeth sank into her left forearm.*

She cried out in shock and pain, adrenaline spiking into terror. She brought her knee up, shoving the zombie away with a forceful kick. Jace arrived a heartbeat later, driving his knife into the zombie's skull. It collapsed in a grotesque heap.

But the damage was done. Becca's arm throbbed, warm blood seeping through her torn jacket sleeve. She clapped a hand over the wound, eyes wide with horror. *Bitten.* The one thing she'd dreaded since this whole nightmare began. She heard the dog barking wildly, as if it sensed something was terribly wrong.

Declan and Jace hovered over her, faces stricken. "Becca—oh, *hell*," Jace muttered, voice trembling.

Declan's expression went grim, the color draining from his features. "We— we have to…"

Becca's mind spun. She'd seen too many people turned from bites. The virus spread fast through direct contact. She was as good as dead, right? Or undead, to be more precise. Still, something in her refused to accept it. The pain, the shock—it was all swirling into a single knot in her chest.

She let out a ragged breath, forcing calm into her voice. "Patch me up," she demanded, wincing. "Just—tie something around it."

Jace hesitated. "Becca, if you turn—"

"Don't. Finish that sentence," she snarled through clenched teeth.

Declan's jaw was tight. "We know how this goes. Anyone who gets bitten—"

Becca saw the flicker in his eyes, recognized the hard decision forming. She'd seen him do the same with other infected survivors who had no chance. She jerked her gaze to him. "Don't you *dare*," she hissed. She could see the tension in his posture, like he was ready to draw his handgun. "Don't you dare try to put me down like a dog."

He inhaled sharply. "If we don't— you could turn, and then you'd kill us. We have a responsibility to—"

She didn't let him finish. Rage and defiance exploded in her chest. Before he could reach for the gun, Becca's free hand balled into a fist, and she *punched him square in the face*. She had some momentum behind it too, so Declan staggered back, cursing. Jace let out a startled yelp.

"I am *not* going out like this," she snarled. Her eyes blazed. "You try to shoot me, and I'll… I'll kill you first!"

Declan raised a hand to his lip, which bled slightly where she'd struck him. His eyes flickered between anger and shock. "Becca, be reasonable—"

"I am being reasonable!" Her voice cracked. She clutched her bleeding arm, grimacing. "We've seen people die from bites, sure. But we've also heard stories about rare immunities, right? Or slower infections. Maybe I'll get lucky. Maybe I'll fight it. We *have* a scientist, for God's sake. Let me at least try!"

Jace looked torn, knife still in hand. "Are you sure? If you turn, we have to stop you from—"

"Then stop me *if* it happens!" she shouted, tears pricking at the corners of her eyes. "But not before. I deserve a chance. And if you try anything, I swear, I'll come back as a zombie just to haunt your asses."

A thick silence settled. The dog whimpered from atop the dumpster, as if asking what the hell was going on.

Finally, Declan exhaled, dropping his gaze. "Fine," he said, voice strained. "We'll do it your way. But if — if it comes to it, I won't hesitate."

Becca swallowed hard, nodding. She felt lightheaded, adrenaline ebbing. "Fair enough."

Jace tore a length of cloth from his shirt, wrapping it tightly around her wound. She hissed in pain, but held still. Blood seeped through the makeshift bandage, but at least it was contained for now.

"You okay to walk?" Jace asked softly.

She tried to stand, heart pounding. The alley spun around her. "I— sure," she lied, knees wobbling.

Declan, nursing his jaw, pressed a hand to her shoulder to steady her. She almost jerked away on principle, but she was too dizzy. "We need to get back to the store," he said. "Dr. Hawthorne might— he could do something."

Becca gritted her teeth. "Yeah. Let's— let's go. Quick." She glanced at the trembling dog, which hadn't moved from the dumpster. "I'm not leaving it here."

"You can't seriously—" Declan began, but caught himself. He sighed. "Fine, I'll get it."

He moved slowly, coaxing the terrified pup with a piece of jerky from his pack. Eventually, the dog let him lift it down from the dumpster. It trembled in his arms, big brown eyes darting nervously. "Got it," he muttered, handing it over to Jace, who accepted it gingerly.

Becca attempted a shaky smile at the sight. "See? Good deed done. Now let's haul ass."

They made their way back to the sporting goods store as fast as possible. Each step jarred Becca's arm, sending waves of pain up her shoulder. A cold sweat drenched her forehead, and her vision blurred at the edges. *Stay awake, stay awake,* she chanted internally, refusing to show weakness.

But the virus was already working, or maybe it was just blood loss. Her limbs felt sluggish, her breathing shallow. By the time they were within a block of the store, the dog's frantic whining was the only sound she could process. Jace kept glancing at her, eyes full of worry, while Declan kept his distance, brow furrowed.

She stumbled across some rubble, heart thundering. A wave of nausea rolled over her. The ground tilted ominously, and she willed herself to keep going. "I'm fine," she mumbled, though no one had asked.

They slipped through the side entrance. Lisa and the others rushed to meet them, faces contorting in alarm when they saw Becca's pale complexion and the bloody bandage on her forearm.

"She got bit?" Lisa gasped, eyes darting between them.

Becca tried to respond, but her voice failed her. She swayed unsteadily, black spots dancing across her vision.

"Help her!" Tasha shrieked. "Where's Hawthorne?"

Marsha ran off, presumably to find the doctor. Edgar cursed under his breath, grabbing a stack of clean cloth. Leslie let out a strangled sob, pressing a hand to her mouth.

Becca's knees buckled, adrenaline finally giving way. Declan darted forward, catching her before she hit the ground. She looked up at him, vision swimming. Part of her wanted to curse him out for even thinking of putting her down. Another part wanted to cling to him like a lifeline. She settled for slumping in his arms.

"Hang on," he murmured, voice strained. "Don't you dare—"

She mustered a weak grin, blood pounding in her ears. "I… told you… I'm not going out like this…" Her world tilted, darkness creeping in. "You— you big jerk…"

And then she passed out.

CHAPTER FIVE

Somewhere between dreams of chocolate-dipped Doritos and nightmares of zombies munching on her limbs, Becca Montgomery blinked awake to the sound of hushed bickering and soft footsteps.

At first, she couldn't figure out where she was. The ceiling overhead looked familiar enough—crisscrossing steel beams, dangling lights. Right, she was in the sporting goods store. But she remembered passing out, blood gushing from a bite on her arm...

Wait. Her eyes snapped open wider. The bite! She jolted upright, expecting waves of feverish agony or, at the very least, a rotted patch of flesh. Instead, she felt... good. Really, really good. Almost *too* good. A hint of confusion flickered in her chest.

Her body, oddly refreshed, offered no protest as she sat up. In fact, she felt an electric buzz of energy zinging through her limbs. Her mouth wasn't dry; her head wasn't throbbing. No aches, no chills, no weird twitching. On a scale of 1 to "I'm about to become a drooling zombie," she was at a zero.

She slowly pushed the thin blanket off and glanced down at her arm. The bandage was still there—someone had changed it, apparently—but no visible blood oozed through. Becca sniffed. *No rotting stench, no pus. Just… normal, if a bit stiff.*

"Hello?" she called, voice surprisingly steady. The room spun slightly, the leftover adrenaline from last night's fiasco flirting with her awareness. But she recovered in an instant.

Her voice must've carried because Jace Carter poked his head around the corner. "Holy *shit*," he mumbled, eyes widening. Then he turned and hollered, "She's awake! And definitely *not* a brain-eater!"

Footsteps thundered, and a whole crowd bustled into the store's makeshift infirmary space: Lisa, Edgar, Leslie, Tasha, Marsha, Dr. Hawthorne, and—after a beat—Declan. They all stared at Becca like she'd sprouted another head. She looked back, blinking in confusion.

"Uh… hey, guys?" she ventured. "You're looking at me like I'm sprouting tentacles or something."

Marsha timidly stepped forward, fussing with her sleeves. "Becca, we— we thought you might not make it. That bite was… you were in bad shape."

Lisa nodded, eyes shining with relief. "You had a fever for a few hours and were in and out of consciousness. Dr. Hawthorne did what he could, but… well, we were preparing for the worst."

Becca's stomach did a somersault. She carefully peeled back the gauze on her arm. Underneath, the skin looked… *pink*, maybe a little tender, but *definitely not* the necrotic mess she expected. She touched it gingerly and felt only a mild twinge.

Hawthorne cleared his throat, stepping closer. His rumpled lab coat had fresh coffee stains on it (or possibly leftover apocalypse grime). He looked both baffled and intensely curious. "You, uh—your vitals are now normal. Actually, better than normal. I… I can't explain it yet." He fiddled with his glasses. "You were delirious last night, then *bam*, this morning you're stable. No sign of infection."

Becca ran a hand through her hair, momentarily startled by its length. *Weird,* it seemed… longer? She stared at a dark strand. She'd never had hair that grew fast, but it looked thicker, shinier. Not to mention, *holy smokes*, her nails—usually brittle—looked smoother. *What the—?*

Jace sidled up, offering her an exaggerated once-over. "Congrats," he drawled, his tone both teasing and awed. "You're a zombie now."

Becca planted her hands on her hips—realizing with a jolt that her hips felt… fuller. *Huh.* She decided not to dwell on that just yet and instead fixed Jace with a smirk. "Then why am I still hot?" she asked, feigning ego. But deep down, genuine bewilderment churned. "Zombies are usually, you know, rotting. Last I checked, my face is *radiant* right now."

Leslie snorted, rummaging in her coupon folder out of habit. "She's not lying; that skin looks like she's been hitting the day spa. Totally not fair. I still have under-eye bags from *pre*-apocalypse."

Becca couldn't help but chuckle. "You guys are messing with me, right?" But as she glanced around, seeing their stunned expressions, she realized they weren't joking. She wasn't the only one noticing her drastically improved complexion, the extra curve in her waist, or the luscious new wave in her hair.

Declan hung back from the group, arms crossed over his chest. A bruised mark decorated his jaw where she'd clocked him in panic the day before. He looked more *concerned* than anything. She locked eyes with him, and something fluttered in her stomach. She remembered the raging argument, the punch. *He wanted to put me down.* Or maybe he just felt like he *had* to. Her mind still reeled with conflicting emotions.

He spoke softly, voice edged with relief but guarded. "How… do you *feel*? Any cravings for… flesh?"

Becca wrinkled her nose. "Ew, no. I mean, I'd kill for a milkshake, but that's about it. Also, I feel like a million bucks." She hopped off the cot, ignoring the wave of dizziness, and promptly stood. She glanced around. "So, yeah, that's weird, right?"

Hawthorne raised a cautious hand. "Weird is an understatement. If you don't mind, I'd like to run a quick exam. Check your temperature, maybe a small blood sample. You're— you're an anomaly, Becca."

She gave a shaky laugh. "Yeah, sure, doc. Whatever. Just— give me a sec, okay?" She turned to Lisa. "So I was out cold all night? Did I try to bite anyone in my sleep?"

Lisa shook her head vigorously. "No. If anything, you just babbled nonsense—something about dog treats and building a chicken coop. We, uh, kept watch in shifts in case you, you know, turned. But you never did."

Becca breathed a sigh of relief. "Great. I'm unbelievably hungry, though. Are there any snacks left, or did we blow through them all?"

Edgar cracked a smile. "We saved you some soup. Marsha heated up a leftover can. It's lukewarm now, but better than nothing."

Her stomach rumbled audibly at the mention of soup. "Bring on the soup. Then, doc, you can poke me with your needles or whatever."

The group parted, letting her move more freely. Tasha offered an encouraging half-smile, handing her a water bottle. Meanwhile, the dog she'd rescued—scruffy and adorable—poked its nose out from behind some boxes. It let out a tiny bark, tail wagging hesitantly. *At least the dog survived,* Becca mused, feeling a wave of relief.

She noticed Dr. Hawthorne's intrigued stare again, so she turned on her heel. "All right, I'll let you run your tests in a minute, but first—food. I almost died, so I think I deserve some soup without being pricked and prodded just yet."

Hawthorne bobbed his head, stepping back. "Of course. Though, if you experience any dizziness—"

"I'll holler," she finished, voice tinged with humor. "Let me just have five minutes of normalcy, doc."

Becca parked herself at a folding table near the store's front windows, sipping from a dented can of soup that Marsha had warmed up. It tasted bland but glorious after her near-death experience. Jace hovered near her, arms crossed, occasionally shooting her these quick, curious glances—like he was expecting her to sprout fangs any second.

She smirked at him over the rim of the soup can. "You keep looking at me like I'm about to peel my face off."

He shrugged, not even denying it. "Can you blame me? You look too healthy, Monty. People don't usually come back from zombie bites *looking better* than before."

She snorted. "Maybe the virus liked me so much, it decided to give me a makeover."

Jace's lips quirked into a half-grin. "Hey, if that's the case, maybe I should volunteer for a nibble. Think it'd give me six-pack abs?"

"Gross," she deadpanned, rolling her eyes. But inside, her mind whirled with questions. *How* was she so fine? She decided to push that aside for a moment and just revel in the fact that she wasn't undead.

Declan approached, clearing his throat. He stopped a foot away, jaw tense as if he had a million things to say but didn't know how to start. Finally, he settled on: "I'm glad you're okay." His gaze flitted to her bandaged arm. "For what it's worth, I— I'm sorry about… y'know."

Becca swallowed, setting the soup can down. "Sorry about wanting to shoot me, or sorry about letting me live?" she asked, her voice intentionally flippant.

His face tightened. "I— you know I was just… doing what I thought was necessary. I can't risk everyone's safety for one person, no matter how—" He stopped short, biting off the words.

"—how *annoying* I am? Or *awesome*? Gotta be more specific, Graves," she teased, though her chest felt tight.

"Both," he said quietly, mouth quirked in a hint of a smile. Then his expression went somber. "But seriously, I'm sorry I tried to— well, I considered— you know."

She mustered a small smile in return, though her heart was pounding. "Yeah, well, good thing you didn't, or we wouldn't be having this conversation."

He nodded. A moment of charged silence passed between them. Then Jace, ever the mischief-maker, loudly slurped from a water bottle. "Aww, group hug?"

Declan shot him a glare. "Shut it, Carter."

But Becca laughed, a genuine laugh that eased the tension. She took another spoonful of soup. "You two are the weirdest comedic duo I've ever seen."

"Dibs on not being the straight man," Jace quipped.

Declan rolled his eyes, and Becca smothered another giggle. Despite everything—the near-death fiasco, the uncertain future—she felt a surprising lightness. Maybe it was just the adrenaline high, or the fact that her body was *buzzing* with energy she couldn't explain.

After the soup break, Dr. Hawthorne cornered her in the store's breakroom-turned-lab. She sat on managed to scavenge.

"All right, I'll just take a small blood sample," he said, voice trembling with a mix of excitement and nerves. "You sure you're okay with this?"

Becca shrugged. "Go for it. Just don't drain me, Dr. Frankenstein."

He chuckled nervously, drawing a few milliliters of blood from her uninjured arm. "Honestly, I'm half expecting you to show some mutated RBCs or bizarre viral markers." He set the vial aside, labeling it meticulously. "If you truly fought off the infection, it might mean you have some form of immunity."

"Or I'm a ticking time bomb," she said wryly, trying to keep her voice light. "But for now, I feel… *great*. Weirdly great. My hair's, like, an inch longer."

Hawthorne nodded, a faraway look in his eyes. "I can run some basic tests—though I don't have advanced equipment. But maybe I can see if your WBC count is elevated or if there's any sign of viral load. It might take a while, and I can only do so much with these supplies."

She hopped off the stool, still marveling at how effortless movement felt. "Whatever. Test away. In the meantime, I want to see if I can still swing a bat without keeling over."

Hawthorne scribbled notes in a small notebook. "No heavy exertion yet, please. Just in case."

Becca smirked. "Sure, doc. I'll keep it light. Maybe just a gentle decapitation or two if we get a zombie visitor."

She left him to his research, feeling a flicker of both hope and apprehension. *If* she was immune— or something close to it—did that mean there was a chance for a cure? Or was she just a freakish anomaly?

Midday arrived, bringing a sweltering heat that seeped through the store's partially broken air conditioning. The group rummaged for battery-powered fans in the camping section, trying to keep somewhat cool.

Becca, restless from her bizarre new energy, wandered toward the store's front entrance. Jace was there, tinkering with a pair of binoculars and keeping watch on the street. The dog—a fluffy terrier mix she'd temporarily dubbed "Chewie," because of its half-growling barks—sat by his feet.

"How's it looking out there?" she asked, leaning over to peer through the glass doors.

Jace shrugged. "Nothing major. A few shamblers down the block. No big hordes."

Becca nodded. The city beyond still looked like a disaster zone—overturned cars, trash everywhere, windows shattered. But with every passing day, it seemed the zombies moved around more aimlessly, scattering in smaller packs. *Or maybe we're just lucky this area's relatively clear,* she thought.

Impulsively, she decided to test something. She pressed her palm to the glass, gazing at a lone zombie about thirty feet away. It stumbled near a broken lamppost, sniffing the air like a confused predator.

"Hey, can you open the door a crack?" she asked, heart thudding.

Jace's brows shot up. "Why on earth would I—oh, no, no, no. You are *not* stepping out there."

Becca flashed a confident grin. "Relax. I just want to see something. I have this *theory*."

"Care to share before I risk letting a zombie waltz in?"

She rolled her eyes. "I think it might not *care* if I step out there. Like, maybe it won't attack me."

Jace gave her a *are you insane?* look. "You're nuts, Monty. Or suicidal. This is a terrible idea."

"Probably, but I gotta know," she insisted, that brashness flaring. "Don't worry, I won't go far. If it charges me, I'll scurry back in and you can slam the door. Sound good?"

Jace looked like he wanted to argue, but curiosity gleamed in his eyes. "Fine," he sighed dramatically. "But if you get gnawed on again, you're on your own."

"I'm touched by your concern," she said sarcastically. Then she gripped the door handle.

He opened it a few inches, scanning the street for immediate threats. When none emerged, he let her slip outside. The dog barked, staying behind with Jace, tail wagging anxiously. She stood on the concrete stoop, the blazing sun on her face, and spotted the lone zombie a short distance away.

Her heart hammered. *This is stupid. This is so, so stupid.* But an inexplicable confidence—or maybe foolishness—propelled her forward.

She took three steps past the threshold, brandishing her baseball bat at her side. The zombie sniffed, turned slowly, as if noticing her. She held her breath, tensing, preparing to dash back in. Jace hovered in the doorway, gun at the ready.

The zombie let out a low moan but… didn't rush her. Instead, it just sort of *stared*. Its milky eyes flicked over her, then away, almost disinterested. *Weird,* she thought, goosebumps crawling over her skin.

She took another step forward, heart in her throat. The zombie swayed, letting out a small grunt. Then it shuffled off, heading down the block like she was no big deal. Her jaw dropped slightly.

Jace's muffled exclamation drifted from behind. "Holy *crap*. It's like it doesn't even see you as human."

She turned, adrenaline flooding her veins, a slow grin stretching across her lips. "I— I think we can mark this down as the weirdest day of my life," she said. Then she hustled back inside, slamming the door behind her.

Jace locked it, staring at her like she was an alien. "So you can waltz around with zombies now?"

She blew out a breath, feeling a strange surge of pride and revulsion. "I guess so. Or at least *some* of them. That might come in handy?"

He nodded slowly. "Yeah, if we ever need a decoy or infiltration. But damn… you sure you're not undead?"

She touched her chest, feeling her heartbeat thumping. "Pretty sure. Still breathing, no rotting. Just a freak of nature, I guess."

Declan marched up, having witnessed the tail end of the scene from inside. "What the hell was that?" he snapped, looking alarmed. "You *let* her walk out there alone?"

Jace shrugged defensively. "Hey, it was her crazy idea. She's apparently Ms. Indestructible now."

Becca waved her free hand. "Chill, Graves. I'm fine. Zombie didn't even try to munch on me."

His eyes narrowed, jaw clenched. "That's exactly what worries me. The rules changed. And I hate not knowing why."

She bristled, arms folded over her chest. "Sorry my existence breaks the rules for you. Next time, I'll do the courtesy of turning into a mindless corpse, just to keep things consistent."

He let out a frustrated growl, rubbing the bridge of his nose. "That's not what I mean. I just… it's a lot to process. If zombies ignore you, it means you're… *one of them* in some way. Or at least partially. Who knows what that could do to you in the long run?"

A tense hush followed. Even Jace looked uneasy. Becca felt her chest tighten. *Am I half-zombie? Is that the truth?*

"Doc will figure it out," she said finally, forcing a breezy tone. "Until then, let's not freak out. I'm still me, okay?"

Declan exhaled, some of the tension leaving his posture. "Yeah. Fine. Just… don't do stunts like that without warning us."

She saluted playfully, though her insides churned. "Aye, aye, Captain Killjoy."

The rest of the afternoon dragged in that lazy, apocalyptic way. The group was abuzz with speculation: some were elated that Becca might be *immune*, others were creeped out by her new zombie-befriending abilities. Hawthorne doubled his efforts to analyze her blood. Jace hovered around, making jokes about her "zombie VIP pass." Leslie asked for skincare tips, half-joking, half-serious. Tasha gave Becca wide-eyed stares, like she was a goddess or a ticking time bomb, or both.

Meanwhile, Becca tried to distract herself by helping re-inventory the store's resources. She and Lisa sorted through boxes of flashlights, lanterns, camping gear—stuff they'd need for the planned exodus to farmland. The dog sat next to them, napping on a fleece blanket. Every so often, Becca would scratch its ears, grateful it was safe.

Around mid-afternoon, Declan found her in the aisle of fishing rods and kayaks, rummaging for anything useful. He paused, watching her juggle a small cooler and a bundle of tarps. Finally, he offered to help, taking the gear from her arms.

"Thanks," she said softly, a wave of awkwardness passing over them. She couldn't help but notice the bruise on his jaw from her punch—evidence of her panic and his near-execution of her. "Sorry about that," she mumbled, gesturing to his bruised face. "I… had a rough moment."

He touched the bruise lightly. "It's fine. I deserved it."

"Eh, maybe just half-deserved," she teased, but the humor fell flat. She shifted her weight, biting her lower lip. "Listen, do you… trust me? Now that I'm… whatever I am?"

He met her gaze. "I want to," he said simply. "It's not easy to unlearn everything we know about bites and infections, but you… you're an exception." He hesitated, then added, "I don't want you to think I'm the enemy. I'm just trying to protect everyone."

A pang of guilt tugged at her. "Yeah, I get it. And you'll protect them from me if you have to."

A grim nod. "Yes. But let's hope it never comes to that."

She exhaled, offering a small smile. "Deal."

They stood there for a beat longer, words unsaid hanging in the air. Then he cleared his throat. "We, uh, have a meeting in half an hour to finalize the plan to leave the city. You should be there."

Becca nodded, her heart fluttering. "Right. Time to build that dream farm with all the chickens, right?"

He chuckled softly, some tension melting from his shoulders. "Something like that."

She watched him go, a swirl of emotions lodged in her chest. She found herself wishing for simpler times—like just a few weeks ago, when the biggest problem was restocking shelves. But if there was one thing she'd learned, it was that the apocalypse had no mercy for nostalgia. She'd have to keep rolling with the punches, or become one of the mindless undead. *Now, apparently, they don't even want to eat me.* She shuddered at the surreal thought.

That evening, everyone gathered around the sporting goods store's central display—once a place to show off new camping gear, now a makeshift conference table. They'd laid out a large city map, plus any other relevant scraps of info they could find on roads and farmland.

Becca, freshly energized despite the day's events, stood near the map, arms folded. Jace lounged next to her, idly spinning a hunting knife. Declan occupied the opposite side of the table, posture rigid, crowbar leaning against a shelf behind him. Lisa, Edgar, Leslie, Tasha, Marsha, and Hawthorne formed a semi-circle, each wearing varied expressions of hope and anxiety.

"All right," Lisa said, tapping a pen on the map. "We're here, on the west side of the city. The farmland we're considering is out here"—she pointed to an area about twenty miles away—"though we're not sure how cleared it is. We might have to pick a path through back roads."

Declan nodded, leaning in. "We have two vehicles that seem workable: the old pickup truck Jace hotwired, and a smaller SUV we found with the keys inside. If we can fuel them both, we can transport most of our supplies and everyone in two trips—assuming we keep them close together on the road."

Edgar cleared his throat. "I can drive one if necessary. I've driven mail trucks all over. Not that it's the same as a pickup, but I'm comfortable behind the wheel."

"Then we just need enough gas," Jace chimed. "We found that small gas station a few blocks away, but it's risky. There might be only a little left. We'll have to scavenge."

Becca pressed her lips together. "We should do that tomorrow morning, early, when the zombies are less active. Once we have fuel, we load up and head out. It's not that complicated—just terrifying."

Leslie sighed, hugging her coupon folder. "And if we get stuck on the highway or a back road?"

"We get unstuck," Jace said with a cocky grin, tapping his knife on the table. "We have *some* ammo, crowbars, knives. We can clear the occasional blockade. And we have Monty here, who apparently can walk past zombies without them blinking."

Becca winced. "I'm not exactly bulletproof. If we come across hostile *humans*, that's a different story."

"We'll handle it," Declan said firmly, meeting her gaze. "Safety in numbers."

Dr. Hawthorne stepped forward, adjusting his glasses. "I'd like to bring my samples, notes… everything I can. If— if we can find a stable place out there, I might set up a small lab area. Keep researching. Maybe replicate your immunity, Becca."

She nodded. "Sure. Whatever you need. Just don't turn me into a pincushion."

He gave a tight-lipped smile. "I'll do my best to keep the pincushioning minimal."

Lisa cleared her throat, finalizing the plan. "So. Early morning, we siphon and scavenge for gas. We come back, load the vehicles, then drive out of the city. Everyone's on high alert. We *stick together.* No last-minute heroics unless absolutely necessary."

The group nodded, tension thrumming in the air. Becca felt it too. This was the big move. Their shot at leaving the city's undead chaos behind for a possibly greener (if uncertain) future. She'd be lying if she said she wasn't nervous. But she was also *ready*—and, for some strange reason, she felt unstoppable.

They decided to rest early, wanting a full night's sleep before the big move. Becca found herself lying in a borrowed sleeping bag near the store's second-floor balcony. Overhead, a broken skylight let in moonlight, illuminating the racks of kayaks and tents in a ghostly glow.

She couldn't sleep. Her mind buzzed with the day's revelations: her bizarre immunity, her newfound *glow-up*, the way zombies basically shrugged at her presence. She tossed and turned, eventually deciding to get up and wander around.

As she reached the store's edge, she spotted a familiar silhouette leaning against the railing, staring out into the night. Declan. Of course. He turned when he heard her footsteps, shadows dancing across his face.

"Couldn't sleep either, huh?" she ventured softly.

He shook his head, gaze drifting to the empty street outside. "Too much on my mind."

She sidled up beside him, resting her arms on the railing. For a few moments, they just stood there, listening to the faint moans of distant zombies carried on the wind, the rustle of debris in the street below.

Finally, Declan spoke, voice quiet. "I'm sorry this happened to you. The bite, I mean. Even if it turned out… well, you know, *positive*, sort of."

She let out a soft chuckle. "Better than the alternative. But yeah, me too." She chewed her lip. "You really think we can make it out there? Find a place, settle down, maybe even farm?"

His lips twitched in a ghost of a smile. "I think we can try. It's better than waiting around here to starve or get overrun."

She exhaled, a flutter of nerves flickering in her chest. "I just… I have this feeling everything's about to change. This immunity thing—whatever it is—makes me wonder if I'm even still *human*. Or if I'm something else entirely."

He turned to her, brow furrowed. "You're still you, Becca. You're still cracking jokes, annoying me… you're still breathing, have a heartbeat." He hesitated, eyes softening. "That's enough for me."

Her heart did a funny little flip. She remembered how close they'd come to a darker outcome. Impulsively, she reached out, placing a hand on his shoulder. "Thanks," she said, voice thick. "For, you know, not blowing my brains out."

A self-deprecating smile tugged at his lips. "You can punch me again if you need to."

She laughed softly, the tension in the air shifting into something warmer. The moonlight caught the bruise on his jaw. She felt a pang of guilt and sympathy. Without fully thinking it through, she gently pressed her fingertips to the bruise, as if that might soothe it. He inhaled sharply, but didn't pull away.

"Sorry," she murmured again.

He shrugged, voice low. "I'll live."

They stood like that for a moment longer, the world outside eerily still except for the wandering dead. Then Becca withdrew her hand, clearing her throat. "I, uh, should get some sleep. Big day tomorrow."

Declan nodded, releasing a breath. "Right. Goodnight, Montgomery."

"Night, Graves."

She turned and made her way back to her sleeping bag, pulse hammering. *Stupid heart, calm down.* She told herself tomorrow would be a big day, full of threats and chaos. She'd need her rest. But the silly grin she couldn't wipe off her face lingered, even as she laid down and drifted off into fitful dreams.

CHAPTER SIX

Despite their grand scheme to leave at the crack of dawn, the group's actual departure from the sporting goods store took considerably longer than planned. Between hunting for more batteries, double-checking ammo, and arguing over which snacks to pack, it was nearly lunchtime before Becca Montgomery and her ragtag crew started loading up their two rickety vehicles.

For once, Becca felt zero lingering pain in her arm from the zombie bite—because, apparently, *she'd beaten the virus.* She still didn't quite understand how, but the bizarre side effects (like her hair's sudden lusciousness) were downright surreal. Her reflection in a cracked side mirror showed smooth skin, bright eyes, and a definite *increase in curves* that practically made her GoodMax polo threaten to burst. She wasn't complaining, but it was *weird*.

Declan Graves, ex-cop and resident brooder, hovered beside the pickup truck, scowling at a city map. "We'll take Route 49 west. With luck, we can bypass those blockades. That is, if we don't run into any new ones."

Jace Carter, ex-con with a penchant for knives, slammed the trunk of the second vehicle (an SUV). "We're all set. Gas is topped off—well, as topped off as we can get. Enough to get us a fair distance, at least."

Becca hefted a final box of supplies, which clattered with cans of tuna, chips, and an assortment of questionable packaged foods. "Can't forget the essentials," she chirped, flashing a grin at Jace. "I'll die for my Doritos, and that's a *threat*."

He waggled his eyebrows. "No one's prying them from your cold, dead hands—assuming your hands can *even* go cold and dead anymore."

She flipped him off, but good-naturedly. "Ha-ha. Keep it up, wiseass."

Lisa, the former store manager, stepped outside clutching her own battered backpack. She cast an anxious glance at the city streets. "Is it just me, or does the area look emptier than usual?"

Edgar, the elderly mailman, nodded. "Might mean the zombies have wandered on. Or it might mean they're waiting to ambush us. Let's not get comfy."

Tasha, wearing her "TEAM NO ZOMBIES" baseball cap, emerged with a smaller duffel bag. "I can't believe we're finally leaving. I mean, I'm excited, but... also terrified." She glanced at Becca, offering a faint smile. "At least we have our... miracle girl?"

Becca coughed, uncomfortable with the label. She wasn't sure if "miracle girl" quite fit, especially given the moral gray area she was about to plunge into regarding controlling zombies. Her gut fluttered with a half-formed realization she hadn't shared yet. That is, until it happened *accidentally* a few hours back.

Because this morning—while rummaging for leftover granola bars—Becca had *accidentally commanded a lone zombie* that had crept near the loading dock. She'd yelled "Sit!" at it out of reflex, like shooing away a stray cat, and... well, the damn thing had slumped onto its butt with a confused moan. She'd freaked, of course, and the others were too busy to notice—but her mind had exploded with possibilities. *Could I... boss them around? For real?*

She'd been too stunned to mention it. But now, a niggling idea itched at her: *If zombies listened to me, we could avoid a lot of trouble.* Yet, talking about it felt borderline insane—*Hey guys, I can do the zombie version of dog training.* She shuddered, deciding to keep it to herself *for now*.

Dr. Eli Hawthorne joined them last, clutching a small case of lab samples and notebooks. He shot Becca a meaningful glance, as if silently reminding her she owed him more blood tests. But for the moment, they had bigger fish to fry. "Ready?" he asked no one in particular.

Declan answered with a grunt, sliding into the pickup's driver seat. "Let's roll."

They set off in a small, two-vehicle convoy, Declan at the wheel of the pickup with Lisa and Edgar riding shotgun and backseat, respectively, and Jace steering the SUV with Becca, Tasha, Leslie, Marsha, and Hawthorne crammed inside. Marsha clutched the rescued dog—whom Becca had named Chewie—on her lap.

The plan: ease out of the city via side streets, rejoin a main road once they got around any major blockades, and—*voilà*—head for farmland. Or so they hoped. But the apocalypse had a knack for spitting on their neat little plans.

They barely made it eight blocks before encountering a line of overturned buses spanning the road. Debris, burned cars, and twisted metal formed an impromptu wall. Clearly, some misguided survivors had attempted to barricade the area, only for it to become a nightmare obstacle.

Jace slammed the SUV's brakes, causing everyone to jostle. "Well, that's not good."

Becca peered out the window at the blockade. "Think we can go around? Check side streets?"

"Worth a shot," Jace agreed, radioing to Declan in the lead truck. They reversed carefully, tires crunching broken glass, then turned onto a narrower road that led behind a row of crumbling brownstones.

The deeper they ventured, the more it felt like a twisted maze. Becca's fingers drummed against her thigh. She was oddly antsy. Possibly because she felt so energized, and confining that energy to the passenger seat gave her a near-compulsive restlessness. Tasha, seated next to her, fiddled with the radio, but only static came through.

"Sure would be nice if we could call up the national guard," Tasha muttered.

Becca snorted. "I'd settle for a pizza delivery guy at this point."

Leslie, in the back, clutched her coupon folder. "Ugh, pizza. Don't tease me like that. My kingdom for a pepperoni slice."

Jace navigated a corner, only to slam on the brakes again. "Son of a— Another blockade!"

This time, it was a massive pile of rubble from a collapsed building, plus a couple of abandoned cars half-buried in the debris. He leaned on the horn—an instinct, which only produced a feeble beep and made Becca wince.

"Dude, don't attract more undead," she hissed.

He grimaced. "Reflex. Sorry."

Declan's truck pulled up behind them, and through the side mirror, Becca saw him hop out, crowbar in hand, to inspect the obstacle. The rest of them piled out of the vehicles, scanning the deserted street. The midday sun baked the asphalt, a swirl of dust tickling Becca's nose.

"Great," Lisa sighed, hands on her hips. "We can't move these cars out of the way. They're practically fused with the rubble."

Edgar poked around the wreckage. "Could we drive over the sidewalk? Might be too narrow."

Declan shook his head. "Too much junk. We risk blowing a tire or getting stuck. We might have to circle back and find an alternate route altogether."

Becca's stomach sank. They'd spent half an hour inching through these back roads, only to get stymied again. She scanned the area. No immediate signs of a horde, at least. "Let's see if there's a smaller alley we can squeeze through," she suggested.

They started exploring on foot. The neighborhood was a patchwork of crumbling storefronts and boarded-up apartments. Broken windows, graffiti, the occasional corpse or two. Grim. But ironically, not *heavily* populated with zombies—just one or two stragglers lurching at the far end of the block.

In typical fashion, Jace whipped out his knife, grin sharp. "I'll handle any biters. You keep an eye out for a route that doesn't lead to a dead end."

Becca found herself wandering near an overturned shopping cart in front of a wrecked convenience store. Her mind drifted back to the earlier moment with the "Sit!" command. *Should I test it?* The idea tingled in her gut, half excitement, half horror. But if it could help them… *maybe it's worth messing with?*

Declan, noticing her paused by the door, frowned. "You good?"

She forced a breezy smile. "Yeah, just… thinking. This store might have some leftover snacks." *Or it might have zombies to test my weird power on,* her mind added silently.

He looked torn between caution and the promise of supplies. "All right. We'll do a quick check."

Lisa joined them, rummaging for a flashlight, and they entered the convenience store. The interior reeked of stale air and rotting produce. Shelves had been toppled, but not entirely looted—some battered candy bars and random canned goods remained, though dust-laden. It was quiet, aside from their footsteps crunching debris.

"Score," Lisa whispered, snatching a couple of intact water bottles. "I miss cold water, though. I'd kill for ice."

Becca poked around the cashier counter, half-hoping to find a Twix or something. Then a shadow moved behind the snack display. She tensed, bat at the ready. Her heart pounded. *This is it.* She caught a glimpse of a zombie.

It was an older man in a torn jacket, hunched over, moaning softly as it pawed at a stuck vending machine. For a moment, it didn't sense them.

Lisa stiffened. "Zombie. We can take it out," she hissed, raising a tire iron.

Becca held up a hand, an idea sparking. "Wait," she whispered. "I have a... new trick."

Lisa blinked. "What do you mean?"

Declan entered from a side aisle, crowbar poised, but Becca motioned him to stop. He shot her a *what are you doing?* glare. She pressed a finger to her lips, stepped forward quietly.

The zombie finally took notice, letting out a low, raspy groan. It stumbled around the corner of the vending machine, arms outstretched. Becca's pulse hammered. *Time to see if that 'Sit!' thing was a fluke or something real.*

She kept her bat raised, locking eyes with the creature. "Uh, hey there, big guy," she murmured, voice shaking slightly. "Stay..."

Amazingly, the zombie froze mid-lurch, looking disoriented. Its milky gaze flicked from her to the snack machine, then back. It let out a whine, as though confused. Declan tensed behind her, ready to strike, but she shook her head subtly.

"Sit," she commanded in a firmer tone, heartbeat roaring in her ears.

The zombie hesitated, then… sank onto the floor. It moaned again, hands limp at its sides. Lisa's mouth fell open, and Declan's expression shifted from alarm to pure disbelief.

Becca swallowed hard. *Holy crap. That actually worked again.* She let out a shaky laugh. "Um. Good boy?" she said, half in jest. The zombie made a weird groan, seemingly docile.

"Becca," Declan warned, stepping closer. "This is messed up."

Lisa's eyes were huge. "How… are you doing that?"

Becca shook her head, adrenaline spiking. "I—I have no clue. They just listen. Or at least this one does." A sudden impulse struck her. "Hey, buddy, open that machine." She pointed at the vending machine next to it, though she had zero idea if a zombie could comprehend such a command.

The older man's reanimated corpse tilted its head. Then it rose in a jerky movement, stumbling to the machine. With undead strength and an awkward yank, it tried to pry the machine's flap. The glass cracked. Becca's heart pounded, half in horror, half in fascination.

"I'm officially freaked out," Lisa whispered. She clutched the tire iron tighter. "But also, this is the *coolest* thing I've seen all apocalypse."

Declan scowled. "This is *not* cool. This is horrifying."

Becca's lips twitched. "Horrifyingly cool, then." She studied the zombie's fumbling attempts. Its fingers scraped the metal frame. With a final grunt, the panel snapped open, and a handful of stale candy bars and chips tumbled out.

The zombie turned, moaning softly like a dog presenting a prize. Becca stared at it, cold sweat gathering under her collar. *Is this ethically messed up? Absolutely. Is it also extremely useful? Heck, yes.*

She forced a wry grin. "Thanks… um, good job." She motioned with her hands, not sure how to release it. "Uh, maybe go away now?" She took a few steps back, heart hammering.

The zombie blinked vacantly, then slouched toward the door as if commanded to leave. It drifted into the street without a second glance at them. Lisa's jaw practically hit the floor, and Declan's knuckles turned white around the crowbar.

Becca exhaled, shoulders trembling. "So… that happened. Anyone want a Snickers?"

Lisa let out a shaky laugh, stepping forward to gather the spilled candy. "I… I don't even know how to process this."

Declan looked downright grim. "We can't let this get out of hand. Using zombies like… *tools*? It's a line we probably shouldn't cross."

Becca's hackles rose. "You'd prefer we keep smashing their heads in whenever we see them? This might help us get out of the city alive." She gestured to the door. "Besides, we'd *still* bash the hostile ones. But if they obey me?"

His frown deepened. "That's not the point. This is messing with the natural order. We're playing with fire."

She tried not to snap at him. "I don't recall a natural order in which corpses roam the earth, but okay, sure. Look, I'm not saying I want a pet zombie. I'm just saying… we need every advantage we can get."

Lisa glanced between them, uneasy. "Let's table the moral debate for now and just gather these snacks. The others are probably waiting."

They packed up quickly, Lisa still rattled, Declan brooding. Becca's mind whirled. She'd just proven that she could *command* a zombie to do something complicated—like smashing a vending machine. And it had listened. *This changes everything.* Yet she also felt a twinge in her gut telling her Declan wasn't wrong about how *freaky* it was.

They returned to the vehicles, distributing the newly acquired candy and chips. Everyone was confused about why the three of them were so spooked.

"Something happen in there?" Jace asked, eyebrows raised.

Becca shifted, glancing at Declan. He gave a tiny shake of his head, which said *this conversation is too big, not now.* She sighed. "Uh, just a random zed. We handled it." She shoved a Snickers bar at Jace to shut him up. He took it with a suspicious grin but let it go.

They maneuvered out of the blocked road and tried another route. Ten minutes later, they hit yet another cluster of wrecked cars. The city seemed determined to keep them trapped.

"Road trip from hell," Tasha muttered as Jace parked the SUV behind Declan's truck. Leslie rummaged for a map. "We can't keep playing labyrinth in these streets. We need a direct path."

Marsha cradled Chewie, the dog, who panted anxiously. "Poor pup. This can't be good for his nerves."

Hawthorne, perched in the corner, scribbled notes. "At this rate, we'll be stuck for days. And with each delay, the risk of encountering more zombies or raiders increases."

Becca chewed her lip, glancing at the half-eaten Snickers in her hand. *What if we used my new ability to clear the path?*

She opened her mouth to propose the idea, but Declan's stare from the rearview mirror stopped her. He gave a tiny, dissuading headshake. She understood—he didn't want them all to freak out about her newly discovered "zombie whisperer" power. At least not yet.

Jace hopped out to talk to Declan. Becca took the opportunity to slip out too. She found them at the hood of the pickup, discussing whether to attempt a major U-turn or try to bulldoze a gap. Leslie and Tasha trailed behind, listening in.

"This is insane," Jace was saying. "We're going in circles."

Declan's jaw clenched. "We can't force our way through. These vehicles aren't tanks."

Becca stepped closer, scanning the area. Sure enough, a row of half-collapsed buildings blocked the route forward, with random cars stacked or crushed. She spied a group of four or five zombies milling about at the far end of the street. Nothing too threatening—unless they caused a racket.

She swallowed hard, heart thumping with that *wild idea* again. "We could, um, see if they'll move some debris for us," she said softly, half-hoping Declan would ignore her.

But Jace heard and cocked a brow. "What do you mean, *they*?"

She exhaled, forced to come clean. "Look, I found out I can... *tell zombies what to do*. Sorta. By, I don't know, commanding them. And they... obey me."

Leslie gasped. Tasha's eyes widened. "Wait, that's *amazing*. Or horrifying."

Declan pressed a hand to his forehead, clearly bracing for the group's reaction. Jace stared at Becca with unabashed fascination. "You *serious*? I'd pay good money to see that in action."

Becca glared at him. "You're not supposed to find this *fun*, you weirdo."

He smirked. "Not *fun*, exactly. But c'mon, that's dope. You can boss around the undead? That's some queen-level stuff, Monty."

A chorus of shock and questions erupted from Tasha, Leslie, and Marsha, who'd come up to eavesdrop. Lisa and Edgar emerged from the truck, also staring in disbelief. Hawthorne, hearing the commotion, hurried over, notebook in hand, eyes lighting up like Christmas. "You can *what*?" he exclaimed, adjusting his glasses.

Declan threw up his hands. "Well, cat's out of the bag. She apparently can tell them to do things, and they listen." He leveled Becca a stern glare. "Don't forget to mention you discovered it basically this morning and that it's not a guaranteed thing. We can't rely on it like it's foolproof."

Becca held up her palms. "Right, yeah, not foolproof. But it might help. Like, maybe we can tell them to shift some junk so we can drive through? Or see if they can open a path."

Hawthorne looked practically giddy with scientific intrigue. "We must study this phenomenon. Take notes on how you give commands, your emotional state—"

Becca gave him a flat look. "Dude, I'm not your lab rat. Let's survive first, *then* you can poke around in my brain or whatever."

He nodded vigorously, scribbling something down. "Of course, of course. Survival first."

Lisa and Edgar exchanged uncertain glances. Leslie piped up, "I mean, if it's an option, and we don't get eaten, I say do it."

Tasha bit her lip. "Is it safe, though? What if they only listen for a while and then turn on us?"

Becca shrugged. "We can keep weapons handy, obviously. But if it works, we might not have to risk ourselves physically moving the debris. It's that or keep wandering aimlessly."

Jace's grin spread. "I'm in. I gotta see this up close."

Declan's scowl deepened, but he didn't outright refuse. "Fine," he grunted. "We'll give it a shot. But the second anything goes south—"

Becca finished for him: "Yeah, yeah, you shoot them in the head, same old drill. I got it."

They walked a short distance from the vehicles to a spot where twisted metal bars and crumpled car bodies formed a mini barricade. Beyond it lay a narrow path that, if cleared, could fit their trucks and lead them out to a connecting avenue.

A cluster of five zombies lurked at the other end of the street, aimlessly swaying. Becca's pulse thudded. She felt hyper-aware of the group's eyes on her. *Don't screw this up,* she told herself. "Stay back," she whispered to the others. "If they rush me, shoot, okay?"

Declan's grip tightened on his crowbar. Jace, next to him, carried a loaded shotgun. The tension was palpable. Hawthorne hovered with his notebook, excitement shining in his gaze.

Becca inhaled, stepping forward. The zombies twitched, heads turning toward her. She raised a hand, voice shaking. "Uh... hi there?"

A low moan passed among them, but none charged. They kind of froze, as if waiting for something. *Weird.* She steeled herself and then said as clearly as she could: "Move... that debris." She gestured at a chunk of metal obstructing the path. Her stomach did flips. Would they do it, or just stare at her like an idiot?

For a beat, nothing happened. Then one of the zombies, a woman with half her hair missing, lurched forward. Another followed. They approached the metal chunk, groaning softly, and began tugging at it. The rest joined in, yanking at twisted beams. Becca's eyes practically popped out of her skull. *They're actually obeying me.* She fought an urge to laugh hysterically.

From behind, she heard Tasha gasp. "No freaking way."

Jace let out a low whistle. "Damn, Monty. That's some next-level wizardry."

Becca swallowed. "Keep it up," she ordered the zombies, injecting confidence into her tone. The creatures moaned but continued prying debris aside. Slowly, agonizingly, they shifted a few large panels of scrap metal enough to create a narrow opening.

Her blood roared in her ears. *This is insane.* Part of her was elated at the help, part of her was deeply disturbed by the sight of rotting corpses following commands like mindless workers. Then a truly unhinged idea popped into her head: *If we can do this, can they fetch other stuff?*

"Uh… hey," she ventured. "Is there, like, a convenience store or something in that direction? Could you… I dunno, find more snacks?" She wanted to smack herself for how *ridiculous* that sounded. *Am I seriously telling zombies to get me chips?*

But the power sang in her veins, and the notion had an undeniable allure. Why risk the living when she could send undead errand-runners?

Jace, apparently reading her mind, leaned in with a mischievous glint. "I want some soda, too. If they can figure that out."

Declan stared at them like they'd grown two heads. "This is twisted," he hissed. "We should not be *using* them like that."

Becca's hackles rose again. "You say that every time, but it's working. And better them rummaging around a dark store than one of *us* going in, right?"

He pressed his lips into a thin line, clearly conflicted, but said nothing.

Meanwhile, one of the zombies, a tall man with an exposed rib beneath tattered clothes, started trudging across the intersection, presumably to follow Becca's "snack" command. Another followed. The rest lingered near the newly cleared path, waiting aimlessly for more instructions. A bizarre hush fell as everyone watched them go.

"God, this is so weird," Lisa muttered, hugging herself.

Hawthorne jotted frantically in his notebook. "Amazing. This level of responsiveness implies some cognitive retention... or at least the virus has rewired them to respond to her specifically. Fascinating."

Becca exhaled, a heady mixture of power and guilt swirling in her gut. "Yeah, well, *fascinating* is one word for it. Let's see if they come back with goodies, or if they just wander off."

Declan paced while the zombies worked. He cast frequent glances at Becca, agitation radiating from him. Finally, he pulled her aside, ignoring the curious looks from the others.

"We need to talk," he said in a low voice.

She folded her arms. "I know, you think I'm diving into the deep end using zombie slaves. But it's helping. We can get out of the city sooner."

His jaw clenched. "You don't see the danger. You're messing with undead creatures that feed on humans. What if controlling them *changes you* somehow? Or what if they turn on you?"

Becca stared him down, stubbornness flaring. "They *won't*. They're basically ignoring me as a target. And controlling them— it's not that complicated. I give orders, they listen, end of story."

He grimaced. "There's more at stake. Hawthorne's drooling at the chance to study you. You think that's not going to cause issues down the line? If word spreads that you can command zombies, do you have any idea how people might use or *misuse* that power? They might try to *lock you up*, exploit you—"

She cut him off, bristling. "Oh, so you think you get to lock me up for *my own safety?*"

He huffed. "That's not what I— I just… This could spiral out of control. I'm worried about you."

An unexpected warmth curled in her chest at his concern. "Well, worry about me all you want, but I'm not letting this go. This might literally save our lives." She pushed a strand of hair behind her ear. "Also, let's not forget that I could have ended up a rotting corpse. If I have a weird advantage, I'm going to use it."

He sighed, tension carving lines into his forehead. "Just… promise me you'll be careful. Don't let Hawthorne or anyone else push you into something you're not comfortable with."

She softened. "I can handle myself, Graves. And if anyone tries to lock me up, they'll have to deal with me —and my new undead army." She said it only half joking, a smug grin tugging at her lips.

He didn't look fully reassured but relented with a nod. "Fine. We'll see how this plays out. Just don't lose sight of who you are, all right?"

Her heart thumped, a swirl of emotion tangling with the comedic absurdity of the situation. "I'm not planning on becoming 'Evil Zombie Queen' anytime soon, if that's what you mean."

Before Declan could respond, Jace's voice rang out: "Heads up! I think they're coming back!"

Sure enough, the pair of zombies reemerged from around a corner, arms loaded with random junk. One carried a half-torn plastic bag stuffed with snack wrappers. Another clutched a battered cardboard box that smelled suspiciously like stale doughnuts. They lumbered toward Becca, moaning softly.

Tasha's jaw dropped. "Holy crap, they're actually delivering snacks?"

Jace clapped his hands in delight, half-joking. "I love this new arrangement. Monty, you're unstoppable."

Becca mustered a wry grin as the zombies stumbled up and dumped their loot at her feet. The box contained a few sealed soda cans, some questionable pastries, and a scattering of protein bars. The plastic bag had half-smashed candy bars. Not exactly a gourmet feast, but in an apocalypse? *Total gold.*

Leslie stared in awe. "I have no words."

Hawthorne crouched, carefully observing the undead. "Remarkable. They followed a multi-step command: leave, retrieve items, return. This suggests a rudimentary problem-solving ability when responding to you specifically."

Marsha wrinkled her nose at the undead stench. "Yeah, well, it's also gross. And how long until they realize *we're* edible?"

Becca cleared her throat, stepping back from the creatures, who now stood slack-jawed, waiting. "Uh, thanks?" She realized belatedly how insane it felt to *thank* a zombie. "You can, um… go away again." She waved her hands. The pair meandered off, presumably searching for more errands to do or maybe returning to their aimless wandering.

Jace watched with open fascination, a slight flush in his cheeks. "That was… I mean, that's kind of hot."

Becca raised a brow. "Watch it, Carter. That's borderline necrophilia territory."

He snorted. "Not what I meant. I meant seeing you boss around the undead like you're queen of the apocalypse. It's… badass."

She rolled her eyes, but her chest fluttered at the compliment. *This is definitely going to my head if I'm not careful.* She forced herself to stay grounded. "Well, let's gather these supplies and see if the path they cleared is drivable."

They hurried to check the newly cleared gap. With the biggest debris moved, the trucks could just squeak through if driven carefully. Everyone hopped back into their respective vehicles, hearts pounding with renewed hope.

Becca slid into the SUV's passenger seat next to Jace. Hawthorne and Tasha sat behind, excitedly chattering about what they'd witnessed. Leslie was behind Tasha, rummaging for snacks, and Marsha held Chewie in her lap, eyes darting between them all with a mix of caution and awe.

As they started the engine, Declan's voice crackled over a walkie-talkie. "We're going in slow. Watch for anything that might snag a tire."

"Got it," Jace responded. With tentative acceleration, they navigated the SUV through the narrow opening. Metal squealed as it scraped the side, but they made it through. The pickup followed suit. A wave of relief washed over the group—progress at last.

They emerged onto a wider avenue that cut across the western side of town. Relief blossomed. The buildings here were more spaced out, promising a clearer path. They could see sunlight reflecting off the distant highway overpass. *We might actually escape soon,* Becca thought, heart soaring.

But as they inched along, the distant moans of undead grew louder, drifting from multiple side streets. A cluster of zombies—possibly a dozen or more—lurched into view at an intersection ahead, drawn by the noise of engines. *So much for no major hordes,* Becca mused grimly.

Jace clenched the steering wheel. "Uh, Monty? We might need your new trick again."

Declan's voice came over the walkie-talkie. "Everyone stay calm. We'll see if we can go around."

But the horde was blocking the intersection, and the side street was littered with abandoned vehicles. Another blockade that would require time—or a miracle—to navigate. The moans grew more frenzied as the zombies scented (or *heard*) the living.

Becca's pulse quickened. She could *try* commanding them to part like the Red Sea, or something equally dramatic. But that many at once? *Could she handle it?*

The SUV and pickup ground to a halt, tension thrumming in the air. Tasha gripped her seatbelt. "We can't fight them all, can we?"

Jace's knuckles whitened on the wheel. "Not without blowing all our ammo. And that'll attract even more."

From behind, Hawthorne spoke up, voice tinged with excitement. "Becca, if you can manipulate multiple zombies, this might be your chance to prove it's not just one or two. But… *be careful.*"

Leslie chewed her lip. "What if it backfires and they swarm?"

Marsha squeezed the dog protectively. "Please don't do anything reckless."

Becca stared at the swirling mass of undead stumbling closer. "But if we don't, we're stuck," she murmured, half to herself. The moral conundrum rattled in her skull: *using* undead as tools or foot soldiers. It freaked her out, yes, but her hunger to get the group to safety overshadowed her doubts.

She exhaled sharply. "Jace, keep the engine running. If this goes south, floor it, or Declan will… figure something out. I'll see if they'll, you know, let us pass."

Jace nodded, adrenaline flashing in his eyes. "Got your back."

Becca gulped, stepping out of the vehicle into the scorching sun. The horde was maybe fifty feet away, moaning and staggering. She raised her bat—though she wasn't sure if that was necessary or for her own comfort—and called out:

"Stop! Don't come any closer!"

Her voice rang across the asphalt. The group of zombies wavered, some tilting their heads. A few in front actually paused. Others continued forward, heedless. Becca's throat went dry. *Come on, focus.*

She tried again, louder, infusing every ounce of willpower into her words. "Stop!"

The effect rippled through the horde. More of them paused, uncertain moans rolling like a wave. A hush fell over the intersection. Heart hammering, Becca took a step forward. She felt a bizarre sense of connection, an invisible thread tugging her toward them. "Let us through," she said, voice trembling. "Move aside."

Slowly—agonizingly—they began to shuffle to the sides, leaving a narrow path in the middle of the intersection. It wasn't graceful or fast, and some stumbled over each other, but they were obeying. *They're actually obeying?* She let out a shaky laugh.

From the SUV behind her, Jace shouted, "Holy *shit,* Monty!" Tasha and Leslie gaped out the windows. She couldn't see Declan's reaction, but she imagined the ex-cop's jaw dropping even further.

Before her, the parted zombies groaned restlessly, but none lunged. It was like they recognized her as some twisted alpha. *I can't believe this,* she thought, near delirious with relief. This was no longer just a parlor trick. She had them forming a corridor.

She beckoned the vehicles forward. Her heart pounded so hard she thought it might burst. The roar of the engines made some zombies flinch, but her invisible hold seemed to keep them from attacking.

Jace inched the SUV up, trailing behind her, while Declan followed in the pickup. The sense of power rushing through her veins was intoxicating. She felt unstoppable… and *terrified* of what that might mean.

Halfway across the intersection, she realized the front row of zombies was still drifting too close, as if unsure. She turned, raising a commanding hand. "Back off!" she barked.

They recoiled like scolded dogs, leaving a wider berth. The SUV rumbled past them, so close that Tasha could have touched one if she'd rolled down her window. But the creatures did nothing—just moaned in confusion.

When the vehicles cleared the intersection, Becca sprinted around to the passenger seat and leapt in, breathing raggedly. Jace wasted no time hitting the gas. She barely registered Leslie's stunned exclamation or Tasha's trembling grin. She heard the pickup rev behind them, presumably following.

"We did it," she whispered, heart in her throat. "We freakin' parted the zombie sea."

Jace whooped, leaning forward on the steering wheel, adrenaline coursing. "That was insane. Hell yes, Monty!"

From the back seat, Hawthorne's pen scratched feverishly in his notebook. "Unbelievable. Controlling a dozen or more undead simultaneously… The implications—"

Leslie choked out a laugh. "The implications are that she's freaking unstoppable. Or maybe unstoppable *and* insane."

Marsha petted the trembling dog, eyes wide. "I'm just glad we got out of that jam. That was the scariest thing I've seen all week. And that's saying something."

Becca forced a shaky smile, hugging her bat to her chest. *They made it,* sure, but every nerve in her body vibrated with the realization of how precarious this was. She wasn't exactly *skilled* with this power, and messing up could be lethal.

But for now, they had a clear path forward. Her phone—useless for calls—showed the time as mid-afternoon. If they stayed on this road, maybe they'd actually reach the outskirts by nightfall. She met Jace's gaze, adrenaline still burning in their eyes. "Let's keep going," she said.

He nodded, gunning the engine. "City can't hold us forever."

In the rearview mirror, the parted horde gradually closed ranks again, stumbling aimlessly as if confused. In the side mirror, Becca spotted the pickup with Declan, Lisa, and Edgar, rolling along behind them. She imagined Declan's face—concern, shock, maybe grudging admiration.

Hawthorne's excited chatter about "neural pathways" and "viral receptors" faded into the background as Becca stared at the city skyline receding behind them. They weren't out *yet*, but they'd inched closer. Her new "zombie whisperer" power was the wild card that might be their salvation or downfall.

The city roads stretched ahead, still littered with potential hazards. But for the first time since the apocalypse started, Becca felt like they had a real chance. *Whether that chance warps me into a weirdo with an undead entourage*, well, that was a problem for Future Becca.

She took a breath, letting a tiny grin sneak onto her lips. *One more blockade, zombies. Let's see you stop me now.* With half the city (unwittingly) obeying her commands, she was too stubborn to back down. *Bad idea? Probably. But what else is new in the apocalypse?*

They pressed on, the engine humming a steady tune of determination. Outside, the sun dipped lower, the sky streaked with orange. Becca felt that electric current inside her, that *buzz* of possibility—like she held the keys to a darker, wilder kingdom than any farmland dream. The question was: how far was she willing to use it?

CHAPTER SEVEN

"It's official," Tasha said with a sigh, adjusting the bright *TEAM NO ZOMBIES* baseball cap on her head. "We've spent more time *almost* leaving this city than, like, actually leaving it."

"Hear, hear," Jace chimed, leaning against the side of the SUV. "I'm so ready for open roads, farmland, and chickens. Can we get some chickens?"

Becca Montgomery couldn't help rolling her eyes as she crunched across the debris-littered pavement. "Yes, we can get some chickens—once we find said farmland. But at the rate we're going, we might be stuck in these suburbs forever, fending off rotting neighbors."

They were about a mile from the main city limits, closer to the outskirts where strip malls and auto shops lined the wide roads. Several hours ago, they'd parted a massive horde in the intersection by using Becca's bizarre new ability to command zombies. That had allowed them to slip through an impassable blockade. Now, the small caravan of two vehicles (the battered pickup and an SUV) idled in a half-abandoned gas station parking lot, gleaning the last fumes of gasoline from a couple of ancient pumps.

Lisa carefully poured the siphoned gas into a red can, scowling. "We'll get just enough to keep going for a bit, but we really have to find a bigger source soon. Maybe a rural station that wasn't looted."

"Dibs on not rummaging alone," Marsha piped up, hugging the scruffy dog named Chewie. "I've had enough near-death experiences for one apocalypse."

"You and me both," Leslie added, adjusting her coupon folder under one arm. "And can we talk about how we're basically living off candy bars and stale chips? Where's a girl gotta go to get some fresh veggies?"

Becca sighed. "Fresh veggies are definitely not on the apocalypse menu yet. But don't worry, once we find a farm, we'll plant the biggest freaking garden you've ever seen. Zucchinis for days."

A few yards away, Declan Graves—ex-cop and resident worrywart—stood with Dr. Eli Hawthorne, discussing the group's next moves. Declan had that permanent crease between his eyebrows, as if the entire world's stress was perched on his shoulders. Hawthorne kept scribbling in a small notebook, occasionally glancing at Becca.

She knew exactly *why* Hawthorne was looking at her. *He wants to do more tests.* The man was borderline obsessed with Becca's immunity and the new "zombie whisperer" talents. But she was still reeling from the moral weight of commanding undead creatures like personal servants.

...Okay, so maybe the moral weight wasn't *that* heavy. She was mostly enjoying it, which was a tad concerning.

"All right, gather up," Declan called, motioning for everyone to huddle near the SUV's hood. "We've got enough gas to keep going another forty or fifty miles. Let's push west. The city sprawls out a bit here, but farmland should start in a few more miles."

Edgar fiddled with a map. "There's a state route that might be less congested. If we find it, we can skirt around the bigger highways."

"Sounds like a plan," Lisa agreed, capping the gas can. "Let's get moving before we draw another horde."

Everyone nodded. They piled into the vehicles—Lisa, Declan, and Edgar in the pickup, Jace behind the SUV's wheel with Tasha, Leslie, Marsha (plus Chewie), Hawthorne, and Becca squeezed in. A comedic fiasco of limbs and gear. And with that, they trundled back onto the road.

Becca gazed out the window, mind drifting to the ragged clusters of zombies they'd periodically seen wandering. They typically left them behind, but occasionally she caught them *looking* at her with something almost like recognition. *Or maybe that's just me projecting,* she thought. *I can't have that many groupies… right?*

They drove another mile through the outskirts, passing a half-crumpled strip mall. The place had once boasted a small grocery store, a dollar shop, and a pizza joint. Now it was a husk of cracked concrete and smashed windows. Most of the undead had presumably moved on, leaving only a few stragglers shambling among the collapsed awnings.

Stragglers that, ironically, perked up when they saw me pass, Becca mused through the SUV window. A chill ran down her spine as two zombies lurched forward and… started following the car. She craned her neck, noticing their blank eyes fixated on the SUV's rear bumper.

"Jace, slow down a second," she said impulsively.

He glanced at her. "Why? You want to invite them to dinner?"

She shrugged, curiosity piqued. "Just… do it."

He sighed but eased off the gas. The SUV coasted to a near-stop. The pickup behind them honked, presumably confused, but Jace stuck his arm out the window to wave them to wait. Meanwhile, the two zombies shuffled closer, moaning softly.

"Becca, what are you doing?" Tasha asked, warily peeking over the back seat.

"Experiments," Hawthorne murmured, eyes lighting up as if he'd been gifted a new lab toy. "Let's see if they respond to your presence."

Becca unrolled the passenger window, her heart thudding. "Uh, hi there. Keep your distance but… follow me," she said, voice cracking slightly. She opened the door and stepped out onto the asphalt. Immediately, the zombies changed course, focusing on her. She tensed. *Are they about to mob me?*

But they didn't. Instead, they paused a few feet away, heads tilted at awkward angles, waiting for instructions. *Just like the other times.* She exhaled shakily, relief flooding her chest.

"C'mon, let's see if we can get them to move around a bit," Hawthorne whispered excitedly, stepping out too. "For science."

Becca snorted. "Sure, for science." She noticed Declan hopping out of the pickup behind them, likely to supervise. She shot him a look that said *don't freak out.*

Declan stayed near the truck, arms crossed, but he didn't stop her. He gave a small nod for her to proceed, though his jaw looked tight.

She turned to the zombies, adopting a mock-cheerful tone. "Hey, you two. Over here." She waved them closer, then hopped up onto the curb near the strip mall. They followed, moaning softly, but not attacking. Hawthorne scribbled furiously in his notebook, while Jace watched from the SUV with a half-grin.

"All right, now, go… there," Becca said, pointing to a broken bench about ten paces away. The zombies looked at the bench, then back at her, as if uncertain. "Go on," she urged. With a few stuttering steps, they shambled over to it.

"You're like their new alpha," Tasha whispered, peeking around the car door. "This is so weird and kinda cool. Also super messed up."

"Agreed," Lisa added from the pickup, though she couldn't peel her eyes away.

"Next you'll have them doing the Macarena," Jace joked. "And I'd pay good money to see that."

Becca couldn't stifle a laugh at the mental image of zombies in a synchronized dance line. But part of her was uneasy. *Is this the right thing to do—bossing them around?* Then she remembered all the times zombies tried to kill them. *Yeah, okay, I don't feel that guilty.* She turned back to the zombies. "Stay there."

They remained by the bench, moaning aimlessly. She gave a final wave, returning to the SUV. Hawthorne followed, nearly bouncing with excitement.

"This is remarkable," he said. "They respond to vocal commands, posture cues—almost like dogs, but with severely limited cognition. Have you tried offering them… incentives? Like raw meat or something?"

Becca made a face. "Why would I have raw meat lying around?"

Jace shrugged. "We do have some jerky or that old steak in the cooler—that stuff is borderline raw, right?"

"Oh, *ew*," Tasha said. "You want to feed them leftover steak?"

Hawthorne adjusted his glasses. "But it might strengthen their obedience. Reinforcement training, so to speak. If you're going down this route, it's worth testing."

Becca wrinkled her nose. "Ugh, fine. Let me rummage." She popped open the cooler in the back seat, searching for anything meaty. Most of their supplies were canned or dried goods. But at the bottom, wrapped in questionable saran wrap, was a chunk of thawed steak that once belonged to a GoodMax freezer. She gingerly lifted it, half-expecting it to smell rancid. "Yeah, this is borderline disgusting."

Jace chuckled. "Perfect for them, then."

Declan walked over, arms still crossed. "You're *feeding them* now? This is crossing a line." His voice was tense with disapproval.

She locked eyes with him. "Look, you said it yourself—my new powers are a risk. Might as well explore them in a controlled way, right? If this helps us keep them docile, that's a good thing."

He opened his mouth to protest, then snapped it shut. "Just... be careful."

"Noted." Becca grabbed the questionable steak, bracing herself, and hopped out again. She approached the two zombies still hovering by the bench. "Uh, hey guys. Snack time?"

She tossed a chunk of raw meat onto the ground. One zombie sniffed the air, crouched, and devoured it with a grotesque enthusiasm. The other joined, nibbling scraps. Tasha squeaked in horror, and Lisa gagged dramatically. But the zombies made no move to attack. In fact, they seemed almost content afterward, gazing back at Becca with slack-jawed docility.

"Okay, so bribes *do* work," she said, both horrified and impressed. "Good to know."

A third zombie emerged from behind a battered dumpster, drawn by the noise and the smell. Becca's pulse sped up. Before it could do anything threatening, she raised a hand. "Stop!" The new zombie froze, then lurched closer in slow motion, as if torn between hunger for flesh and the compulsion to obey.

She eyed the cooler, but they had no more raw steak left. *Well, guess I'll wing it.* "Stay there," she ordered.

The creature moaned, shifting from foot to foot, but remained mostly stationary.

Behind her, Hawthorne leaned to Jace, whispering, "It's like a half-baked dog training session."

Jace let out a snort. "Yeah, except the dogs might eat your face if you slip up."

Becca glanced around at the half-dozen people staring at her, plus three somewhat obedient zombies. *This is my life now.* She plastered on a grin. "So… that's that. We done?"

Declan sighed, stepping forward. "Yes, can we *go* now? This is too big a crowd to linger. We have a mission: find farmland, remember?"

"Right," Becca said. She turned to the small congregation of undead. "Um… go away?" They stared vacantly. She made a shooing motion. They shuffled off behind the mall as if they had somewhere else to be, leaving her both relieved and spooked.

They piled back into the vehicles and resumed the drive west, leaving the strip mall behind. But tension buzzed in the SUV. Even though Jace was clearly fascinated by the "zombie whispering," Tasha, Leslie, and Marsha seemed unsettled. Hawthorne couldn't wait to talk more about it. He was practically bouncing in his seat.

"This might be a game-changer," Hawthorne said eagerly. "If you can control enough of them, we could potentially keep entire areas clear. Or gather them in one place, away from us—maybe even test cures more safely. The possibilities are endless!"

Leslie frowned, hugging her coupon folder. "And is that not just... extremely messed up?"

Marsha shuddered. "Feels like playing God. We're using them like slaves."

Becca glanced at them in the rearview mirror, feeling a pang of discomfort. "I get that it's messed up. But you've all seen how dangerous it is out here. If we can make them less of a threat—shouldn't we? We'd save human lives."

Tasha tugged her cap lower. "What about the people they *were* before? Is it disrespecting them to treat them like dogs?"

Silence fell. That was a question Becca didn't have a neat answer for. *In an ideal world, we'd have a cure or a way to put them to rest peacefully.* But this was the apocalypse, and survival often overshadowed ethics. She stared out the window, jaw tight.

Hawthorne cleared his throat. "Morals aside, it's a valuable resource. If the virus truly destroyed their consciousness, then we're dealing with... reanimated shells. Minimizing harm to ourselves might be the priority."

Leslie pursed her lips. "Still doesn't sit well with me. But I guess none of this is easy."

Jace reached over, patting Becca's shoulder. "Don't sweat it too much. We do what we have to. Beats getting eaten or shot by raiders."

She nodded mutely, though a storm brewed in her mind. *Was she crossing a line she couldn't uncross?* She remembered how *good* it felt to part that horde, to direct them like puppets. Power was intoxicating. Maybe she needed to be cautious not to let it overshadow her humanity.

But as they cruised on, weaving around a wrecked delivery truck, she also recognized a piece of her that didn't care. She liked the feeling of control in a world gone mad. *I'd rather be the one commanding them than be their lunch.*

Late afternoon found the two-vehicle convoy rolling through a half-flooded side road. They were forced to detour again—yet another collapsed overpass blocked the main route. The day's heat shimmered off the cracked pavement, and everyone was cranky from hunger and stress.

They paused near a cluster of battered houses to stretch their legs and figure out a route from an old AAA road atlas Edgar found in the pickup. Most of the houses looked ransacked, windows broken, doors ajar. The entire block felt eerily deserted, with no moans echoing. *A small blessing,* Becca thought.

While Jace, Edgar, and Declan argued about directions, Becca wandered toward a nearby yard, scanning for anything useful. A battered barbecue grill caught her eye. She was about to dismiss it as junk when she noticed something inside—slabs of meat? Possibly rancid, but worth checking.

"Really going for that raw meat angle, huh?" Tasha teased, trailing behind with a cautious expression.

Becca shrugged. "If I'm going to train these zombies further, might as well get some tools. The doc was right—food motivation is a thing."

Tasha scrunched her nose. "Seriously messed up, but I won't stop you."

They popped open the grill. The stench was *awful*. Some leftover ribs or steaks had been left to rot. Flies scattered as the lid lifted. Tasha gagged, turning away. Becca coughed, eyes watering.

"Ugh, that's vile. But maybe salvageable if I wrap it up?" She rummaged in her backpack for a plastic bag. "This is next-level disgusting, even for me."

Tasha stared in morbid fascination. "Can't believe you're doing this. The apocalypse changes people, I guess."

Becca chuckled darkly, scooping the half-mummified hunk of meat into the plastic bag. "If it helps keep the undead docile or helpful, it's worth it. Just… please do not let me get any of this in my mouth. Or on my clothes."

She sealed the bag, fighting the urge to vomit. Then she shot Tasha a grin. "Zombie training treats: acquired."

"You're insane," Tasha said, but with a shaky laugh. "Let's get out of here before I pass out from the smell."

They returned to the vehicles, and Jace raised a brow at the bag. "Dare I ask?"

Becca smirked. "You'll see."

They drove on, eventually finding a side route that seemed promising. Shadows lengthened as twilight approached, painting the sky in pastel oranges and pinks. The group decided it was best to keep going a bit longer before camping—somewhere outside the immediate sprawl of civilization.

They rolled past an abandoned hardware store, a salvage yard, and more half-collapsed homes. Along the way, they spotted a handful of scattered zombies lurking near a field. Becca's curiosity flared again. *Time to practice this weird skill.*

She signaled Jace to stop. Declan's truck also halted behind them, confusion evident. Becca hopped out, raw meat bag in hand.

"Okay," she announced to the group, half-joking, half-serious, "time for Zombie Training 101. I need to see if we can do… group commands, or something. Y'all can stand guard, obviously."

Declan huffed in exasperation. "Must we do this now?"

"Yes," she insisted, crossing her arms. "If we want them to keep a safe distance or help us clear debris, I need to figure out how to handle more than one or two at a time. This is safer while we're still near empty fields, not in the thick of a city center."

He sighed but nodded reluctantly, stepping aside. Hawthorne looked thrilled, notebook at the ready.

Becca scanned the field. Three zombies ambled aimlessly near a crooked fence. "Hey, you guys!" she called, striding forward. They turned, moaning, drawn to her voice. A thrill shot through her—equal parts fear and excitement.

"All right, no biting," she commanded, as though that were a real possibility. The zombies drifted closer but didn't lunge. She held out the plastic bag, grimacing. "Got a… treat for you if you behave."

Jace snorted from a safe distance. "You sound like a preschool teacher, but for rotting corpses."

"Shut it," she hissed, opening the bag. The smell wafted out, making her eyes water. She brandished a hunk of rancid rib. "Sit?"

One zombie promptly collapsed to its knees, moaning. The other two wobbled uncertainly. Becca tossed the rib to the kneeling one, which devoured it with disgusting fervor. "Good… boy?" she said, feeling insane.

"Try to get the others to do the same," Hawthorne suggested, scribbling notes.

Becca pointed at the second zombie, a woman with half her scalp visible. "Sit," she repeated. The zombie stared blankly, letting out a guttural sound. Becca stepped closer, hand still holding the plastic bag of meat. "Sit!"

This time, it hesitated, then sank to a crouch, arms slack. Becca tossed it a small chunk. "Atta girl. Good —uh—zombie." Her voice dripped with sarcasm, but inside she was reeling. She was *training them like dogs.*

The third zombie, an older man missing an arm, just drooled, ignoring her command. She frowned, stepping forward. "Sit, I said." Nothing. "Sit!" She stomped a foot, brandishing the bag. Still no reaction except a mild tilt of the head. She realized with a jolt that not all of them responded the same way. Maybe it was too far gone?

She shrugged, tossing a piece of rancid meat on the ground near it. The zombie pounced on it, chomping with gusto, but didn't attempt to follow her command. "Huh. So… some are more receptive than others," she mused aloud, glancing at Hawthorne.

He nodded eagerly, enthralled. "Yes, yes! This suggests varied brain damage or virus progression might affect obedience."

"Told you it wouldn't all be sunshine and daisies," Declan grumbled from behind.

Becca turned, stepping away from the enthralled zombies, wiping her hands on a spare rag. "Well, it's a start. Two out of three is something." She looked at the others, a shaky grin tugging her lips. "I guess we need more practice—like, maybe I can teach them basic tasks if I bribe them enough."

Lisa's expression was a mix of horror and amusement. "Next you'll have them rolling over."

Becca raised a brow. "Don't tempt me."

Marsha, hugging the dog protectively, muttered, "Chewie's one thing, but rotting corpse pets? I'm not sure how to feel."

Leslie half-laughed. "If it keeps them from attacking us, I'll take it."

By nightfall, the group managed another few miles, eventually pulling off the road to camp in a relatively open field dotted with dying grass and a couple of scraggly trees. The battered vehicles formed a loose circle, headlights illuminating the area while they set up meager sleeping arrangements—mostly tarps, blankets, and one battered tent from the sporting goods store.

Becca sank onto a folding chair, exhausted but too wired to sleep. She stared up at the starry sky, listening to the quiet bustle of her friends rummaging for supplies. The dog curled up at Marsha's feet, dozing. The air smelled of dust and the faint tang of burnt rubber from the highways.

A soft moan drifted from the darkness. Becca jolted, reaching for her bat. Another moan, closer this time. Her adrenaline spiked, until she saw silhouettes emerging from the gloom. *Oh, no.* It was a small group of zombies—maybe four or five. And they were… ambling toward her, but not in a typical "let's devour your brains" manner. More like *"we've arrived, boss."*

She stood, heart pounding. "Uh… guys?"

Declan was at her side in seconds, crowbar raised. Jace and Tasha also emerged from behind the tent, flashlights ready. The zombies stopped a few yards away, moaning softly. One looked vaguely familiar—was that the scalp-missing woman from earlier?

Hawthorne popped his head out of the tent, eyes wide with curiosity. "They followed you?"

"Are you freakin' kidding me?" Lisa groaned, rummaging for her tire iron. "This is a camping trip, not a zombie con."

Becca swallowed hard, stepping forward, bat in hand. "What do you want?" she asked, half expecting an answer. The undead just stood there, swaying.

"Try commanding them," Jace whispered. "Send them away?"

She inhaled. "Go away," she ordered, making a sweeping motion. The zombies… moaned, but lingered.

One stepped forward with a jerky shuffle, causing Tasha to squeak in alarm. But it didn't attack—just stared at Becca like a lost puppy. She recognized it as the one that had refused to sit earlier. Now, it seemed more docile.

Declan's face darkened. "They're waiting for directions, aren't they?"

Becca's stomach twisted. "Looks like it. They want me to tell them what to do."

Marsha, near the vehicles, shot them a terrified look. "That's horrifying. Are we about to be stuck with a… a zombie entourage?"

"Zombie entourage?" Leslie echoed, half-laughing in disbelief. "We can't have them trailing us everywhere. People will think we're insane."

Becca exhaled, feeling the weight of a decision. "We can either chase them off forcibly—like, kill them. Or maybe let them hang around if they're not hostile. Maybe they could be… I don't know, an early warning system?"

"Or a walking advertisement that we're messing with dark forces," Lisa grumbled. "In normal times, I'd call a mental institution on all of us."

Hawthorne rubbed his chin thoughtfully. "If they're truly subordinate, we might harness them as guards. *But* there's the risk they'll attract more, forming a larger group. That could become a hazard."

Declan scowled. "A *horde* is always a hazard. The bigger it gets, the more likely it'll draw attention from raiders or other survivors who'll see us as a threat."

Jace nudged Becca gently. "What do you think, oh fearless zombie queen?"

She hesitated, scanning the dull eyes of the undead waiting for her. "I think… if they're not hurting us, we can keep them around for a bit. At least until we figure out how to manage them. We can try leading them away from camp at night, so they're not right on top of us. Then in the morning, if we need them to move debris or scare off raiders, well… we have muscle. Gross muscle, but muscle."

Lisa covered her mouth, as though stifling a curse. "This is insane."

"Welcome to the apocalypse," Jace said with a cheeky grin.

"Fine," Declan muttered, clearly torn. "But the first sign of trouble, we put them down."

Becca nodded, trying not to feel stung by his cynicism. She turned to the zombies, chest tight. "All right, you, uh… follow me." She motioned for them to move around to the far side of the field, away from the tents. They obeyed, stumbling along behind her in a small knot of undead.

Hawthorne followed at a distance, scribbling notes in the moonlight like a mad scientist. *At least he's enthusiastic,* she thought wryly.

"Stay here," she told the zombies, pointing at an open patch of grass. They halted, moaning softly, forming a little cluster. She rummaged out a small chunk of the rancid grill meat, tossing it near them. They dove at it with hungry snarls. *Disgusting, but effective.* At least they wouldn't wander off in search of living flesh if they had a treat.

When she returned to the campsite, Tasha gawked. "Did you just bribe them to stay put?"

Becca shrugged. "I guess. Let's see if it works all night."

The group tried to rest. Jace and Declan took first watch, patrolling the perimeter while the others dozed fitfully. The hum of insects and the occasional distant moan of undead played in the background. Becca lay on a flattened sleeping bag, staring up at the stars. Could she—a random grocery store clerk a few weeks ago—really command an entire horde? That idea sent her mind spinning with equal parts terror and excitement.

Hours later, around midnight, a startled yelp tore Becca from her half-sleep. She grabbed her bat, heart pounding. Lisa and Edgar had been on watch, apparently. She scrambled up, scanning for threats.

Near the far edge of the field, she spotted a group of silhouettes—more zombies. And the smaller group she'd corralled was shuffling around excitedly, as though welcoming new members.

"Crap," Becca muttered, racing over with the others. "What's going on?"

Lisa clutched her tire iron. "They just… came out of nowhere! The group was five earlier, now it's, like, ten. And some are edging closer to us."

Indeed, the undead numbers had nearly doubled. They formed a loose circle around the "originals," who moaned in recognition. The new ones also seemed drawn to the campsite. A horrifying thought dawned on Becca: they might be hearing the moans or sensing her presence, like a beacon.

Declan arrived, brandishing his crowbar. "This is exactly what I was worried about. They're forming a bigger group." He looked at Becca, eyes flashing with anxiety. "You have to do something before we're swarmed."

Jace nodded. "Yeah, Monty, talk them down."

Becca swallowed, stepping forward. She tried to ignore the rancid stench wafting from so many corpses. "Stop," she commanded, voice trembling. The new zombies hesitated, as though listening. The older ones moaned softly, turning to her. *They're definitely waiting for me to say something.*

"Stay back," she added, making a pushing motion. The undead moaned again but didn't approach further. Some wavered uncertainly, drool dripping from their slack jaws. Others just stared as if enthralled.

"Now, uh... any chance you guys want a snack?" she ventured, rummaging for more raw meat, but realized she was nearly out. She tossed them a few scraps from the grill bag. Several pounced, snarling. Others seemed satisfied just being near her. *This is beyond weird.*

"Great," Lisa muttered, eyeing the scene with a mix of horror and fascination. "We're basically luring them here with a barbecue buffet."

Becca bit her lip, feeling sweaty and overwhelmed. "I didn't *invite* them. They're just... following me. If I can lead them away from camp, we'll be safer."

Declan's brows knitted. "Where do you plan to lead them? We're surrounded by open fields for miles in each direction."

She closed her eyes, thinking rapidly. If she took them far enough in the other direction, they might stay there, waiting for her return. *But that means traveling alone with a horde at night.* That idea sent chills down her spine.

Jace laid a hand on her shoulder. "I'll go with you, if you do that. No way you're wandering off alone with these freaks."

Declan looked torn. "I can come too."

She shook her head. "No, we need someone to guard the camp. Plus, you and me together in a field of zombies? I can't handle your meltdown if something goes wrong."

He frowned but reluctantly nodded. "Fine. But be careful."

Hawthorne piped up, "I can accompany you for observational data—"

"Nope," Jace interjected, flashing a sharp grin. "You stay here, doc. We can't babysit both you and the zombies."

Hawthorne pouted but acquiesced. "All right, fine."

Armed with minimal raw meat, a couple of flashlights, and their weapons, Becca and Jace set off across the field. The newly enlarged group of undead—ten or so—followed them in a ragged line under the moonlight. It was surreal, a twisted parody of the Pied Piper leading rats. Except the rats were decaying corpses, and the piper was a snarky ex-grocery clerk.

Jace walked beside Becca, shotgun slung across his back. "So, this is the weirdest date I've ever been on."

She snorted, tension easing slightly. "We have very different definitions of 'date.' But hey, at least there's a full moon."

"Romantic," he said, winking.

They reached a gentle slope leading down to a small wooded patch. The farmland beyond was visible in the distance, a faint silhouette. Becca paused, turning to the moaning horde. "All right, guys, stay here. I mean it. Don't move unless I say so."

The zombies milled around her, moaning. She tried tossing a final piece of meat. They lunged, snarling, then settled. Jace held the flashlight steady, watching in fascination. "So, they're basically your groupies."

She gave a lopsided grin, wiping sweat from her brow. "Seems like it. I'd love a normal fan club, maybe fans who buy me coffee, but here we are."

He chuckled. "At least no one else can claim to have zombie minions. That's gotta count for something."

She stepped back, beckoning Jace to follow. The undead stood there, moaning softly, but didn't follow. "They're listening," she said, relief flooding her. "Okay, let's hurry back to the others. With luck, they won't wander off tonight… or wander back to camp."

Jace nodded, throwing one last wary glance at the horde. Then they turned and jogged across the field, heartbeats pounding. A few times, Becca risked a glance over her shoulder, terrified that the zombies might be shambling after them. But no—they stayed put, like loyal foot soldiers waiting for commands.

When they returned to the campsite, the others let out a collective sigh of relief. Hawthorne peppered them with questions, which Becca deflected, exhausted. "Doc, can we do the Q&A tomorrow? I need sleep."

Declan studied her in the flickering flashlight beam. "You okay? Everything go all right?"

She forced a tired grin. "Yeah, I'm good. They're parked in that field over there, hopefully for the night."

"That's… good," he said, relief evident in his eyes. "I guess."

"Don't look so glum, Officer," Jace teased. "We just saved your butt from a zombie rave."

Declan rolled his eyes, but tension left his shoulders. "Fine. Let's just hope they stay put. Because if we attract more—"

Becca cut in, "We'll figure it out. One crisis at a time, yeah?"

He nodded, stepping back to resume watch. The others settled into a wary calm. Exhausted, Becca finally crawled into a half-assembled tent. She curled under a thin blanket, mind swirling with questions about how she'd handle this growing undead following. *We're forming a horde,* she realized with both dread and a sneaky thrill. She drifted off to the muffled sound of moans in the distance, feeling the sweet ache of power in her veins.

CHAPTER EIGHT

Becca Montgomery woke up with a crick in her neck, a knot in her back, and a strange sense of impending doom. She'd slept in a half-collapsed tent that made her yearn for the old world's worst motel bed. At least the dog —Chewie—had kept watch at the entrance, although he offered no solution for the stiff breeze that had whipped through the night.

Her eyelids felt heavy, but the persistent moan drifting across the campsite snapped her fully awake. *Zombies.* Right, she was leading a ragtag group of survivors across the apocalypse. And, oh yeah, she'd somehow acquired an undead horde—like a suburban soccer mom who'd accidentally fostered 200 dogs. Only these were drooling, rotting corpses.

"Ugh," she muttered, forcing herself upright. "Morning breath in the apocalypse is the *worst.*"

Tasha, the pastel-haired cashier, was zipping up her own sleeping bag a few feet away. She rubbed bleary eyes. "Morning, Becca. Or whatever time it is."

"Could be noon," Becca joked, "but time is meaningless. So is morality, apparently, since I'm the puppet master of the undead." She rubbed her face, heart pounding with the memory of last night: leading a small group of zombies into a field, bribing them with rancid meat, and hoping to keep them from overwhelming the camp.

Tasha gave a half-laugh. "Don't get me started. Everything's upside down."

Outside the tent flap, Lisa and Leslie were already stirring, rummaging through supplies to see what pathetic breakfast they could muster. Possibly more stale crackers or a can of cold beans. A wave of sorrow for her pre-apocalypse life—complete with Starbucks cappuccinos—hit Becca. *I'd kill for some coffee.* She sighed dramatically, reaching for her tennis shoes (one size too big, courtesy of raided sporting goods).

She stepped out into the crisp morning air—and froze.

In the distance, across the field, a massive crowd of zombies loomed. Her stomach dropped. "Oh, no," she whispered. "Please tell me that's not all mine."

"Hey, you're awake," Jace said, strolling up behind her. He looked oddly cheerful for a guy who probably got two hours of sleep. "Uh, you see that, right?"

Becca pointed. "Yeah. I see it. Do you see it?"

He let out a low whistle. "Sure do. Looks like your fan club had a growth spurt."

"Fan club" was putting it mildly. Last night, there'd been a dozen, maybe fifteen zombies lurking in that field. Now, she counted *at least* four or five dozen, possibly more, forming a loose semicircle as though waiting for a rock concert. Or worshiping some weird undead deity—her.

Declan Graves—ex-cop, moral compass, and general grump—marched up with a scowl etched deep into his features. "Becca, we have a problem," he said, gesturing at the crowd. "All the zombies you commanded or interacted with—since the day you found out you could do this—are apparently gathering. They must have tracked us overnight."

Lisa, clutching a tire iron, looked ready to pass out. "How are we supposed to handle *that many*?"

Dr. Hawthorne jogged over, notebook in hand. His eyes sparkled with a mix of terror and fascination. "This is… extraordinary. They've come from miles, presumably. Maybe they're connected telepathically or sense you somehow?"

Becca inhaled sharply, fighting a wave of panic. *So every time I told a zombie to sit or fetch or "Shoo, go away," they eventually came back? Great.* She squared her shoulders, forcing humor into her tone. "Well, guess my morning agenda involves greeting the entire undead population. Starbucks, who?"

Edgar looked up from the map he'd been studying. "Whatever you do, do it carefully. We can't just pack up and leave if they're blocking our path."

Tasha muttered, "This is insane. Absolutely insane."

It *was* insane—especially because at the forefront of this undead throng sat the very first zombie Becca had accidentally commanded. She remembered the half-faced man who had accepted her "sit" command in a grocery store aisle. Now, he crouched near the head of the group like a loyal dog, moaning softly.

As if that weren't weird enough, in the zombie's lap was… a tote bag. Another zombie to his right clutched a plastic grocery sack. And a third one, missing half its scalp, clung to something cylindrical. With each step, they emanated that familiar rotting stench. But they seemed to be *presenting* these items.

"What in the world?" Tasha breathed.

Jace snickered under his breath. "It's like they brought you breakfast."

Becca's heart pounded as the undead horde parted slightly, allowing the *original* zombie to shuffle forward. The half-faced man slowly rose, moaning, and placed the tote bag on the ground a few yards from Becca. Then he stepped back, vacant eyes locked on her. The other two zombies followed suit, dropping their sacks. *What is this, a door-to-door undead Amazon delivery?*

"Should we be backing up?" Lisa hissed.

Declan tensed, crowbar at the ready. "If they rush us—"

"They won't," Becca said firmly, stepping forward. She swallowed her fear. *Time to lead.* The moans intensified as she approached, but none of the zombies lunged. They almost seemed reverent, if an undead creature could manage that expression.

She carefully nudged the tote bag with her foot, leaning down to peek inside. Sure enough, it was loaded with *snacks*—some battered, but evidently collected from ransacked stores or vending machines. Candy bars, crushed chips, even a box of stale donuts with a half-torn label. They must've remembered how she demanded snacks in the past.

Her stomach flipped. *They're bringing me offerings.* She turned to the second bag, discovering more random goodies—crumpled soda cans, a few packs of crackers, a jar of pickles. And that third zombie had a *very* dented can in its hand. Becca carefully pried it away, reading the label.

"No way," she whispered, eyes going round. "*Espresso Double Shot.* That's... coffee. Sort of."

Jace let out a bark of laughter. "They must've heard you complaining about needing caffeine."

Tasha shook her head in disbelief. "That is the single weirdest gift I've ever seen. A zombie offering coffee."

Becca blinked down at the can. It was caked with who-knows-what, but she recognized the brand. "I can't decide if I'm grateful or creeped out." She snorted. "Maybe both."

Hawthorne scribbled notes again, muttering, "Incredible. They're retrieving items they know you find valuable. This suggests memory or at least recognition of prior commands."

Declan, arms crossed, watched the scene with a pinched brow. "So they're basically your personal scavengers now? Great. Because we definitely needed a bigger moral quagmire."

"Look at it this way," Jace drawled with a wicked grin, "free breakfast."

Lisa coughed. "I, uh, think I'll pass on the zombie donuts. But you do you."

Becca gazed at the offering-laden zombies—there had to be a couple dozen behind them, moaning softly. The odor was atrocious, like a mass grave at low tide. But they *hadn't* attacked. Instead, they'd hauled half-rotten coffee and random snacks across the city to deliver to her. The comedic absurdity made her want to laugh and cry at once.

"All right," she said, voice wavering, "um… good job, guys?"

The horde moaned in unison, as if responding to her. A few in the back shuffled restlessly, drawn by the possibility of raw meat bribery or some new command. Others stared blankly, drool pooling at their chins. It was a post-apocalyptic assembly line of loyal—if smelly—minions.

Unbeknownst to Becca or anyone else, within that horde lurked a figure who was *not* fully mindless. Zane Walker, a tall, lean man with tousled dark hair, lingered near the middle of the crowd. He had a faint greenish pallor and a bite mark on his forearm, half-hidden by a torn hoodie sleeve.

His eyes were not blank, though. He observed everything with a keen intelligence, quietly blending in among the moaning, drooling zombies. For weeks, he'd been caught between life and death—*some* mixture of the virus that never fully turned him. He'd survived. And now, stumbling across Becca's bizarre "zombie queen act," he found a glimmer of hope.

He could sense the other zombies' meager consciousness—flickers of thought that mostly revolved around hunger, confusion, and an inexplicable pull toward

Becca. He, too, felt that pull, but his mind remained intact enough to question it. *Why does she have this effect on us?*

As the group of survivors laughed and argued, Zane drifted closer, ears tuned to their conversation. He yearned to speak up, to let them know *he* was different. But paranoia kept him silent for now; how would they react to a "zombie" that talked? *They'd probably blow my head off.* So he hung back, letting the crowd conceal him, gleaning information like a spy in a ragged hoodie.

He heard Hawthorne mention "viral mutation," Declan rant about "morality," and Becca crack jokes at her own expense. Something about her voice made him feel… more alive. The constant dull ache in his chest lessened, and his mind cleared. *Fascinating—and terrifying.* For now, he remained a silent observer, biding his time until he could reveal himself safely.

"Okay," Becca announced, gathering her crew by the SUV and pickup, out of direct earshot of the moaning horde. "This is… a lot. We've got an entire undead population bringing me gifts, and apparently, they won't take a hint to back off. We need a plan."

Marsha, cradling Chewie the dog, shuddered. "Maybe we just accept the snacks, say 'Thanks, but no thanks,' and quietly drive away?"

Lisa shook her head. "They'll follow us. We saw how some of them traveled miles to find her. There's no guarantee they'll stop."

Hawthorne tapped his notebook. "We could attempt to lead them to a remote area, away from any major roads or survivors. If we keep them docile, they might not wander."

Jace raised a brow. "So we keep them around as, what, an undead army for whenever we need them? Because that's both awesome and horrifying."

Declan exhaled, pinching the bridge of his nose. "I've said it before, but this is dangerous. The bigger the horde, the bigger the target on our backs—rogue survivors might see us as a threat or assume we're controlling zombies for some evil plan."

Becca tried not to bristle at the "evil plan" reference. "I'm not trying to build a personal empire. I just want to… survive. Maybe having them is an advantage—like, if raiders approach, we could direct the horde to scare them off."

Lisa frowned. "And if the horde goes rogue? We risk hundreds of zombie kills on our conscience, not to mention if they break free and devour some poor family."

A hush fell, moral dilemmas swirling. Even Edgar, typically quiet, spoke up softly: "We're dealing with something unprecedented. If we do it, we must do it carefully."

Becca let out a frustrated sigh. "I never asked for a zombie fan club. Blame the virus. But ignoring them won't make them vanish."

Tasha lifted her cap, ruffling her hair. "Look, I don't like it either. But maybe we can keep them behind us as we move west? Then, I don't know, gradually peel off so they lose interest?"

"That might be possible," Hawthorne said, half-pondering. "If they're truly attuned to Becca's presence, though, they might keep a fixed radius unless forcibly turned away."

Declan scowled. "Let's just see if we can lead them to a big empty field, form some kind of barrier, and slip out. The fewer we have trailing us, the better. I can't believe I'm even suggesting a plan to 'park' a zombie horde."

Becca nodded, ignoring the pang of annoyance. "All right. Let's try that. I'll see if they'll stay put or guard some random area. If they keep ignoring us, great. If they catch up… we'll figure it out."

Jace clapped his hands together. "Cool. Another day, another insane plan. Let's do it."

Becca approached the horde, which parted to let her through like a bizarre red-carpet reception. Some moaned hungrily, others just stood there drooling. The "original" zombie from the grocery store was front and center, almost wagging an imaginary tail. She mustered a wry smile. "Hey, buddy. Good morning to you, too."

In the back, Zane watched, heart pounding. He saw how the group parted for Becca, how each moan carried faint echoes of gratitude and curiosity. *Interesting,* he thought. *They're not just ignoring her; they're... devoted.* The virus inside him pulsed with recognition, intensifying that strange sense of connection. *She's the cause of all this. But she's also their anchor.* He steeled himself. Maybe he could approach them if the moment was right.

Becca cleared her throat. "All right, guys… thanks for the coffee and, uh, candy. But we need to move on. I want you all to stay here." She made a downward gesture. "Stay."

The horde moaned. A few zombies took shuffling steps forward, but she repeated firmly, "Stay." They halted. *So far, so good.* She glanced at the group behind her. Jace gave a thumbs-up, Lisa watched nervously, and Declan hovered with a crowbar at the ready.

"Now, we'll be back if we need you," Becca said, feeling silly for using that phrase. "But for now, don't follow us." She stepped back, wanting to test if they'd remain in place. The horde fidgeted but mostly stayed put, as if waiting for further instructions.

A stirring in the back caught her eye—one zombie parted from the rest, stepping forward with a more *purposeful* gait. He wore a ragged hoodie, hair falling over his forehead, and though his skin was pale, he had an odd vitality in his eyes. Could just be a random partially fresh corpse, but something about him made her heart flip. He seemed… *aware.*

He walked right up to her, ignoring the tension from Declan, who lifted the crowbar threateningly. The rest of the group braced for a potential attack. But the figure just raised his hands in a non-threatening gesture. Becca's pulse hammered. *What is happening?*

Then the zombie spoke, voice low and raspy but *very much* coherent: "Don't. I'm not... like them."

Her jaw dropped. *A zombie that can talk.* Everyone froze.

Jace's eyes went wide. "Holy—did that corpse just speak?"

Lisa actually squeaked, and Tasha pressed a hand to her mouth, stepping back. Hawthorne nearly tripped over his own feet in excitement. "Fascinating," he breathed.

Declan flinched but didn't lower the crowbar. "Stay back. You're one of them, but you can speak?"

The man—zombie?—nodded, throat bobbing. "I'm... *Zane,*" he said haltingly, as if the words felt foreign. "Not fully turned. Been... stuck like this for weeks." He raked a hand through his tangled hair. "Didn't know if you'd kill me on sight."

Becca found her voice. "Zane, you said? Are—are you infected?"

He let out a rueful half-laugh, lifting his hoodie sleeve to show a single *healed bite mark*. "Yeah. I got bit.

Should've died or turned. But I didn't. Kinda like you, I guess."

Her breath caught. "How do you know about me?"

He shrugged. "Heard the others... *talking* in their moans. They don't have full speech, but there's a sort of... communication. They're drawn to you. Some appreciate what you're doing—giving them direction. Or maybe just controlling them. Either way, it's better than aimless hunger."

Hawthorne perked up, scribbling even more frantically. "Wait, you *understand* them?"

Zane nodded wearily. "In a sense. Their thoughts are mostly impulses: hunger, confusion, following the alpha. But there are a few—like me—whose minds linger. We're caught between living and dead."

Becca's mind reeled. The entire group looked shell-shocked. "So, you're... half-zombie?" she asked, the question hanging awkwardly in the air.

He huffed a bleak laugh. "Yeah, guess so. Half-zombie. My body's mostly dead, but my brain's functional. I need less... 'food' than them, but still some. I can smell living flesh and want it sometimes, but not strongly enough to kill."

Declan's grip on the crowbar remained tight. "That's... unbelievably messed up."

Zane shot him a wry glare. "Tell me about it."

Marsha whispered, "Does that mean you're... dangerous?"

He hesitated, scanning the group's tense faces. "Not intentionally. But... I won't lie, sometimes the hunger flares. Being near you people helps me remember who I was. The hunger fades around her." He nodded at Becca, who blinked in surprise.

Jace scratched his temple. "A half-zombie that gets *less* monstrous around Monty. That's new."

Hawthorne was practically jumping out of his skin. "This is incredible. Two examples of partial immunity: Becca, who overcame the infection entirely, and you, who remain half-turned but retain higher cognition. The potential for research is mind-blowing."

Zane snorted softly. "Research me all you want, doc, but I'm not volunteering for dissection." His gaze flicked to Becca. "I'd rather stick with you, if that's okay."

She swallowed. "You... you want to join us?"

He shrugged, the motion oddly casual. "I've been drifting for weeks, neither fitting in with the undead nor the living. But *they* follow you. You calm them. And you're still human. Feels like a safer bet."

Declan narrowed his eyes. "So we let a half-zombie roam around our camp?"

Becca turned to him. "He can talk, reason, and wants to be here. We're not about to run him off if we accepted the entire horde for errands."

Declan looked like he wanted to protest, but Lisa spoke up first. "If he's truly not going to harm us, we can at least keep an eye on him. Just… no biting, please."

Zane smirked, though it came off weary. "Don't worry, not my preference."

Hawthorne, still scribbling, approached carefully. "Zane, you mentioned hearing them communicate? Can you… can you translate anything they're saying right now?"

Zane cast a glance at the moaning crowd behind him. "Most are content. Some are hungry, but they sense that you can feed them meat if needed. They also sense your… anger and fear, which keeps them at bay. They're basically waiting for commands."

Tasha shuddered. "That's so creepy."

Becca pushed down a tremor. "So they're not people, right? *Most* are just mindless, yes?"

Zane nodded somberly. "Exactly. Only a rare few can think—like me. They're all relieved not to be aimlessly wandering in hunger, though. Your presence soothes them." He paused, scanning her face. "I guess we're all thankful for that."

She inhaled, feeling a wave of conflicting emotions. Relief, pity, fascination. This was... insane, but also gave her a sense of purpose. For the first time, maybe controlling them *wasn't* purely about survival. Maybe she was *helping* a few lost souls find peace. Or that was a dangerously naive thought.

After some tense discussion, the group decided to let Zane stay—and keep traveling. The plan to lead the main horde away still stood, but maybe they'd keep a smaller "guard" of those who insisted on following. Declan insisted on a watchful eye on Zane, while Hawthorne wanted daily checkups. Jace, somewhat annoyingly, kept joking about the "half-dead pretty boy" in the group.

Zane, for his part, mostly kept quiet, standing at the fringes with a guarded expression. He didn't join in the banter, uncertain if they truly welcomed him. But each time he drifted near Becca, he felt a subtle warmth in his veins, like a faint pulse returning.

"Let's try to move the big group out of our path," Becca said, stuffing the gifted coffee into her backpack. She'd clean the can later, maybe get a single, if revolting, sip. "We'll keep heading west. If some want to follow at a distance, fine, but we can't have this many near us."

They formed a small expedition: Becca, Zane, Hawthorne, and Jace—the latter two insisting on tagging along for "safety" and "research," respectively. The others stayed back to pack the vehicles and keep watch for raiders. Lisa gave them a withering look, as if to say *please don't unleash a thousand zombies on us.*

With Zane's help, they approached the massed horde in the field. Zane half-whispered translations of the more complicated groans. "They sense your presence. They want instructions… or meat. Or both."

Becca mustered her "confident zombie queen" posture. "Hey, everyone, thanks for the gifts," she said, voice echoing across the field. The moans shifted, almost an acknowledgment. "I need you to go that way—" She pointed off toward a far corner, where farmland stretched. "Stay there, okay? No following."

The moans swelled. Some zombies, especially the "originals" who had run errands for her, took hesitant steps in the indicated direction. Others stood, uncertain. Zane nodded at a few stragglers, murmuring commands in a raspy tone that sounded half like moans. Slowly, the horde began trudging away from the camp, forming a loose line in the distance.

Jace whistled low. "Holy crap. They're actually obeying."

Hawthorne's eyes shone with unbridled excitement. "This is the largest controlled movement of zombies I've ever witnessed. *Incredible.*" He turned to Zane. "You said they sense relief under her guidance?"

Zane shrugged. "Yeah. They hate the confusion of not knowing what to do. This gives them a kind of… purpose. It's twisted, but… better than them attacking the living, right?"

Becca let out a breath, tension easing. "Yes. We're definitely not complaining if they follow instructions."

A handful of stragglers lingered, including the half-faced "original" and a couple who'd delivered coffee. Zane translated their moans: "They want to stay near you. They fear losing the 'alpha.' They'll keep some distance if you insist, but they—uh—they basically worship you." He said it awkwardly, shooting her an apologetic look.

Becca gave a strangled laugh. "Great, so I'm an undead goddess now."

Jace snorted, clapping her on the shoulder. "Hey, if the shoe fits."

Hawthorne scribbled furiously. "We can manage them. Let them follow maybe a quarter mile behind. That way they won't bother us, but remain close enough if we need them. The rest can stay in that field or wander off. Does that sound feasible?"

Becca nodded, exhaling with relief. "Yes, that's perfect. Everyone happy?" She shot a glance at Zane, who offered a small nod. She forced a grin. "Fantastic. Let's go."

Returning to the camp, they relayed the plan to the rest of the group. The vehicles were loaded, and the sun had climbed higher, bathing the farmland in golden light. The group formed a caravan again—Declan, Lisa, and Edgar in the pickup; Jace, Tasha, Leslie, Marsha, plus Zane (and dog Chewie) in the SUV with Becca. A comedic overcrowding, but they'd manage.

"Zane, you smell kinda… undead," Tasha pointed out apologetically, making a face. He gave a rueful shrug. "Yeah, sorry. Soap helps a bit, but not much. I can sit in the far back if you want."

Marsha waved him off. "It's fine. We're used to the smell, thanks to rotting *everything* these days."

Leslie gingerly cracked a window, hugging her coupon folder. "Maybe we can do a little stop for air fresheners."

Becca snorted, sliding into the front passenger seat. "Sure. Next strip mall we see, we'll do a Bath & Body Works run."

Declan walked over, crowbar in hand. "So… you're letting the half-zombie ride with you?"

She gave him a look. "He's more docile than half the psycho survivors we've met. If he acts up, Jace can cut him down, right?"

Jace brandished his knife with a mock flourish. "You bet."

Zane just rolled his eyes, climbing into the SUV quietly.

Declan's frown didn't fully lift, but he stepped back. "Fine. But I'm not letting my guard down." With that, he hopped into the pickup, revving the engine.

Becca sighed. "He'll come around eventually," she muttered, more to herself than anyone else.

Hawthorne, leaning in through the open window, shot her a meaningful look. "We'll need to do daily check-ins on Zane's vitals, see if he reverts or stabilizes. And you, too. Don't forget."

She forced a smile. "Right, doc. We'll schedule a spa day for the undead. Thanks." With that, they started the SUV, and the caravan rumbled along a rural road that cut through fields and sparse trees.

It was weirdly peaceful—no more city rubble or corpse-littered parking lots, just open space under a bright sky. Tasha fiddled with a half-broken radio, picking up only static. Leslie rummaged for snacks, grimacing when she found a smashed Twinkie. Marsha dozed with the dog in her lap, and Jace hummed tunelessly.

Becca, enjoying the breeze from the cracked window, spotted a few zombies trailing in the far distance. *The stragglers,* she thought, half-laughing. *Who would've guessed I'd be a zombie Pied Piper?*

She couldn't resist making a joke to lighten the mood. "So, is it too early to start brainstorming horde T-shirts? 'Becca's Undead Army—We Aim to Displease'? Might help with morale."

Tasha giggled. "I'd wear that."

Leslie giggled too, then frowned. "Wait, that's morbid, but… weirdly funny. I'd want a discount, though."

Zane, silent until now, let out a surprisingly human chuckle from the back seat. The sound startled Becca—he had a pleasant laugh, low and warm, that belied the half-zombie state. She turned to see him fiddling with his hoodie, trying to hide the decaying patch on his arm.

"Sorry," he said, voice still raspy. "Didn't expect to find jokes in the apocalypse."

Jace flashed a grin in the rearview mirror. "Stick with us, buddy. We're the comedic relief in this world of nightmares."

Becca felt a small surge of satisfaction hearing Zane laugh. *Half-zombie or not, he's still got a sense of humor.* Then the thought flickered: *He gets more human around me?*

They traveled another hour or so before spotting a cluster of small farmhouses up ahead. The vehicles pulled off the road to investigate, hoping for supplies or a place to rest. The farmland stretched endlessly, dotted with barns and overgrown fields. A single windmill creaked in the distance.

They approached the first farmhouse cautiously. A few stray zombies lurked, quickly dispatched by a well-placed crowbar swing from Declan or a knife thrust from

Jace. The interior was ransacked but had a few surviving items: canned peas, boxes of pasta, and some dusty jars of pickles.

Marsha squealed in delight at discovering an unopened jar of peanut butter. Leslie found a small stack of old newspapers—she liked reading them for nostalgia. Becca rummaged for anything else useful. Tasha and Lisa stood guard outside.

Meanwhile, Zane hung back, half-lurking near the door. He clearly didn't want to rummage with them, probably mindful that any raider weirdo might see a "zombie" and shoot first. Hawthorne lingered near him, occasionally sneaking questions about the virus. Zane answered tersely, uncomfortable under the scrutiny.

Eventually, while the others packed up the newly found supplies, Becca stepped outside to stretch and found Zane leaning against a battered fencepost, watching the horizon. He turned as she approached, offering a faint smile.

"You okay?" she asked, half-awkward.

He shrugged, gaze distant. "Better than I've been in a while. It's… nice not to be alone, or stuck with the mindless ones. Even if I smell like roadkill."

She forced a laugh. "We can solve that if we find a working shower or, like, a pond."

He half-smiled, meeting her eyes. "I might do that. I—uh—just wanted to say thanks. For letting me join. I know it's weird."

Her chest fluttered. "We're *all* weird now. I mean, I command zombies like a bossy toddler at a daycare. You're half-dead. Jace is an ex-con with a knife fetish. Declan is basically an armed guilt-trip machine. Hawthorne's a science nerd on steroids. And Lisa's… well, she's Lisa. So, yeah, you fit right in."

That earned another amused chuckle from him. The tension in his shoulders eased. He looked at her with something akin to admiration. "I sense the virus inside me is… calmer around you. I'm not sure how or why, but the hunger fades. The more I'm near you, the more I feel… human."

Becca swallowed. "That's wild. Maybe there's something about me—like my blood, or those immunity factors. Or maybe it's magic, I don't know." She kicked at the dirt. "But if it helps you keep your mind, I'm glad. Gotta admit, I was worried we'd wake up with you gnawing on our arms."

He grimaced. "Believe me, I worried I'd do it too." He took a shaky breath. "But I won't. Not if you keep letting me… *exist* around you. That's all I ask."

She gave him a crooked smile. "Deal. Just promise not to judge me too harshly if I keep making wisecracks about the undead. That's my coping mechanism."

He pressed his lips together in a sort of grin. "Fair enough."

Moments later, the rest of the group emerged from the farmhouse, arms loaded with random supplies. They stashed the goodies in the vehicles. The dog, Chewie, barked excitedly at the scent of something in a half-open can of tuna Tasha found. The afternoon sun beat down mercilessly.

Declan called for everyone's attention: "We'll keep heading west. Might find a bigger farm or something suitable for a longer stay. We'll do a scouting stop soon, see if it's defensible. That's the priority—finding a place we can actually settle."

Everyone nodded in agreement. Tasha looked hopeful, Lisa rubbed her weary eyes, and Marsha patted Chewie's head. Jace hopped behind the SUV wheel with a mischievous grin, clearly itching to drive again. Hawthorne hovered near Zane, half-hoping to corner him for more questions, but Zane politely sidestepped, giving Becca a grateful nod.

"Let's roll," Becca said, forcing a bright tone. "The farmland awaits, and maybe we'll find an actual cow that's not a zombie. Imagine real milk."

Leslie brightened. "Don't tease me with dairy dreams."

And so the caravan set off once more. Through the rearview mirror, Becca saw a handful of her loyal undead trailing far behind, refusing to be fully abandoned. The bigger horde, she hoped, had stayed put in that distant field. She tried not to think about how she'd manage them if they caught up.

As the SUV rumbled down the dusty road, Tasha fiddled with a cracked phone for music, Jace hummed nonsense, and Zane stared pensively at the passing countryside. Lisa, from the pickup behind them, occasionally radioed with route updates. Edgar dozed. Marsha joked about how she missed iced tea. Meanwhile, Declan undoubtedly mulled over moral dilemmas from the driver's seat. And Hawthorne, riding with them, scribbled notes whenever Zane so much as twitched.

Becca couldn't help but grin at the absurdity. They had:

- A science experiment (Hawthorne's obsession).
- A cop who wouldn't shut up about morality (Declan).
- A knife-happy ex-con (Jace).
- A half-zombie hottie (Zane), slowly reclaiming his humanity around her.

And me, she thought wryly, *the accidental queen of the undead.* She might not have asked for these powers, but if they let her keep the people she cared about safe, maybe it was worth the cosmic weirdness. *Or,* she considered with a smirk, *maybe this is karma for all the snack hoarding I did pre-apocalypse. The universe saw me munching Doritos for breakfast and said, "Yes, let's make you the undead overlord."*

As the road stretched on, she let out a small laugh at that mental image. If this was karma, well, she'd own it. Because in an apocalypse of rotting nightmares, she'd rather be the unstoppable comedic anti-hero than the victim. And apparently, the half-living hottie at her side was on board, too.

The farmland passed in a blur of golden fields and dilapidated barns, the sun inching lower in the sky. The group pressed forward, searching for the next potential safe haven, unaware of the new challenges that might wait around the bend—human raiders, mutated undead, or simply the chaos of forming a new civilization among the rotting husks. But for now, at least, they had coffee (sort of), plenty of jokes, and a growing sense of camaraderie.

And a giant horde of zombies that recognized only one alpha: the sassy, snack-loving, half-crazy woman named Becca Montgomery.

CHAPTER NINE

"Smell that country air, folks," Becca Montgomery declared, stepping out of the SUV into the crisp dawn. They'd pulled up to a *potentially* perfect farmhouse nestled behind a modest grove of trees. The property was fenced in on three sides, and beyond that lay open farmland that stretched for miles. "If this place has fewer than two undead lurking in the barn, I'm calling it a win."

The rest of the ragtag group—Jace, Declan, Lisa, Tasha, Leslie, Marsha (with dog Chewie), Edgar, Dr. Hawthorne, and half-zombie Zane—piled out of the vehicles, stretching sore limbs. They'd been driving, scouting, and occasionally fleeing random undead for days, searching for a defensible home base.

Lisa scanned the farmhouse exterior: chipped paint, a sagging porch, but intact windows and a sturdy-looking fence line. "I like it," she said cautiously. "Quiet. And there's a well out back, apparently."

Declan Graves, ex-cop and resident scowler, nodded. "We should do a sweep inside, see if there's any leftover supplies. Then check the barn, see if it's stable. If it's clear, we can settle here at least temporarily."

Becca's heart fluttered at the thought of an actual *home*, even if it was a dusty old farmhouse in the middle of apocalypse farmland. She surveyed the orchard, noticing half-wild apple trees and a few patches of overgrown vegetable beds. *We could actually grow food,* she realized, a surge of hope warming her.

But, of course, the apocalypse had a knack for comedic timing.

Just as they started toward the porch, Tasha hissed, "Uh, guys, do you hear that?"

A distant cacophony of moans drifted on the wind. Becca's stomach dropped. "Please tell me that's not what I think it is."

Jace snorted. "Oh, I'm sure it's exactly what you think it is. Your loyal fans are back."

Sure enough, beyond the fence line, a disorganized mob of zombies lurched into view. They were led by a smaller cluster—a dozen or so undead who'd insisted on following at a distance. Now, however, they had *even more* behind them. *Again.* But the weirdest part? They seemed to be dragging a makeshift crate. Inside it, a small, wide-eyed calf blinked in terror, letting out panicked mooing.

"What in the…?" Lisa murmured, tire iron in hand.

"Is that a *baby cow*?" Tasha asked, voice squeaking.

Becca rubbed her eyes like she was waking from a bizarre dream. "I should probably be freaking out, but I'm mostly confused. They're bringing us a *cow*?"

Zane, the half-zombie hottie who had joined them a day earlier, tensed. He could sense the group's mixed excitement and dread. "I'll see if I can figure out what they're up to," he offered in that raspy half-alive voice. Pushing open the creaky farmhouse gate, he strode toward the moaning congregation.

Hawthorne grabbed his notebook, eyes shining. "Fascinating. Another instance of zombies retrieving living creatures as a gift? This is unprecedented."

Declan just scowled. "So first, they brought coffee. Now a baby cow. I can't decide if we should be impressed or horrified."

Marsha, hugging Chewie, sniffled. "Poor calf. It looks terrified."

Becca swallowed hard, stepping up beside Zane as he reached the fence line. The zombie at the front—one with half a face missing—hoisted the crate forward with guttural moans. Another behind him held a battered tote bag full of random produce that might have come from a raided greenhouse or store's vegetable aisle. She recognized wilted lettuce, some carrots, and half-crushed tomatoes.

As if that weren't enough, a third zombie rummaged in a plastic bag and presented a new can of *Double Shot Espresso*, slightly dented but less filthy than the last. They all stood there, moaning, as if awaiting her reaction.

Zane cleared his throat, focusing. He'd explained earlier that he could interpret some of their moaning patterns. "They're basically saying… they found more 'food' and 'things' you like. They're proud of themselves. They want your approval." He lifted his gaze, flicking between the undead and Becca. "They also mention they saw a baby cow lost in a field, so they put it in a crate, thinking *you* might want it."

Becca felt her heart melt despite the absurdity. "They're delivering livestock now? This is… bananas."

"Carrots, actually," Jace quipped, peeking over her shoulder.

Hawthorne scrawled notes, eyes alight. "A new stage of behavior. They're not just scavenging items;

they're capturing living animals. This is complicated ethically."

Becca inhaled, taking a cautious step forward. The calf let out a distressed *moo*, but seemed otherwise uninjured. The zombies simply… *brought* it here? "That's… unbelievably weird, but kind of sweet in a horrifying way. Thanks, guys," she ventured, voice thick with hesitation. She turned to Zane. "Anything else they're saying?"

He tilted his head, listening to more groans. "They say they also found fresh coffee and vegetables—like you wanted fresh food, right? They figure the cow can produce milk eventually. Or maybe you can eat it. They're not sure which humans do. They, uh, want to make you happy."

Becca's jaw slackened. "That's both touching and disturbing. I appreciate the generosity, but we can't keep collecting random farm animals. Or can we?" She shot a desperate look at Declan, who was crossing his arms in that *seriously?* Manner.

He sighed. "If we're making this farmhouse our home, I guess a cow might be useful. But it's not healthy to rely on zombies for groceries. This is insane."

She sighed, exasperated. "I know, but I can't *stop* them. They come back even if I say no. If you want me to handle it, then let me figure out how, okay?"

His scowl deepened. "Fine. But either you get rid of them, or you find a way to keep them in line. Because I'm not sharing our new home with a thousand rotting freaks."

"Seconded," Lisa muttered. "We can't have them crowding the fence day and night."

Becca nodded, biting her lip. "All right, I'll do something. I guess… I'll train them? Or keep them around but out of the way? Let me think." Even as she said it, she half wanted to laugh. *Training zombies?* Next thing, she'd be filming a tutorial on "How to Tame Your Undead."

Deciding they needed a safe base, the group performed a thorough sweep of the farmhouse. Marsha found a half-stocked kitchen with dusty mason jars. Leslie discovered a small generator in a side shed, though it lacked fuel. The barn, surprisingly, had fewer than three zombies—two to be exact. They were easily dispatched or *calmed* by Becca, who commanded them to "go outside." They complied, trudging off to join the bigger horde.

Even Chewie, the scruffy dog, seemed content sniffing around the porch, tail wagging. Meanwhile, the calf let out fretful moos in its crate near the fence, uncertain about its new environment. Tasha and Lisa tried to calm it with handfuls of weeds.

"Yes, this'll do," Declan declared, standing near the living room window, scanning the yard. "Fences, open sightlines, decent condition. We can patch holes. We've got a barn for storage or livestock. Some orchard trees for fruit. We can actually make a home here."

Becca smiled, ignoring the swirl of stress about the undead. "So we're officially farm owners?"

He nodded reluctantly, sparing her a tight-lipped half-smile. "I guess so."

Jace, who'd helped clear the barn, ambled in, tossing a leftover pitchfork aside. "I say it's cozy enough. Let's call it the *'Why Not Ranch'*. Because *why not* invite half the apocalypse to our doorstep?"

Becca snorted. "If we're naming it, I vote for 'Zombie Acres.' Or maybe 'Caffeinated Cattle Farm' since these undead keep bringing coffee."

Leslie giggled. "Goodness, you two. Let's just keep it simple: *The Farmhouse.* We're not open for business or anything."

Hawthorne, rummaging in a corner, muttered, "I'll need a spot for my lab, or at least a table to do bloodwork. With both Becca and Zane around, there's so much to study."

Zane, standing by the door, tried not to look uncomfortable. "As long as you don't dissect me, doc."

Hawthorne offered a sheepish grin. "Promise. *Minimal* stabbing." Then he jotted more notes.

After they took a quick break to snack on some newly found produce (and, ironically, a few *canned* beans nobody really wanted), Becca stepped outside with Jace, Tasha, and Zane. The rest started unpacking the vehicles, settling into the farmhouse. The moaning from beyond the fence grew louder; evidently, more undead had arrived or lingered, forming a half-moon around the property.

Tasha wrinkled her nose. "This is too many. They're basically a crowd."

Zane nodded. "They're waiting for instructions, but it's also like they're… excited to be near you. The longer they stay, the more alert they become. Some are even starting to think in basic ways."

Becca arched a brow. "Basic ways like… what?"

He closed his eyes, focusing on faint moans. "They want tasks. They want direction. They say the more you command them, the easier it is to fight the hunger. They… appreciate it." He looked a bit sheepish relaying zombie gratitude.

"That's bizarrely sweet," Tasha murmured. "I mean, still creepy, but sweet."

Becca flicked her gaze to Jace. "Well, if we can't chase them off, maybe we can train them to do chores or guard duty. That'd solve some of Declan's concerns." She raised her voice in a dramatic flourish. "Yes, let's harness the undead for manual labor. *Mwahaha.*"

Jace snorted. "I'm so in. Let's do it. 'Zombies R Us: Farmhands for Hire.'"

Tasha giggled. "We can pay them in raw meat."

Becca puffed out her chest. "But seriously, let's see if we can at least get them to patrol the perimeter or something. Keep other random undead away. Or fetch supplies if we need them."

Zane shrugged. "They'd do it if you give them direct commands, especially with bribes. But training them systematically might take, well, effort."

Becca peered at the mass of moaning figures, a swirl of determination igniting. "Let's try. Right now. *Jace*, come with me. Tasha, can you watch from a distance, maybe keep an eye on the baby cow if it tries to wander?"

She nodded quickly. "On it.

Out by the fence, Becca faced down a small group of undead volunteers—maybe a dozen who'd stepped closer in response to her beckoning. Jace stood at her side, knife ready if anything went sideways.

"All right, guys," she announced in a mock teacher's voice. "We're going to practice some simple commands: 'Stay,' 'Patrol,' 'Bring coffee… you know, the basics.'"

Jace cracked up. "I can't believe we're doing this. We need a whistle or something."

Becca stuck her hands on her hips. "Nah, I'll just use my commanding presence." She cleared her throat. "Hey, you—sit!"

A tall zombie with ragged overalls moaned, tilting its head. After a beat, it plopped onto the ground with a wet *squelch*. She suppressed a gag. "Good… job. You get a carrot, I guess." She tossed a limp carrot from the produce bag they'd brought out. The zombie sniffed, then gnawed on it uncertainly.

"Um… next," Jace said, pointing at a short female zombie with half a scalp. "You, patrol that fence line." He waved an arm to indicate the yard's perimeter. Becca repeated it with more authority, "Go patrol." The zombie let out a rasping moan, then shuffled off along the fence, as if on a slow, meandering guard duty.

"Holy crap," Jace murmured. "It's actually doing it."

Becca grinned, adrenaline surging. "We might be onto something." She turned to a cluster of three more, all moaning softly. "You guys… pick up that trash." She pointed to a scattered pile of old packaging near the fence. "Clean it up."

Miraculously, they did—albeit clumsily, dropping scraps multiple times before depositing them in a half-broken crate. She and Jace exchanged astonished looks. "We're basically creating an undead cleanup crew," Becca said, half-laughing. "I regret nothing."

Zane wandered closer, smiling faintly. "They're quite receptive if you keep it direct. They, um, can't handle too many instructions at once, though."

"Got it," Becca said, turning back to the group. "We'll keep it simple."

For the next fifteen minutes, she and Jace ran a bizarre boot camp, instructing random zombies to "stand guard," "fetch logs," or "sit quietly." The undead moaned in confusion sometimes, but each small success felt like a mini-victory. Jace offered comedic commentary, praising them like a coach on a sports field. Becca found herself giggling in ways she hadn't since the apocalypse began.

At one point, Jace stepped behind her to correct her stance—*like that even mattered.* She turned abruptly, nearly colliding with him, and they both laughed. The moment felt surprisingly intimate—this weird teamwork, forging a new world order. Then, spontaneously, Becca found her face inches from his. Perhaps it was the adrenaline, or the insane relief at progress, or the fact that Jace had that roguish grin. Before she knew it, their lips collided in a sudden, heated kiss.

It lasted a few seconds—maybe longer. Time blurred. She smelled his sweat, felt his chest against hers, heard the distant moans of zombies who probably were confused as to why their fearless leader was now smooching. She tasted salt and something sweet, maybe old gum. Whatever it was, a spark shot down her spine.

Then they broke apart, breathing heavily, both wide-eyed.

"Oh," she managed, voice trembling. "That... that happened."

Jace's grin spread slow and confident. "Yeah, it did. I regret nothing either."

A strangled noise from behind made them both whirl. Declan stood there, crowbar in hand, wearing an expression of *extreme judgmental scowling.* Tension radiated off him in waves, like he'd just witnessed a crime scene.

Becca's cheeks burned. She coughed, stepping back from Jace. "Declan, hi. We were, uh— training the zombies."

He raked a hand through his hair, jaw set. "Clearly," he muttered, voice clipped. "I see you're... very thorough about it."

Zane appeared off to the side, face thunderous. He looked *almost* livid, though he tried to hide it. A faint flush colored his pale cheeks, making him appear more alive than ever. *Jealous?* Becca thought, heart pounding. The half-zombie parted his lips to speak but said nothing, just glowered.

Hawthorne scurried over, oblivious to the tension. "Did I miss something? Because I see you're commanding them to do tasks, which is incredible—" He cut off, noticing Jace's and Becca's flushed faces and Declan's scowl. "Uh, everything okay?"

Becca forced a laugh, glancing at the moaning undead. "Yep, we're good. Just got carried away with the, you know, coaching technique." She shot Jace a look that said *we'll talk about this later.*

Jace winked at her, stepping back to retrieve his knife. "Right, yeah, training. That's all. Nothing to see here, folks."

Declan's jaw tightened. "Anyway," he said curtly, "glad your session is going so well. Next time, keep it professional, maybe?"

An awkward hush descended. The zombies, sensing the shift, just moaned. Zane fidgeted, gaze flicking between Jace and Becca with a wounded look. Hawthorne scribbled notes, presumably about the "make-out effect on leadership morale."

Finally, Becca cleared her throat. "So, yeah, we've taught them some tasks. A few can patrol the fence, some can gather junk. This is workable."

Declan grunted. "Great. Then maybe keep at it… minus the lip-locking. We have real work to do too—like repairing fences, storing supplies, and dealing with that cow."

Becca exhaled. "On it, boss. Sheesh."

They reconvened by the barn, where Lisa was organizing scavenged nails and boards to patch up holes. Leslie fed the calf some leftover veggies, and Tasha sorted through random farm tools. Meanwhile, Hawthorne cornered Zane for a quick Q&A session.

"How do you feel right now, Zane?" Hawthorne asked, pen poised. "Seeing as you look more, well, *alive* than before."

Zane's jaw clenched, his eyes darting to where Becca was half-listening to Jace's wisecracks. "I— yeah, I feel a bit warmer, less numb. The hunger is... quieter."

Hawthorne scribbled. "That's consistent with the phenomenon we've seen. Being near Becca must be boosting your dormant immune system. Fascinating." He adjusted his glasses. "And earlier, you seemed... upset?"

Zane huffed. "Not upset. Just... Surprised." *Jealous*, his mind screamed, but he refused to say it aloud. "I barely remember my human emotions some days, but seeing them... *together* brought something out."

Hawthorne nodded sympathetically. "Understandable. If your emotional centers are reawakening, you might experience typical human feelings —like jealousy."

Zane let out a bitter laugh. "Don't read too much into it, doc." He shot another glance at Becca, who was busy delegating tasks to the newly trained undead. *It's not like I have a claim on her.* She was free to kiss whoever. That didn't stop the pang in his chest, though.

Hawthorne made a final note. "Take it slow. Emotions can be intense. And do let me know if you experience any physical changes—like your pulse returning or your wound healing further. We should track that data."

Zane nodded, biting back his turmoil. "Sure, doc. I'll keep you posted."

Later that afternoon, they all gathered in the farmhouse's main room, an old living area with mismatched chairs and a dusty fireplace. The donkey-brown sofa sagged under Tasha and Leslie, who rummaged through a crate of produce. Declan leaned against a wall, arms crossed, shooting occasional glances at Becca and Jace. Marsha petted the dog, Lisa fiddled with ration counts, Edgar perused a tattered local map, and Hawthorne sat at a rickety table, scribbling notes about everything.

Becca sauntered in, plopping onto a wooden chair that groaned under her weight. She spotted Jace smirking from across the room. With a forced cough, she turned to the group. "So, status update: the fence is partially patched, the barn is decent, and the zombies are basically acting like weird farmhands. They brought random lumber from a collapsed shed down the road. That's… helpful, I guess."

Lisa snorted. "Yes, they're basically doing manual labor. Creepy but effective."

Declan nodded tersely. "Still don't like it, but if it keeps them occupied and away from the house, fine. We can do watch shifts overnight to ensure no uninvited corpses slip in."

"Agreed," Tasha said. "Besides, we have that baby cow to feed. Maybe we can name it? Something like 'Latte'? Since the zombies keep bringing coffee?"

Becca snorted. "Latte the cow. I dig it." She avoided Declan's gaze, but she felt it boring into her. *He's probably still mad about the Jace thing.* She didn't regret it, though. Not one bit.

Zane, lurking near the doorway, forced a casual tone. "I can help with watch. Doesn't matter if it's dark out—I see okay at night." Some half-zombie perk, apparently. He avoided eye contact with Becca, but his posture screamed tension.

Jace chimed in, smirking. "Yeah, *Zane* can be our night guard. Saves me from missing beauty sleep."

Becca shot Jace a playful glare. "You need it, trust me."

He grinned, winking at her. She felt her cheeks warm again. *Stop it,* her mind chided. She cleared her throat. "Anyway, any other pressing issues? Because I have some new commands for the zombie crew tomorrow—like building a real perimeter."

Lisa frowned. "Are you sure we want them building stuff? That might require more skill than rummaging for coffee."

Hawthorne tapped his pen on the table. "They might not be dexterous enough. But if you break tasks down, perhaps they can carry lumber, hold posts. You'd need living folks to do the actual hammering."

"Yeah, or we might witness the undead version of an OSHA violation," Tasha quipped. The room rippled with uneasy laughter.

Marsha gently raised a hand. "Since we're planning to stay here long-term, do we… have a *leader*? Because no offense, but we can't have chaos forever."

Declan glanced at Becca, then averted his gaze. "Someone needs to coordinate daily tasks, watch schedules, resource management."

Lisa cleared her throat. "I was a manager once, but this is different. And let's be honest, everyone's basically looking at Becca to manage the… undead portion."

Becca's eyes widened. "What, me? I'm not exactly leadership material— I'm just the one who got bitten and ended up with freak powers." *And who occasionally kisses knife maniacss while zombies watch.* "I'd, um, prefer to share the responsibility. We're all in this together, right?"

Declan relented a bit. "We can form a small council, maybe. But we *do* need you to keep the zombies in line. That's not optional."

She shrugged, trying to hide her relief. "Fine. I'll run the undead department. You handle, like, moral policing and structure. Lisa can do supply management, Tasha can do communications if we ever get a radio working, Edgar can do scouting, etc."

A chorus of nods filled the room, tension easing. They made a few more jokes, hammered out a watch schedule for the night, and parted ways to handle chores. Zane volunteered for the late-night shift, as promised, not meeting Becca's eyes.

A couple hours later, Becca ventured outside to retrieve some water from the old well, thinking the fresh air might help clear her head. She found Jace there, leaning against the well's crumbling stone, flipping a knife with casual ease.

"Hey," she said quietly, approaching. The sky glowed orange and pink as the sun dipped behind a line of distant trees.

Jace glanced up, tucking the knife away. "Hey yourself. Coming to fill a bucket or something?"

She nodded, fiddling with the rope. "Yeah, plus I… wanted to talk about earlier." Her stomach did a little flip. "The, uh, training session kiss."

He smirked, though it looked surprisingly gentle. "You regret it?"

She blew out a breath. "I said I didn't regret it, and I meant it. I just—didn't see it coming. Also, Declan looked about ready to kill us."

Jace shrugged. "He can scowl all he wants. We're all adults. The apocalypse is short, might as well enjoy life. Right?"

She managed a wry grin. "That's one way to see it. I just… can't handle drama on top of controlling a zombie horde, you know?"

He stepped closer, eyes gleaming. "No drama. If you want to do it again sometime, you know where to find me." His voice dropped, flirting with playful confidence.

Her cheeks flushed, and she let out a small laugh, flustered. "Wow, you're persistent."

"Guilty," he teased. "Anyway, no pressure. We've got a farm to run, zombies to train. But I'm not exactly sorry it happened." He gave her a light tap on the chin, then strolled off.

She stood there, heart racing. "I regret nothing," she murmured, echoing her earlier line. She turned back to the well, ignoring the swirl of complicated feelings. Part of her was *definitely* attracted to Jace. Another part kept noticing Zane's wounded expression, and something about Declan's broodiness tugged at her. She mentally cursed the apocalypse for turning her love life into a bizarre comedic mess.

Near twilight, a cluster of zombies loitered around the barn, moaning softly. They'd gathered scraps of wood, presumably to help with tomorrow's perimeter project. Becca approached with caution, carrying a small bundle of raw meat they'd salvaged from an abandoned convenience store. The undead perked up, drooling at the prospect of meaty bribes.

Zane hovered at her side, offering translations. "They're excited to build tomorrow," he said, voice subdued. "They also mention how they can 'think' better the longer they're near you. Like the virus that clouds their minds is clearing slightly."

Becca paused, letting that sink in. "They want me to keep giving them tasks so they can keep… *thinking?* That's unbelievably weird, but kind of sweet." She tossed them small bits of meat. "Here, for your dinner, or whatever."

Moans of gratitude rose, and a few zombies even attempted clumsy gestures that might have been the undead version of a thumbs-up. "They also say some are enjoying the fact they're not mindlessly hunting. They have a direction. It's a relief to them," Zane added.

She felt a pang of compassion. "I never thought I'd empathize with zombies. But if they're grateful… I'm not complaining." She turned to Zane, searching his face. "What about you? Do you want tasks too?"

He gave a rueful half-smile. "I'm more advanced than they are. But I guess… yeah, having something to do keeps the hunger away. Focus on living, or half-living." His gaze flicked away. "And sorry about earlier. I know I was… well, I reacted badly."

Becca softened. "It's okay. I get it. Tensions are high. And I know this is all new for you, too." She paused, feeling an urge to reassure him. "We'll figure it out, okay? If you need me to… *do something* to help you feel more human, let me know."

His eyes glimmered with a faint spark of hope. "Thanks." He cleared his throat, reverting to that guarded tone. "For now, let's keep them fed so they don't wander off looking for random cows or more coffee."

She barked a laugh. "Agreed. My coffee addiction doesn't require that many Double Shot Espressos. But keep the produce coming, I guess."

Darkness settled over the newly claimed farmhouse. The group gathered for a late meal—some rehydrated pasta and the last of the fresh veggies. Zane took the first watch shift along the fence line. Jace retired to the barn loft, presumably to watch the night sky. Declan insisted on bunking near the front door, crowbar in arm's reach. Lisa, Tasha, Leslie, and Marsha shared the second-floor rooms. Edgar dozed in a small side room. Hawthorne set up a makeshift "lab" corner to store his notes and test supplies, leaving a space for Zane's future check-ups.

Becca, exhausted from the day's emotional roller coaster, curled up on a worn couch in the living room. She was half asleep when she heard faint moans from outside. She peered through a window, seeing silhouettes of zombies patrolling the perimeter—like a night guard. The sight, bizarrely, made her feel… safer. *They're our watchers now,* she mused, stifling a laugh. *Never thought I'd rely on undead bodyguards.*

Her mind wandered to the earlier kiss with Jace, the flicker of jealousy in Zane's eyes, and Declan's stern scowl. *What am I doing?* She also recalled the comedic chaos of training zombies to pick up trash, retrieve coffee, and even bring them a baby cow. Her life had become an absurd comedic apocalypse, and somehow, she kind of loved it.

She let out a weary chuckle, whispering to no one, "I regret nothing." Then, with a final exhale, she drifted into a surprisingly peaceful sleep, cradled by the knowledge that a horde of undead minions stood guard. *Zombie queens never sleep alone,* she thought ironically before the darkness claimed her.

CHAPTER TEN

A month had passed since Becca and her ragtag group of survivors claimed the old farmhouse. Somehow, they had turned a crumbling property into a functioning (if eccentric) homestead. The once-broken fence now stood mended—partly by actual living hands and partly by the shambling undead who followed Becca's commands. The orchard, previously overgrown, was trimmed and fruitful. Even the barn had been cleaned out to store their modest supplies (and to house a very puzzled-looking calf they'd named *Latte*).

Most bizarrely, the surrounding farmland teemed not with wild animals but with an organized (or somewhat organized) zombie workforce. Any passing survivor or local would do a double-take at the sight of reanimated corpses hauling supplies, patrolling fence lines, or performing menial tasks like clearing brush. That vision alone was enough to spark rumors: that a "witchy zombie queen" lived here, commanding the dead like dogs. Rumors that might attract the wrong kind of attention.

And, oh, did it. But that part comes later.

For now, Becca woke up feeling more rested than she had in *years*. Her once-chronic nightmares of rotting hordes had been replaced by semi-humorous dreams of teaching zombies to line-dance—no doubt an influence of her real-life escapades. She stretched on her makeshift cot in the farmhouse living room, blinking at the early morning light streaming through half-repaired windows. On the couch, Tasha dozed with Chewie the dog sprawled over her feet; across the room, Dr. Hawthorne sat at a table, scrawling in his ever-present notebook, glasses perched on his nose.

She managed a lazy wave. "Morning, doc. Up early again?"

He glanced up, eyes gleaming behind the lenses. "I've been cataloging data about Zane's condition. You wouldn't *believe* the improvements. He's nearly fully human in vitals—pulse, breathing, temperature."

Becca perked up, rummaging for a half-eaten bag of chips. "Seriously? So the virus is… receding?"

Hawthorne nodded eagerly. "Yes, he's regaining color in his skin, normal appetite, even sleeping better. I think your presence is accelerating some kind of immunological response—like the partial immunity in his bloodstream is merging with your aura or something. It's mind-boggling."

She let out a snort. "I don't think I have an aura, doc—maybe just an overabundance of sarcasm. But that's awesome news. I can't wait to see him fully back to normal."

Hawthorne scribbled a final note. "At this rate, he might pass for a healthy human in another week. I'll keep monitoring. But it's… incredible, Becca. You're a living anomaly."

She popped a stale chip in her mouth. "Me and anomalies go way back. Thanks for the update." She stuffed the chip bag away, yawning. "I'm going to see if Jace wants to do a morning run in the orchard."

The doc peered over his notes. "Would that be a 'morning run' or 'flirting with the knife maniacs' run?"

Becca choked on her spit, cheeks flushing. "Dude!"

He chuckled. "Hey, I'm just observing. For science."

She threw an old sock at him, which he dodged with a grin. "You're incorrigible, doc."

Outside, the morning air was crisp, carrying the scent of earth and budding flowers. Summer was on the horizon, and the orchard trees rustled with a gentle breeze.

Becca found Jace in the vegetable garden behind the barn, sorting through a basket of weeds the undead had pulled overnight. He wore that lazy grin of his, hair disheveled, a knife always within reach.

"You look way too cheerful for 7 AM," she teased, approaching him.

He shrugged. "Gotta love early chores. Beats rummaging for scraps in the city. Plus, I get to watch reanimated corpses pluck dandelions—comedy gold."

She snorted. "Right?" She gestured at the orchard. "You up for a quick jog around the trees? I need to burn off some energy before we do fence checks."

He eyed her suspiciously. "You sure it's a jog you want, not a chance to show off your thighs?"

She rolled her eyes, a playful smirk tugging her lips. "Please, these thighs are *all business*. But yes, I'm feeling antsy. Let's race."

She set off at a sprint, Jace on her heels. Through the orchard, they darted between rows of blossoming trees, occasionally leaping over fallen branches. The morning light filtered through leaves, painting the ground in shifting patterns. She heard him breathing hard behind her, but his laughter rang clear.

Out of nowhere, he yelled, "Zombie tag!" and lunged at her in mock pursuit. "You're it, Monty!"

She shrieked, half-laughing, stumbling through a row of half-ripened tomatoes. "Oh, you jerk!" Adrenaline spiked as he sprinted away with surprising speed. She chased him, weaving through a cluster of undead "garden helpers" who paused mid-task to watch them with blank stares.

One zombie, struggling with a hoe, let out a low moan as Jace bounded past. Becca laughed breathlessly. "You see that? Even the zombies think we're crazy." She cut around a wheelbarrow, nearly colliding with a second undead carrying a bucket of mulch.

Jace cackled. "I stand by my choices." He vaults over a low fence post, trailing mud.

Becca pumped her legs, determined not to let him escape. With a burst of energy, she tackled him from behind, sending them both sprawling into the soft grass near a wild raspberry patch. They tumbled in a flurry of limbs, laughter, and mild cursing.

When they finally stopped, breathless, she lay on top of him, hair in disarray, mud smeared on her elbows. He gazed up with that rakish grin. "Couldn't resist, huh?"

She rolled her eyes, but her cheeks felt warm. "You deserved it, tagging me 'it.'"

He laughed, brushing a stray lock of hair from her face. "No regrets?"

She smirked. "None," then pushed herself off him, ignoring the flutter in her chest. "We should get back. I gotta check on the fences before Declan yells at us for slacking."

He stood, dusting off his pants. "Yeah, yeah, Ms. Zombie Queen. Lead the way."

On the walk back, they passed Zane in the clearing near the barn, supervising a small group of zombies who were hauling planks for fence repairs. True to Hawthorne's update, Zane looked nearly *alive*—his skin had color, his eyes sparkled with awareness, and the decaying patch on his forearm was all but healed. He was still on the pale side, but if you didn't know better, you'd never guess he'd been half-dead a month ago.

He offered them a wave. "Morning. You two look… sweaty."

Becca wiped her forehead. "We were playing around. Testing our cardio, y'know? How're the repairs going?"

Zane smiled—a genuine, human smile. "Good. The zombies are responding to hand signals now. I just show them where to put a plank, and they do it. Less moaning, more action."

Jace shot him a grin. "Nice job, man. Soon we'll have the best-fortified farmland in the apocalypse."

Zane nodded, a flicker of pride in his expression. Then his gaze lingered on Becca, an unspoken warmth there. She felt a small squeeze in her chest. *He's come so far.* She offered him a wry grin. "Thanks for pulling your weight, Zane. We'd be lost without your zombie-translating skills."

He dipped his head. "Thanks for… well, everything. I owe you." He held her gaze a beat longer, then turned back to the undead planksmen, calling a raspy, "Over here," that made them shuffle to place boards along the fence line.

Becca exchanged a brief look with Jace, who arched a brow teasingly. She ignored his silent commentary—there was enough complicated tension swirling in her life. Right now, she just wanted to keep the farm running smoothly, keep the group safe, and maybe enjoy small moments of normalcy among the comedic undead mania.

By midday, the sun climbed high, and Becca found herself cornered near the barn by Dr. Hawthorne, who clutched his notebook like a lifeline. His eyes shone with scientific zeal. "Can I ask you some routine questions, Becca?"

She sighed good-naturedly, wiping sweat from her brow. "Sure, doc. Lay it on me."

He flipped pages. "How have you felt physically since your last check? Any fatigue, sudden bursts of strength, weird cravings?"

"Nothing beyond the usual. I'm normal—unless you count occasional Dorito cravings, which might just be me being me."

He scribbled. "Emotional changes? Enhanced confidence controlling the undead? Episodes of mania?"

She snickered. "No mania, doc. Just the normal adrenaline rush from commanding zombies to do chores. Confidence-wise, yeah, I guess I'm more comfortable giving them orders now."

He nodded, humming. "Interesting. And your relationship with Jace, Declan, Zane… any changes or, er, tension that might affect your mental state?"

She nearly choked on her spit. "Wow, you're prying."

Hawthorne cleared his throat, looking sheepish. "Purely for research, I promise. Emotional stress could affect your neurochemistry, which might influence your immunity factor. That's all."

She rolled her eyes but couldn't help smiling. "I'm fine, doc. Just… balancing a weird love pentagon with an knife maniac, a half-zombie, and a broody ex-cop is par for the apocalypse course, right?"

He scribbled furiously, muttering, "Indeed, indeed." Then he snapped the notebook shut, giving a satisfied nod. "Thanks. You're doing well, Becca. Please don't hesitate to note any strange symptoms."

She patted his shoulder. "You'll be the first to know if I grow wings or shoot lasers from my eyes." She strode off, leaving him flipping pages with an exasperated but amused sigh.

Afternoon arrived in a golden haze. The group bustled around the farm, stashing supplies, tending to the orchard, feeding Latte the calf, and occasionally instructing zombies to haul compost or fill gaps in the fence.

Declan patrolled the perimeter with Lisa, scanning the fields for any signs of trouble. Edgar helped Tasha set up a rudimentary radio kit in hopes of contacting other survivors. Marsha busied herself inside, sorting dried goods. Everything felt *almost* domestic—like a surreal countryside retreat, if you ignored the moaning undead labor force.

But that peace was doomed to end. Because beyond the horizon, a rival human group had been watching for weeks. Rumors had spread of a "witchy zombie woman" controlling a horde, amassing power. Some saw it as an abomination, a threat that must be eliminated. Others wanted to harness her powers themselves.

Late in the day, a small band of armed survivors approached the farmhouse's wooded edge. They spotted the undead patrolling and waited for a moment to strike. A deadly plan brewed: capture the so-called witch, intimidate the farm's residents, and end her unnatural hold over the dead.

The farmhouse still lacked reliable plumbing, and the battered outhouse out back was basically defunct. So any time nature called, folks found a patch of woods or used a bucket. Becca, in particular, loathed the claustrophobic, spider-ridden outhouse. She'd once described it as "the entrance to a Stephen King novel."

So, as dusk approached and she felt the call of nature, she grabbed a roll of toilet paper from a shelf, calling to Tasha, "Back in five—just gotta pop a squat. If you see a zombie standing in the orchard, that's probably me."

Tasha laughed. "Got it. Watch out for ticks. And, y'know, random apocalypse threats."

Becca waved off the warning with a smirk. "Please, ticks are the least of my worries." She weaved through a gap in the fence, heading into the cluster of trees. She found a secluded spot near a mossy log, ensuring no undead lurked nearby. Pulling down her pants, she muttered, "Only psychos use the house bathroom. Or, well, *one day* I'll fix the plumbing, but not today."

Mid-relief, she felt a chill creep up her spine. The hair on her neck prickled. The woods had fallen oddly silent. She hastily finished, yanking her pants up. "Hello?" she called softly, scanning for movement. *Probably just a rabbit,* she told herself.

She was dead wrong. A hand clamped over her mouth before she could scream. Another arm wrapped around her waist, hauling her backward. Her heart thundered in her chest.

"Gotcha now, you freak," a gruff voice snarled in her ear. She thrashed, trying to bite the hand over her mouth. Adrenaline surged, but she was outnumbered. Three or four armed individuals loomed—she caught glimpses of dirty clothes, wild eyes, rifles. "Shut up," one hissed, pressing a gun barrel to her temple.

Becca's mind spun. *Oh God, oh God.* She clawed at the arms restraining her, but they tightened. Another voice sneered, "We've heard about your witchy powers, controlling the dead. That stops now, b*tch."

Panic welled in her throat. She wanted to scream. *If I can just make noise, the zombies will come.* She forced down terror, managing a muffled shout that turned into a raw scream when a fist connected with her side. Pain lanced through her ribs, but it fueled her desperation.

She screamed again, louder, "HELP! ZOMBIES — JACE, DECLAN, ANYONE—!" The gun jammed against her head, but she refused to stay silent.

All at once, the moans in the orchard changed pitch—like a howl of rage. The nearby zombies, attuned to Becca's voice, felt her panic and pain. They lurched into a collective frenzy, racing toward the woods. Even the ones scattered around the farm sensed something and began converging. The rival humans, dragging Becca out of the tree line, froze at the sight of a large group of undead surging forward.

Her group—Jace, Zane, Dr. Hawthorne, Tasha, Lisa, Declan—rushed outside, weapons drawn, alarmed by the changed moans. But before they could intervene, the zombies turned from docile helpers into savage protectors. They shoved Becca's friends aside, ushering them back to the farmhouse, moaning furiously, determined to keep them safe. A few rotting arms even blocked Jace from advancing, dragging him away so he wouldn't get shot.

Becca's mind reeled. *They're protecting everyone else, but I'm still in the enemy's grasp—this is bad.* One of the rival humans yanked her hair, forcing her to her knees. "Stay still," he barked. Another aimed a rifle at her temple.

She heard them snarl, "We kill the witch, we kill her hold over the dead. They'll scatter. This farmland's ours."

Her heart hammered. *No, no, no.* The farm. Her group. She refused to die here, in the dirt, under these maniacs. She tried to scream again, but a palm smashed against her mouth, cutting her lip. Blood filled her taste buds.

The moans grew deafening. The zombies closed in from all sides like a dark tide. The rival humans yelled commands. One fired a warning shot into the horde, but that only spurred them into a frenzy. Then the gore started.

Zombies lunged, grabbing at limbs. The humans fired, bullets shredding undead flesh. Some zombies collapsed, but more took their place, eyes burning with rage. The farm's orchard transformed into a battlefield of thrashing bodies and shrieks. The smell of blood and rot filled the air.

Becca watched, horrified, as one zombie sank rotted teeth into a man's shoulder, ripping a chunk of flesh. He screamed, dropping his gun. Another was tackled by a cluster of undead, pinned under a pile of gnashing jaws. It was brutal, primal. The air rang with guttural growls and terrified shrieks.

Minimal brain-eating was *not* on the menu. The zombies, enraged by Becca's distress, showed no mercy. They tore into the rival group with a horrifying efficiency, limbs flailing, blood spraying. Only one or two humans managed to flee, stumbling away with panicked cries. The rest were devoured or torn apart on the spot.

Becca's captor, the one holding the gun to her head, froze in terror as the horde closed in. She felt his grip slacken for a split second. She seized the moment, slamming her elbow into his gut. He stumbled, and she wrenched free, gasping. A zombie lunged at him, jaws snapping. Becca flinched as the man's scream cut short. *Dear God.*

Becca tumbled to the ground, shaking, covered in blood that wasn't entirely hers. The orchard resembled a slaughterhouse—rival humans torn asunder, chunks of flesh scattered in the grass. A few zombies lay re-killed by bullets, but most still stood, panting with savage satisfaction. The few living attackers who escaped were long gone, fleeing into the dusk.

She lifted her head, delirious with relief. *I'm alive.* She didn't see any sign of Jace or Zane, or the doc—her protectors had been herded away for safety. She tried to stand, knees wobbling. Two zombies approached, arms outstretched. She instinctively recoiled—only to realize they were gently helping her up, not attacking.

Tremors ran through her body. Her ribs throbbed where she'd been punched. One of the zombies let out a crooning moan, sliding its hands under her arms. Another stood on her other side, supporting her shoulder. They were... carrying her?

She let out a shocked laugh, tears welling. *I guess we're at that level now.* Her undead guardians carefully guided her through the orchard. Each step squelched on blood-soaked grass. The moans around her softened from murderous frenzy to concerned whimpers. A wave of weird gratitude swelled in her chest. *They saved me. And damn, it was horrifying, but... they saved me.*

At the farmhouse edge, her group stood with wide-eyed horror, pinned back by a ring of protective zombies. The moment they saw Becca being carried out of the carnage, relief flooded their faces.

Jace shoved past the undead barrier, sprinting to her. "Becca!" He grabbed her, pulling her away from the zombie arms. "Oh God, you're bleeding."

She managed a weak grin. "Not all of it is mine," she croaked. "Relax, I'm... alive, mostly intact."

Declan strode up, scowl deeper than ever. But beneath that scowl glimmered relief. Zane hovered behind him, jaw clenched with concern. Hawthorne rushed forward, rummaging for bandages. "What in the *hell* happened?" Declan demanded, voice tight. "We heard you scream, then the horde went berserk."

Becca sank to her knees, letting them fuss over her. "Rival group… wanted me dead," she gasped between breaths. "Zombies… lost it. Killed them. So messy."

Tasha's eyes brimmed with tears. "Oh God, are you okay? Let me clean that cut."

Marsha, pale, pressed a cloth to Becca's lip. Lisa hovered, wringing her hands. Edgar scanned the perimeter with a rifle, making sure no more threats lurked.

Zane knelt beside her, eyes flicking over the blood on her clothes. "Thank God you're all right," he murmured. She felt a warmth in his gaze that betrayed his reawakened humanity.

Dr. Hawthorne, trembling with adrenaline, whispered, "They tore those attackers apart like rag dolls. Must have been 10 to 15 of them. I— I can't even comprehend the gore."

Becca, still shaking, forced a wry smile. "I did promise minimal brain-eating. Guess we only half-delivered."

They helped Becca inside, away from the carnage. The zombies remained outside, milling around with subdued moans. Jace half-carried her to the living room couch, ignoring the blood-smeared path she left behind. Tasha got fresh water, Lisa grabbed blankets, Hawthorne hovered with medical supplies, and Zane offered silent support, hand on her shoulder.

Declan paced, arms rigid. "This changes everything," he said, voice low. "Word will spread that you have an army of zombies who kill anyone who threatens you. Locals will call you the Zombie Queen for sure."

Becca gave a tired snort, wincing at her bruised ribs. "They already do, apparently. Guess it's official. I didn't ask for it, you know."

His gaze flicked to her battered form, then away. "I know. But after this… I trust you even less. People died—this is a new level of violence. If you can't keep them from butchering folks, we're in deeper trouble than I thought."

A pang of hurt hit her. "I didn't *tell* them to kill. They reacted to me being attacked." She swallowed. "Yes, it was brutal, but it saved my life. Sorry if that's not squeaky clean enough."

He grimaced, torn. "I'm not saying I want you dead. Just… your hold over them is more dangerous than I realized."

She wanted to snap back but felt too drained. Instead, she nodded weakly, "We'll figure it out, Declan."

Jace placed a comforting hand on her arm. "Enough. She's hurt. We can worry about politics later." He and Tasha gently peeled away her bloody jacket to tend to bruises.

Zane hovered, fists clenched. "That group was planning to kill her. We can't blame the zombies for protecting her."

Declan's scowl deepened, but he said nothing more, stalking off to guard the front door.

Becca sighed, closing her eyes as Tasha dabbed at a cut on her forehead. Hawthorne took her vitals, quietly noting each bruise. She felt exhaustion creeping in, overshadowing the adrenaline. *This is my life now,* she mused hazily, *leading an undead horde, fending off psycho humans, and dealing with a suspicious ex-cop plus a newly human half-zombie. Great times.*

But as she drifted, she couldn't help feeling a surge of fierce gratitude toward her rotting minions. Sure, they were terrifying. Sure, it was a moral gray area. But they *saved her.* She felt a strange warmth in her chest—like pride. *Is this what it means to be a queen?*

Hours later, the chaos settled. They disposed of the attackers' remains in a mass grave far from the farmhouse (with some of the zombies' help, ironically). Only two or three of the rival group had escaped, presumably to spread stories of the horrifying "zombie queen" whose undead slaughtered their companions.

In the farmhouse, Becca rested on the couch, her group huddled around, quietly passing a lantern for light. Lisa handed around cups of watered-down juice, Tasha petted Chewie's trembling form, and Hawthorne fussed over Zane's final check-ups for the day. Jace lounged near the door, occasionally meeting Becca's gaze with a reassuring nod. Declan hovered on the outskirts, eyes locked on her with a conflicted mix of worry and mistrust.

Despite the thick tension, there was also an undeniable sense of unity. They'd survived another horror. The farm—still standing, still guarded by reanimated defenders—had become an oasis in the madness. The price? Becca's blood, some shattered illusions, and a body count that might haunt them. But in this grim apocalypse, survival always had a cost.

Becca stared into the flickering lantern flame, letting the day's events swirl in her mind. The playful morning in the orchard, the comedic zombie workforce, the savage rescue from kidnappers... and the knowledge that her "witchy powers" just grew more infamous.

Zombie Queen. The locals would whisper that name with a mix of awe and terror. She exhaled shakily, deciding that if she had to wear that crown, she'd do it her way—*with minimal brain-eating, maximum snark.* And maybe, just maybe, she'd find a way to prove that leading undead didn't have to mean losing her humanity.

A half-smile tugged her lips as she drifted into uneasy sleep. No regrets.

CHAPTER ELEVEN

One week after the violent showdown with the rival human group, *Zombie Acres*—as some had jokingly dubbed the farm—seemed surprisingly tranquil. The orchard leaves rustled in a gentle breeze; the half-wild orchard grass swayed; and somewhere in the distance, Latte the calf mooed plaintively for her breakfast. Even the zombies, arrayed around the yard doing menial tasks, offered a subdued chorus of moans.

Becca Montgomery, self-appointed (and sometimes reluctant) *Zombie Queen*, cracked open the rickety front door, stepping outside. She wore a pair of cutoff jeans and a flannel shirt tied at the waist—farm chic meets apocalypse. The sun's warmth kissed her cheeks. She inhaled the crisp air and allowed herself a brief moment to appreciate the quiet. *I hope no one tries to kill me today,* she thought wryly.

Sighing, she surveyed the yard. A half-dozen zombies lumbered near the fence line, "guarding" or simply standing in slow-motion. Another trio had wandered by the barn, where Zane was showing them how to stack some leftover lumber. She spotted Tasha and Leslie rummaging in the orchard for fresh fruit, laughing. And out by the refurbished water pump, Jace teased a pair of undead who'd apparently forgotten how to hold buckets.

"Morning, Monty," Jace called, spotting her from across the yard. He waved a battered straw hat he'd found somewhere, looking annoyingly handsome in a sleeveless shirt that showed off every swirl of his tattoos. "Sun's up, chores are calling, and I believe the local undead want your attention." He pointed at a huddle of zombies who had gathered with expectant moans.

Becca rolled her eyes with a grin. "They always do. Fine, I'll see what they want." She trotted down the porch steps, hearing the boards squeak underfoot. On the other side of the yard, she glimpsed a familiar silhouette—Declan Graves, stoic ex-cop, leaning against the fence with arms crossed. He was clearly keeping an eye on her, as he did every morning, but refusing to approach.

Her stomach fluttered. *Damn him,* she thought. *We had that big blow-up after the last attack, but I swear there's something in his gaze—anger, tension, maybe... longing?* She shook off the distraction, forcing her attention to the moaning zombies who brandished a random haul of broken pots, as if offering them to her. "Hey, guys," she said with a sigh. "Thanks for the, uh, shards of pottery? Very sweet. Let's not gather trash for me to trip on, okay?"

The zombies moaned, uncertain. *Time to be a nice queen, or something.* She gave a soft command to deposit the junk by the barn, and they shuffled off in compliance, groaning their typical guttural "Yes, queen" moan (or so she liked to imagine). Another day on the weird farm. Another day to keep people safe.

Declan's presence tugged at her mind. She decided to take a breath and cross the yard to him, ignoring the swirl of tension that always flared when they were alone. He stiffened at her approach but didn't bolt.

"Morning, Graves," she said lightly, stopping a few feet away. The air between them crackled with the intangible tension. His gaze flicked over her face—she still had faint bruises from the kidnapping fiasco, though they'd mostly healed.

"Morning," he returned, voice low. He toyed with the crowbar at his belt, his perpetual security blanket.

"How are we on watch rotations?" she asked, feigning business. "Any sign of those bastards returning?"

His jaw tightened. "No. We've got the undead patrolling at night. And Zane's been helpful with that, too." He hesitated, then added, "It's working… somehow."

She lifted a brow. "You sound surprised."

He exhaled, crossing his arms more tightly. "I still don't like it. The whole *zombie army* thing. But… it *does* keep us safer." His eyes flicked up to meet hers, unwavering. "I can admit that."

A prickle of warmth blossomed in her chest. "Wow. That's a big admission from Mr. Morals over here."

His cheek twitched with irritation. "Don't push it, Montgomery. I said I don't like it, not that I endorse it."

She snorted softly. "Right, of course. Wouldn't want to ruin your brood fest." But inside, she couldn't hide a small spark of relief. *He's not outright condemning me.* After a tense moment, she ventured carefully, "Look, I know you used to think I was, like, a monster controlling them. But… do you still?"

His shoulders relaxed a fraction. The silence stretched. Then, quietly, he said, "No. I don't think *you're* a monster." He looked away, as if the words cost him something. "You're just doing what you have to, I guess."

Her heart gave a little flip. *Finally.* She forced a smirk, though her voice sounded breathier than intended. "Well, I appreciate the half-endorsement. One day, you'll love my undead minions. Mark my words."

A muscle feathered in his jaw. "Don't push your luck." But he let out a resigned huff, almost… amused?

They stood there, tension buzzing. She realized abruptly how close they were, how the morning light highlighted the faint stubble on his jaw. Her gaze lingered on the scar near his temple. She recalled the times he'd threatened to kill her if she turned into a zombie, and how that threat was long behind them now. Something electric hummed between them—annoyance, attraction, or both.

Her pulse kicked up. She parted her lips, uncertain if she wanted to provoke him or appease him. He must've sensed it too, because he immediately frowned and stepped back, eyes darkening. "I should check the perimeter." He spun on his heel, striding off before she could respond.

"Sure, yeah," she muttered to no one, heart pounding. "Run away, big guy." The unresolved tension simmered like an unanswered question in the humid air.

Leaving Declan to brood, Becca strolled around the barn and found Zane finishing up some fence-lugging with the zombies. The transformations in him were undeniable—his complexion healthier, his dark hair no longer limp, and he barely moaned anymore. If you didn't know about his half-zombie state, you'd guess he was just a slightly pale, attractive dude with a sad backstory.

He glimpsed Becca, that small, shy smile crossing his lips. "Need any help?" he asked, brushing sawdust from his shirt. "We're nearly done with the fence repairs."

She waved a hand. "Nah, I'm good. But thanks. You sure you're not overexerting yourself?"

He chuckled softly. "I barely feel the old fatigue. Honestly, I'm stronger than ever. Maybe it's your immunity rubbing off on me."

She shifted her weight. "That's great, though, right? You're practically normal now."

A flicker of something crossed his eyes—relief, but also conflict. "Yeah, 'normal.' It's what I wanted. But it's… I don't know. I got used to the mental connection with the other zombies. Now I feel more… separate." He ran a hand through his hair. "But I can still sense them somewhat. They're calmer when you're near."

Becca nodded, empathy tugging at her. "So you're stuck between living and undead, mentally?"

He hesitated, gaze flicking around. "Kinda. Some of me misses feeling that universal hunger, ironically. Now I just… crave normal stuff, like hot food and, um…" He trailed off, cheeks coloring.

She teased gently, "What, you want a big steak? Or maybe you're craving a different appetite?"

His cheeks flushed deeper, voice unsteady. "I'm not… *I just*—" He fumbled, stepping closer. "Sometimes I — when I see you with Jace, or you bantering with Declan, I feel an urge to… I don't know, kiss you? Or at least be near you." He swallowed thickly, looking half-ashamed. "It's confusing. I spent so long half-dead, now these emotions are slamming into me."

Becca's heart fluttered. The sincerity in his voice tugged at her. She placed a light hand on his forearm, ignoring the swirl of guilt. "Zane, it's okay to have feelings. I can't blame you. This entire apocalypse fosters weird bonds."

He exhaled shakily. "Yeah, but I'm not sure what to do with it. Or if you'd even—like if you want me around that way?"

She flushed. *I have, like, three men swirling around me, each with different baggage.* "Look, you're sweet, and I like you. You're so… gentle. But things are complicated, you know?" She tried to smile. "I don't want to lead you on if I can't promise… well, more. Yet."

He nodded, forcing a half-grin. "Got it. I guess I'll just… keep being your friend, unless you want more."

A surge of warmth and pity welled up. "I do want you here, Zane. You're important. Let's just… keep it open?" She realized how vague that sounded but hoped he wouldn't push. He nodded, quietly relieved, but that longing shadow remained in his eyes.

Late morning found Becca sitting near the orchard, munching on an apple she'd snagged from a freshly harvested basket. She watched as a pair of zombies ambled by, arms loaded with branches for compost. Life had become so bizarre, she sometimes forgot how unnatural it was.

Jace ambled over, dropping onto the grass beside her with a groan. "Phew, orchard's all tidied up. Our rotting minions are surprisingly good at yard work, if you don't mind a few bone fragments in the mulch."

She snorted. "Lovely. We'll have the creepiest but most well-maintained orchard in the apocalypse." She offered him half the apple, which he declined with a grin.

They sat in companionable silence for a moment, until he bumped her shoulder playfully. "So, Monty, you got hot cop drama on one side, half-zombie heartbreak on the other. You living your best soap-opera life or what?"

She gave a mock groan. "Oh, shut up. Everyone's reading too much into my personal life."

He laughed, that mischievous twinkle in his eye. "Hey, you're the one who made out with me in the orchard last week. Don't think I forgot. I'm just enjoying the chaos."

Her face heated. "You were the one who— oh, never mind." She huffed, though a smile tugged her lips. "It was a moment of adrenaline, you jerk."

"Sure, sure." He leaned in conspiratorially. "No regrets, right?"

She wanted to smack him but ended up rolling her eyes with a reluctant grin. "None. But no repeating it until I sort my head out. That's all I'm saying."

He shrugged, unabashed. "Fine by me. I'll wait. I'm patient. And in the meantime, I get to watch you juggle Mr. Grumpy and Mr. Confused. Pure entertainment."

She punched his arm lightly, but she couldn't help laughing. "You're impossible."

"I try," he said, smirking. Then he stood, offering a hand to pull her up. "C'mon, Zombie Queen. We've got chores, and I hear Dr. Hawthorne is itching to do a 'group check-up.' Lucky us."

Sure enough, early afternoon found everyone herded into the farmhouse's large living room—an impromptu medical station set up along the walls. Dr. Hawthorne, brimming with academic fervor, insisted on taking vitals, checking wounds, and updating his notes on both Becca's immunity and Zane's progress. He also roped in Tasha, Leslie, Marsha, and Edgar for general check-ups, though the real interest centered on the undead-adjacent phenomena.

Declan hovered near the window, arms folded, scowl firmly in place. Jace lounged on the couch, occasionally flipping a knife between his fingers. Zane sat perched on a stool, looking anxious, and Becca paced near the fireplace, feeling caged.

Hawthorne started with Zane, measuring heart rate, lung capacity, temperature. "Astounding," he murmured, shining a flashlight in Zane's eyes. "Pupils reactive. Heartbeat in normal range. Next to no sign of necrosis." Zane gave a relieved half-smile, though he squirmed under the doc's scrutiny.

Then Hawthorne turned to Becca, beckoning her over with an excited wave. "Your turn, oh queen of the undead."

She rolled her eyes at the dramatic nickname but complied. He checked her pulse, peered at her pupils, asked about any odd symptoms. "None," she insisted. "I'm fine, doc. Just sometimes a headache if I give too many commands at once, but that's normal, right?"

He frowned. "A headache, interesting. Possibly mental strain from controlling them. Do you feel them more intensely now than before?"

She shrugged, noticing Declan's gaze boring into her from across the room. The tension bristled. She refused to give him the satisfaction of glancing away. "They do seem more… linked to me. If I'm upset, they're upset. If I'm happy, they're calmer. It's like an emotional echo chamber."

Hawthorne nodded, scribbling vigorously. "Fascinating. Possibly a psychic bond or advanced empathy from the mutated virus. Keep me posted if it gets worse."

Jace piped up from the couch, flipping his knife. "Or if you start hearing their thoughts. Then we'll have a real horror flick on our hands."

Becca shot him a playful glare. "Don't jinx me." She turned back to Hawthorne. "Anything else?"

Hawthorne shook his head. "That's all. Thank you, folks. I'll compile these notes. Might isolate a new theory soon."

Declan cleared his throat, obviously restless. "We done here? We have actual security matters to address. The last group that tried to kill us might not be the only ones." The gruffness in his tone was edged with a hint of worry.

"Security, sure," Jace teased. "Maybe we can teach zombies to set booby traps next."

Becca suppressed a giggle. "One step at a time."

As the group dispersed, Becca moved to the porch, intending to check if any undead needed her attention. She was halfway down the porch steps when Declan stepped out behind her, clearing his throat. She turned, heart thumping. "Yes, Graves?"

He stared at her, face a tumult of emotions. For once, he seemed uncertain. Finally, he blurted, "I said earlier you're not a monster. I meant it." His voice held a heated undercurrent, something that sent a zing down her spine.

She folded her arms, trying for nonchalance. "I appreciate the sentiment. So why do you still act like I'm going to, I don't know, raise an undead army to conquer the world?"

A muscle in his jaw twitched. "Maybe because you *could* do that. And it scares the hell out of me. But—" He sighed, stepping closer. She caught the faint scent of soap and gun oil. "But I know you're not evil. You've protected us, time and again."

Her pulse skittered. She arched a brow. "You're not going soft on me, are you?"

He almost laughed, though it came out as a tight scoff. "Don't push it, Montgomery." A beat passed, the tension swirling. Their gazes locked. His mouth opened as if to say something more, but he pressed his lips shut, wrestling with unspoken feelings.

Becca felt heat pool in her belly, confused desire sparking. She took a step forward, close enough that she could see flecks of gold in his dark eyes. "You know," she said softly, "it'd be easier if we could just… talk without you scowling, or me deflecting with jokes."

He inhaled sharply, fists clenched at his sides. "I'm not scowling, this is just my face." Then, quieter, "But you're right. We should talk."

Her breath caught. The late afternoon sun cast a warm glow on the porch. The hush between them brimmed with unsaid words, sizzling tension. She could almost imagine leaning in, bridging that distance, but an old fear prickled. *He's complicated. We have so much friction. Would we kill each other or…?*

Before either could act, a sudden shout from the side yard broke the moment. Tasha yelled, "Hey, guys! We found another stash of seeds—someone help me carry these to the barn!" The interruption shattered the quiet like glass.

Declan exhaled, tension retreating behind a stoic mask. "Duty calls," he muttered, turning abruptly. "We'll talk later, maybe." He strode off, leaving Becca throbbing with unresolved longing. *Damn it,* she cursed, stomping a foot on the porch.

The rest of the day rolled on with typical farm tasks: feeding the calf, gathering apples, sorting seeds, mending fences. Zombies shuffled about, some on guard duty, others hauling materials. The group functioned like a bizarre cooperative—half living, half undead, all comedic.

Late afternoon, a small comedic crisis erupted: the zombies assigned to orchard cleanup apparently started "tagging" each other with rotten fruit, mimicking the game Becca and Jace played earlier. She discovered them lobbing squishy peaches at each other in a slow-motion fruit fight.

Marsha, wrinkling her nose, scolded, "They're making a *mess*! And that fruit is half-rotten, they're flinging mush everywhere!"

Becca tried not to laugh. "Oh my God. They're literally copying our orchard tag. This is insane." She stepped in, commanding them to drop the peaches, and they obeyed, moaning apologetically. She stifled a giggle as one zombie, peach pulp dripping from its bony fingers, looked almost contrite. "Good grief. You can't make this up."

From behind her, Jace called, "You can train them to do yard work, but you can't stop them from partying, Monty!" He gave a thumbs-up, clearly amused.

The fiasco ended with a sticky orchard floor and a dozen undead looking sheepish. Another day in paradise.

As twilight draped the sky in dusky purple, the group gathered around a crackling fire pit in the front yard. Someone had rigged up a spit to roast some veggies and maybe the last of the dried meat. The zombies, for the most part, milled near the edges of the property, moaning softly as they patrolled or simply stared into space.

Becca sat on a low stool near the fire, Tasha beside her, Lisa rummaging in a supply box for condiments. Leslie and Marsha teased each other about the orchard fiasco. Jace sprawled on the grass, carving random designs into a piece of scrap wood. Hawthorne flipped through a half-tattered magazine, occasionally scribbling in his notebook. Edgar dozed, leaning against a fence post. And leaning against the porch railing were Declan and Zane, sharing an uneasy silence, each occasionally casting glances at Becca. Tension simmered.

She cleared her throat. "So, Tasha, any luck with the radio kit? Might be nice to hear if there are friendlies out there who don't want to kill us."

Tasha shrugged. "Not yet. Some static, but no stable signal. I'll keep trying tomorrow."

"Cool," Becca said, staring at the flames. She felt the weight of multiple gazes flickering over her. *Am I the center of everyone's weird romantic radius?*

Jace, noticing the tension, smirked and decided to poke the bear. "So, Monty, you want to tell us about your orchard tackle with me? Or about that porch conversation with Declan? Or maybe your barn fence talk with Zane? Because the sparks are flying, and I want to roast marshmallows in the aftermath."

Becca inhaled, nearly choking on air. Tasha giggled, Hawthorne raised a brow, and Lisa hid a snort. Zane stiffened, and Declan turned to glare at Jace. "Are you always so unsubtle, Carter?"

Jace shrugged, eyes dancing with mischief. "Unsubtlety is my specialty, Officer." He turned back to Becca, winking. "So? Fess up."

Becca fought the urge to throw a flaming log at him. *But maybe this is a chance to blow off steam.* She shot him an unimpressed look. "My orchard tackle with you was just me kicking your butt in an impromptu race. Porch conversation with Declan was him not calling me a monster, which is progress. Barn fence talk with Zane was him being sweet. That's all."

Zane flushed, refusing to meet her gaze. Declan scowled deeper, and Jace feigned a dramatic sigh. "Oh, the tension kills me. It's like living in a soap opera, but with zombies. I love it." He rolled onto his back, staring at the twilight sky, laughter spilling out.

Declan pushed off the porch railing, expression thunderous. "Some of us are busy trying to protect this place, Carter, not turn it into a circus." The anger in his tone sparked fresh friction.

Becca jumped in, voice sharp, "Don't start. We can have a sense of humor, or do you want us all to brood 24/7?"

He glared at her. "You're the queen, you tell me." The sarcasm bit deeper than usual, but behind it lay genuine frustration. She bristled, feeling her own temper rise.

Zane, discomfort radiating, stepped forward. "Declan, don't be harsh. We all want to keep the farm safe. Jace is just joking."

Declan's gaze snapped to Zane. "You're new to being human, so I don't expect you to understand. But jokes won't protect us from the next group that storms in."

Zane's eyes flickered with a trace of old undead anger. "I understand survival just fine. I also understand that you're angry about something else." Tension soared.

Becca leapt to her feet. "Okay, enough. We're all on edge, I get it. But let's not tear each other apart." She shot Declan a pointed look. "You and I can talk tomorrow or whenever you want, away from the peanut gallery."

He grumbled, turning away. "Fine." But the longing in his eyes before he stormed inside said a million contradictory things.

Jace sat up, whistling. "That's the most drama I've seen all day. My job here is done." He winked at Becca. She groaned, wanting to either murder him or hug him.

Eventually, the tension settled, and folks drifted off—some to stand watch, others to claim corners of the house to sleep. The zombies remained stationed around the property, moaning in the gentle night breeze.

Becca found herself in the orchard again, leaning against a sturdy apple tree. She breathed in the nighttime scents: earth, grass, distant hint of decay from the undead. *This is my life now,* she thought. *Zombies, chores, heart-pounding arguments with men who can't decide if they want me or want to kill me. Great times.*

She heard footsteps. Zane approached, hands in pockets. "You okay?"

She nodded, offering a small smile. "Just needed fresh air."

He stopped a few paces away, gaze soft. "If I can do anything to help you… or if you need to talk, I'm here."

Her heart clenched. The earnestness in his voice was undeniable. She stepped closer, letting her hand rest gently on his forearm. "Thank you. I appreciate that." His eyes flicked to her lips, a fleeting moment of longing. She felt a spark in her belly. *So many sparks. I'm a damn fireworks factory.* She stayed still, though, not wanting to lead him on.

With a resigned half-smile, he pulled back. "Good night, Becca." He wandered off, shoulders slumped. She exhaled, sadness twinging. *I can't fix everyone's feelings at once. Or my own.* But at least he wasn't half-dead anymore. That was progress.

A short time later, she headed inside, stepping over Jace's sprawled form in the hallway. He snored lightly, arms behind his head, a faint grin on his lips. She sighed, shaking her head affectionately. *That guy…*

Upstairs, she paused near Declan's door. It was closed, but a sliver of lantern light glowed beneath it. She lifted a fist to knock, then lowered it, reconsidering. *Not tonight.* She wasn't sure if they'd talk or start fighting again. Or worse—something else that might shred the tension in ways she wasn't ready for. Her heart hammered at the thought. *Tomorrow, maybe.*

Settling into her own makeshift bed—a few blankets in a corner of the second floor—Becca stared at the flickering lantern shadows on the wall. She felt the swirl of sexual tension with Declan, the gentle confusion with Zane, the carefree banter with Jace. It was a trifecta of chaos in her personal life. Meanwhile, she commanded an undead horde, trying to keep a farm afloat in a violent, post-apocalyptic world.

Yet, amid all the confusion and comedic anarchy, she found a strange sense of belonging. She had people who cared for her, zombies who would literally kill for her, and a decent orchard orchard to boot. She let her eyes drift shut, letting the day's madness fade, deciding that tomorrow she'd handle the next wave of drama. She always did.

CHAPTER TWELVE

It was midmorning at the farm, and Becca Montgomery was already feeling the press of a hectic schedule:

1. Check on zombie patrols.
2. Figure out why Latte the calf was mooing incessantly (again).
3. Possibly go for a run, *unless* a sudden crisis popped up.

But first, there was Dr. Eli Hawthorne—the group's resident scientist—who had insisted on gathering more in-depth data about Becca's "powers." He'd set up a small lab station in what used to be the farmhouse's dining room, complete with test tubes, a battered microscope, and notebooks crammed with scribbled observations. She'd been dodging his request for days, but apparently, today was The Day for *Science*.

She stepped into the makeshift lab area, wearing cut-off jean shorts and a tank top (the summer heat was no joke). Eli stood by a rickety wooden table, glancing at some carefully labeled vials. His dark hair was slightly messy, and he wore a white shirt with the sleeves rolled up, exposing surprisingly toned forearms. *Wow, that's new. Or have I just never looked?* She blinked, feeling a sudden flush. *Get it together, Monty.*

He turned, catching sight of her. A small smile flickered on his lips. "Morning. Ready to collect some data?"

She tried to sound breezy. "Yeah, doc. Lay it on me. You want a blood sample? Saliva? Another round of weird reflex tests?" She mentally told herself *not* to stare at his arms, but damn it, they were right there, flexing as he rearranged glass tubes.

He pushed a pair of glasses up the bridge of his nose—apparently newish reading glasses, which looked far too good on him. "All of the above, though let's start with a baseline exam: heartbeat, blood pressure, that sort of thing." He gestured at a stool near the table, inviting her to sit.

She hopped up, ignoring the flutter in her stomach. *He's your friend. This is just science.* "Sure thing."

He carefully wrapped a makeshift blood pressure cuff (salvaged from who-knows-where) around her arm. "Relax your shoulder," he murmured, leaning in. She inhaled, catching a faint whiff of soap and mild aftershave. *He smells... nice.* She forced her gaze away, attempting to focus on the peeling wallpaper instead of his biceps.

He finished pumping the cuff, eyes flicking to a gauge. "Blood pressure's slightly elevated, but that might be normal for you, or—"

Declan Graves—the ex-cop and perpetual brood machine—poked his head in through the doorway. "Hawthorne. You seen Zane? He was supposed to help me with fence checks."

Eli blinked, setting down the cuff. "Uh, not recently. He might be out back with Jace?"

Declan's gaze shifted to Becca, perched on the stool. His brows knitted suspiciously. "What's going on?"

She waved a hand. "Relax, Graves, I'm just getting my usual doc check. For *science*."

He scowled, stepping inside. "Fine. Don't let me interrupt." But the tension in his posture said otherwise. He crossed his arms over his chest, glaring at Eli like the man had personally offended him. Something about that irritated Becca. *He's the one who's always uneasy with my zombie powers—why does he get to judge me for letting Eli do some tests?*

"Look," she told Declan, "I'm busy. Go ask Jace where Zane is, or check the orchard. We've got enough watchers for one science project." The challenge in her voice sparked in the air.

Declan glared, jaw tight. "Sure. I'll go. But watch your back. The doc's got a habit of taking... intense notes." He stormed out, leaving the door half open.

An awkward silence followed. Eli cleared his throat. "He's worried about you," he offered.

She huffed. "He's always worried, or scowling, or both. Let's not talk about him, okay?"

Eli nodded, fiddling with the stethoscope around his neck. "Sure. Next step: I'll check your heartbeat." He stepped closer, pressing the stethoscope to her chest, just above the curve of her tank top.

Her pulse jumped. *Focus, Monty.* She forced a laugh. "Heh. Don't mind the thudding."

He smiled softly, focusing on his watch. "It's, um, a bit rapid." There was a note of humor in his voice too. *He knows.* She felt heat creep into her cheeks. *Of course he knows—my heart's racing.*

Just as Becca was about to say something sarcastic to cover her flustered state, Jace breezed in, a smirk on his face. "Whoa, doc, you're getting real cozy with Monty there." He eyed the stethoscope placement. "Should I come back later?"

She rolled her eyes, sliding off the stool. "Jace, you have the worst timing."

He laughed. "I specialize in comedic timing, actually." He leaned against the door frame, arms crossed. "So, doc, you learn anything fascinating? Like, is she part alien, or does she just have a weird virus thing?"

Eli, unflappable, pulled out his notebook. "Still a virus thing, but I'm identifying new markers in her blood. Possibly a mutated strain of the original zombie pathogen. I'll do more tests after I get a sample." He motioned to a tray of syringes, then looked at Becca. "If you're up for it?"

She forced a grin, ignoring the quickening thrum of nerves. *Needles, yuck.* "Sure, doc. Let's do this." She perched on the stool again, thrusting out her arm.

Jace sidled up, eyebrow cocked. "You sure, Monty? You're not squeamish?"

She shot him a glare. "I handle zombies tearing limbs off. I think I can manage a little syringe." *Though I might faint if I keep noticing Eli's biceps.* She took a steadying breath.

Eli prepped the needle, glancing at Jace's hovering form. "Maybe you can stand back so I don't accidentally poke you too?"

Jace grinned. "I'm not opposed to a little poke here and there, but sure, doc." He stepped aside, winking at Becca. "You got this, Monty."

She clenched her jaw, letting Eli slide the needle into her arm's vein. A quick sting, then the tube filled with her blood. She tried to keep her eyes on the wall, determined not to flinch. As he finished, she caught a glimpse of his forearm muscles flexing, and a swirl of warmth shot through her lower belly. *Down, girl.*

Eli gently placed a bandage on the puncture site. "All done," he said softly, his voice unexpectedly soothing. "You okay?"

She nodded. "Yeah, thanks." She forced a laugh. "If you needed more, let me know—but not too much, I need my blood."

He chuckled, capping the vial. "I'll start some basic tests now. With better equipment, I could do more, but we'll see how far this old microscope gets us." He turned to rummage through his supplies.

Jace cast Becca a teasing look, leaning in to whisper. "You're not drooling, are you?" He eyed her up and down, amusement glittering in his eyes.

She smacked his arm. "Shut it. Go see if you can, I don't know, help the zombies practice their breakdancing or something." She tried to sound exasperated, but a grin tugged her lips. "Give us some peace, will you?"

"Fine, fine," he sing-songed, heading to the door. "Don't do anything I wouldn't do." He disappeared, leaving a faint echo of laughter behind.

Now alone with the doc, Becca hopped off the stool, rubbing her bandaged arm. "So, do you want me to do anything else? A mind-control demonstration? I could command a zombie to do jumping jacks or fetch your lab equipment."

He flashed a genuine smile. "I'll need to measure some data while you give commands, actually. Maybe see if your heart rate or temperature spike." He lifted a battered notepad. "We can do it outside, though. I'd like to observe you in action. If... that's okay?"

She bobbed her head, trying to ignore how her chest fluttered at the mention of "action." "Sure, doc. Let's see if we can find a willing zombie volunteer."

They stepped out into the midday sun, heading around the side of the house. She noticed him discreetly flexing his shoulder, probably from carrying lab gear earlier. Her mind traitorously zeroed in on the subtle ripple of muscle. *Stop, Monty, get it together.* She exhaled. *He's not that hot... okay, maybe he is. But it's the apocalypse—I shouldn't be thirsting over the one science guy left alive. Also, he's definitely giving me weird vibes. Or am I imagining it?*

They found a cluster of four zombies near the orchard fence. Perfect test subjects. Eli pulled out a small handheld device that measured heart rate (cannibalized from old medical equipment). "I'll hold this to your wrist while you command them, see if your pulse spikes."

She grinned. "Alrighty." She stepped up to the zombies, who turned their milky eyes toward her. "Hey, guys. Over here." Their moans rose in that familiar tone of *Yes, queen?*

Eli positioned the device on her wrist, scribbling notes. "Go for it."

She cleared her throat. "You, uh… pick up that broken chair and move it near the barn." One zombie moaned, shambled over to a collapsed wooden chair, and hoisted it—mostly competently—then trudged off.

Eli's eyebrows shot up. "Incredible. Your pulse jumped from 78 to 82 BPM. Slight, but noticeable."

She giggled. "Adrenaline from giving orders? That's silly."

He shrugged, eyes dancing with fascination. "Could be a subtle link between your emotions and their actions." He turned to the second zombie. "Try a more complex command, maybe multiple steps?"

She pursed her lips. "All right, big guy, you… pick up that bucket, walk it to the orchard, then come back." She pantomimed the steps. The zombie moaned, grabbed the bucket, stumbled toward the orchard, and eventually returned, empty bucket in hand.

Eli all but beamed. "Your heart rate hit 90 BPM during the second step. Might be that mental strain or just a normal reaction." He scratched notes, stepping closer. "This is so—"

Declan suddenly strode up, arms crossed, eyes narrowed. "What's going on here?"

Eli startled, turning. "Just data collection, measuring her vitals while she commands them. Why?"

Declan glared at him, then at Becca. "Don't push her too hard. She's still recovering from the last fight." The concern in his voice was overshadowed by a tense, almost protective vibe.

Becca bristled. "I'm not a fragile flower, Declan. I'm fine. Let the doc do his research."

He huffed. "Fine," and stepped back a few paces, but remained watchful, arms folded. *He's basically giving us the stink-eye,* Becca thought.

Then Jace arrived, apparently drawn by the zombie demonstration. He took one look at the standoff and grinned. "Ooh, is the doc giving you a physical, Monty? Bet that's fun. Need a volunteer for anything?"

Becca rolled her eyes. "You're incorrigible, Jace. We're measuring data, not hooking up."

He spread his arms dramatically. "I'm just saying, apocalypse dating can be a group sport if you're open-minded." He shot an impish wink at both Becca and Eli.

Eli flushed, stepping back. "Uh, no, no, that's not… I'm purely collecting data, obviously." He shot Becca a startled look that was half shy, half intrigued. She stifled a laugh.

And as if the tension wasn't thick enough, Zane approached from the orchard path. He took in the scene—Becca, Eli close together, Declan's scowl, Jace's grin—and frowned, concern evident. "Everything… okay here?"

Becca spread her hands. "Just a science experiment. No biggie."

Zane nodded stiffly, gaze lingering on Eli's proximity to her. "All right. Let me know if I'm needed." She felt the worry radiating off him—fear of being replaced, maybe? She offered a reassuring smile. He gave a tight nod and shuffled off.

Declan cleared his throat again. "Well, if you're done with the zombie demonstration, we have real chores —"

Eli cut in politely, "We're not quite done, actually. I'd like to measure one more command, possibly more physically demanding—like making them run, if that's possible?"

Becca blinked. "Uh, sure. They can hustle a bit if I order them. Might be hilarious to watch." She turned to the remaining two zombies. "Hey, can you, like, jog around the barn and come back?"

The zombies moaned, looking bewildered. She gestured with her arms. "You know, run—like a faster walk?" They took a halting shuffle, then sped up to a clumsy lurch. The result was a comedic near-jog. She and Jace burst out laughing. Even Eli stifled a grin, though he dutifully watched the data tracker.

She glanced at Declan, expecting him to scowl, but he wore a half-smirk. *Progress.* Then, noticing her looking, he swiftly masked it with his usual stern expression. *Never mind.*

Once the zombies finished their awkward jog, Becca lowered her arms, exhaling. "All right, guys, good job. Grab some, um, orchard brush or something." They ambled off moaning. The comedic sight made her giggle.

Eli jotted final notes, eyes shining. "That was… extremely helpful. Thank you, Becca. I have a ton of data to process."

Her heart pounded from the exertion—or from the tension swirling around them. "No prob, doc. Glad to help." She tried not to stare at his rolled-up sleeves, or the way sweat beaded on his temple. Apocalyptic thirst was a real thing.

He gave her a crooked smile. "You mind if we talk more in the lab? I want to run a quick test on your reaction speed, maybe get a second blood sample for comparison post-exertion."

She swallowed. "Another needle? *Sigh.* If it helps your research, fine." She turned to see Declan, Jace, and Zane all eyeing them with varying degrees of interest. "You guys can go do your chores or whatever. I'll be with Eli."

Jace winked. "Have fun, Monty. Don't break the doc's beakers… or his heart." He swaggered off, chuckling.

Declan looked like he wanted to protest, but instead, he mumbled, "Just be careful," and walked away, tension rolling off him. Zane lingered, meeting Becca's gaze with a worried smile, before sighing and trailing after the others.

Eli, oblivious to half the subtext, motioned for her to follow him inside. "Shall we?"

She squared her shoulders. "Lead the way."

Back in the "lab" (the farmhouse dining room), the afternoon sun slanted through a dusty window, illuminating motes in the air. Becca perched on the stool again while Eli prepared another syringe. Her heart hammered for reasons unrelated to fear of needles.

He took her arm gently. "Give me your left side this time, so I'm not hitting the same vein." His voice was low, soothing.

She swallowed, eyes flicking to his chest. *He's definitely in decent shape under that shirt.* She forced herself to stare at the table. "Sure, doc."

He tied the improvised tourniquet, leaning in. She felt the warmth of his proximity, smelled that subtle soap again. "This might sting," he whispered.

"Yeah, I know," she muttered, voice coming out husky. He slid the needle in, drawing fresh blood. She bit her lip, trying not to notice how his forearm brushed against her knee. *Focus, Monty, you're a grown woman, not a schoolgirl.*

The moment stretched, thick with tension. Finally, he withdrew the needle, capping it carefully. "Got it." He pressed a cotton pad to her arm. "You okay?"

She nodded, exhaling shakily. "All good." She attempted a laugh. "If I faint, blame your biceps."

His eyes widened, a hint of red coloring his cheeks. "What?"

She realized she'd spoken out loud. *Oh, damn.* She coughed. "I—I mean, I blame the needle. Blood loss or something." *Smooth recovery, Monty.* But the flicker of a grin on his lips said he wasn't buying it.

He carefully bandaged her again. "So you, uh, notice my arms?"

She cleared her throat, feeling that unstoppable wave of embarrassment. "I might have noticed you're more… fit than when we first met. Apocalypse workouts, right?" Her forced casualness sounded ridiculous to her own ears.

He ducked his head, smiling. "I've been lugging gear around, rummaging for supplies, helping with farm tasks. I guess it shows." He placed the blood vial on a tray, eyes lifting to meet hers. "I'm not complaining if you're— you know, noticing." A quiet beat of mutual attraction lingered.

She let out a frazzled laugh. "Weird times, doc. We're in an apocalypse. I guess… we gotta find bright spots where we can." *Bright spots or biceps. Same difference.* The tension in the room soared.

A wave of heat pulsed between them. She glanced down at his lips, then forced herself to look away. *We can't. It's… we're colleagues, right? Allies.* But the room's stillness tugged at her, urging a step forward.

He swallowed, taking a half-step closer. "Becca, I — I'm glad you're letting me do this research. It's… important. And you're…" His voice dropped. "You're important."

Her heart thumped. "Thanks," she whispered. She half wanted to lean in, half wanted to run. *So complicated.* Instead, she placed a hand gently on his forearm. "Hey, we'll figure out how all this immunity and zombie control works, right?"

He nodded, gaze flicking to her mouth. "Yes. That's… the plan."

A few seconds of loaded silence passed. The tension sizzled, a heartbeat away from tipping into something more. Then footsteps clomped in the hallway, shattering the moment. Lisa called from the other side of the door, "Hey, doc, we need you to check a stash of medical supplies Tasha found. Some bandages might be salvageable."

Eli blinked, stepping back. "Sure! I'll be right there." He shot Becca a fleeting, almost regretful smile. "Another time, I guess."

She forced a grin, swirling with relief and frustration. "Yeah, sure. Another time. I should go check on, uh, stuff." She bolted out of the makeshift lab, cheeks burning. *Whew.*

She escaped to the porch, gulping fresh air. The entire day had been a rollercoaster of tension. *Is it always going to be this insane?* She wondered if she could handle flirting with a scientist *and* dealing with moody Declan, charming Jace, and sweet but confused Zane.

But it seemed fate wasn't done with her. Declan was there, leaning against a post, arms folded. He shot her a piercing look. "Done playing lab rat?"

She bristled. "It's research, not 'play.' If it helps me understand my powers, that helps all of us, right?"

He shrugged, gaze simmering. "Sure. Just… keep your guard up, is all." The words dripped with jealousy or concern—maybe both.

She crossed her arms. "I can take care of myself, Graves." She glared, stepping past him to the yard. "And if I want to… talk with Eli, that's my business."

He stiffened. "Never said it wasn't." A muscle ticked in his jaw. She couldn't decide if she wanted to punch him or drag him inside for a heated confrontation. The tension was suffocating.

Suddenly, Jace walked by, whistling a tune. He threw them a knowing look. "You two lovebirds done fighting? Or do I need popcorn?"

She whipped around, exasperated. "We're not lovebirds, Jace."

Declan muttered something under his breath, then stalked off. Jace chuckled, strolling over. "I love this. Seriously, Monty, your love life is better than TV. You got big bad ex-cop jealous, the doc flailing with his test tubes, and Zane pining like a puppy. Drama, drama."

She smacked his shoulder. "It's not funny! I'm stuck in the middle of an apocalypse with a bunch of guys who can't decide if they like me or hate me… or both." She sighed dramatically.

He smirked, patting her back in mock sympathy. "Apocalypse dating is complicated, indeed. I say lean into it."

She rolled her eyes but let out a reluctant laugh. *He's not entirely wrong.*

At that moment, Zane emerged from the barn, noticing her conversation with Jace. He looked torn, scuffing a boot in the dirt. "Hey, um, Becca. Want to… help me feed Latte? She's been restless."

She forced a smile, ignoring Jace's mocking grin. "Yeah, sure. Let's go." As she followed Zane toward the barn, she couldn't help thinking about Eli's arms, Declan's glare, Jace's teasing, and the swirl of chaos that was her life.

By the time twilight settled over the farm, Becca had managed to avoid any more awkward collisions with people she might or might not be interested in. The zombies continued their evening patrols, moaning softly in the gathering dark. Tasha and Leslie worked on dinner, a stew of random canned goods. Jace teased them from the sidelines, offering no real help. Marsha fussed over Chewie, while Edgar hammered a loose board on the front porch. Declan and Zane scanned the perimeter, each lost in their thoughts.

Dr. Eli Hawthorne hovered at his makeshift lab table, eyeing the blood samples under a dim lantern. Becca stood at a distance, watching him from the doorway. Part of her wanted to approach and see if he needed help. Another part was too frazzled after the day's tension to handle more flirting. She decided on a middle path—slipping away to the orchard for a moment of solace.

She found a quiet spot under a gnarled apple tree, the same place she often escaped to. The night sky above twinkled with more stars than she remembered in the old world. She sank to the ground, hugging her knees. *So I'm attracted to the doc... but I also have these unresolved feelings with Declan's protective scowl. Then there's Jace's carefree charm, Zane's sweet confusion...*

She let out a soft laugh at the absurdity. *Who would've guessed the apocalypse would come with a side of romantic chaos?*

A gentle moan startled her. A single zombie had wandered close, perhaps sensing her mood. It approached hesitantly, then sank to a kneel as if wanting to keep her company. She exhaled, tension easing. "Hey, buddy. You okay?"

It moaned softly in response, not aggressive, just present. She patted its shoulder, an odd wave of affection welling up. *Maybe that's the real secret: building a weird new family—living, undead, everything in between.*

After a few minutes, she stood, heart calmer. Tomorrow, she'd face more science tests with Eli, more suspicious glares from Declan, more teasing from Jace, more longing stares from Zane. And, ironically, she found she didn't mind. Because at least life was interesting. She ruffled the zombie's tattered sleeve. "Come on, buddy, let's get you back to the yard. It's bedtime."

CHAPTER THIRTEEN

It started with a single rumor.

Some wandering survivor had escaped a horde in the nearby countryside, raving about how certain zombies had spared him because he'd spoken Becca's name out loud—like it was a magic password. The rumor spiraled into tales that there was a farm, run by a "zombie queen," where the undead followed commands and protected humans. It sounded impossible, but in a world of rotting corpses and freakish immunities, maybe it wasn't so far-fetched.

Over the next week, small trickles of ragtag survivors began stumbling to the farm's perimeter, eyes wide with disbelief at the docile undead patrolling the fences. Some came seeking shelter, others curious about rumors of an apocalyptic "cult" that worshiped a woman who controlled zombies.

Becca Montgomery never intended to start a cult. She didn't even want the title of "queen." But one morning, she woke to find half a dozen strangers outside the farmhouse gate, clutching backpacks and improvised weapons, begging for sanctuary. She exchanged a nervous look with Declan, who let out a long-suffering sigh. "This is a *terrible* idea," he muttered.

But Becca glanced at the hopeful, desperate faces beyond the fence and couldn't bring herself to turn them away. "Let's see where it goes," she replied softly, ignoring Declan's glare.

Jace, who'd been eavesdropping, quipped from the porch steps, "Are we getting matching jackets? Maybe with a 'ZQ' logo for 'Zombie Queen'? I'm in favor of cult merch, just saying."

Declan groaned, arms folded. Becca shot Jace a playful glare. "Shut up, you knife maniac." But she felt an odd swirl of excitement. *If these survivors can integrate peacefully, maybe we can do more good... or it might blow up in our faces. Let's find out.*

Over the next few days, more stragglers arrived. Some had heard direct rumors about "Becca the Zombie Queen," others had simply stumbled upon the farm. Word spread that the undead here wouldn't attack you if you respected the rules. That they'd even protect you if you got threatened. It sounded like a miracle in the apocalypse.

Lisa and Tasha struggled to manage the influx of anxious newcomers, making them turn over weapons, checking them for bites, assigning them to a corner of the property. Zane, still mostly human but with a lingering half-zombie sense, hovered near the gates to sense if anyone had ill intent. Jace called them the "Zombie Queen's Royal Reception Committee," which earned him more than a few exasperated eye-rolls.

The newly arrived survivors ranged from a middle-aged teacher looking for safe harbor to a young couple with a toddler, plus a group of grizzled scavengers who claimed they'd "seen the horde kill bandits on sight." They all stared at Becca with an odd mix of reverence and fear. Some even brought small offerings—canned goods, seeds, or random supplies.

Becca tried to quell the awkwardness. "Look, we're not a cult," she told one wide-eyed woman who knelt in the dirt, calling her "Holy Mistress." *Holy Mistress, seriously?* "We're just… a community trying to survive. The zombies are my friends, not— not gods or anything."

But rumors had a life of their own. The more she denied it, the more people whispered about her "humility." It was borderline comedic. Dr. Eli Hawthorne took endless notes on the sociological phenomenon, shaking his head in disbelief at how quickly a rumor could birth a proto-religion.

Declan, for his part, was in a perpetual state of "This is a bad idea." He patrolled the farm's perimeter with a grim scowl, arms folded over his chest, occasionally barking commands at the newly arrived survivors. "You can't just wander into the orchard without permission," he snapped at a young man who nearly got head-butted by a curious zombie.

Whenever Becca tried to reason with him, the conversation inevitably ended with him scowling and muttering about security risks. She tried not to take it personally, but the tension between them built like a storm cloud overhead. They never fully resolved their mutual annoyance—nor the electric undercurrent of attraction that flared whenever they argued.

One afternoon, as they stood by the barn discussing how to allocate chores among the new arrivals, the tension boiled over.

"We can't just let them roam the property unescorted," Declan insisted, pacing near a stack of feed bags.

Becca folded her arms. "We can't treat them like prisoners, either. This is a farm, not a fortress. They came for safety."

He shook his head, eyes stormy. "They came because you have some freakish hold over zombies, and they think you're their savior. That's not normal, Becca."

She bristled, fists clenching. "I never asked to be some damn savior! I'm just trying to help people. Or do you prefer we turn them away to die out there?"

He glowered, stepping closer. "You're letting them worship you, fueling their delusions. That's how cults start. *You're* the one encouraging them to stay."

She jabbed a finger at his chest, heart pounding. "Don't pin this on me. They're free to come or go. I'm not forcing them to do anything except abide by basic rules."

He grabbed her wrist, voice a low growl. "You're naive. This many people in one place, plus an undead army? We're a giant target. Mark my words."

Her pulse thundered. She yanked her wrist free, glaring up at him. "Stop manhandling me. I'm sick of your gloom-and-doom." Anger simmered under her skin, but also… that *pull*. The tension that had crackled between them for weeks, threatening to ignite.

His eyes burned with frustration. "I'm trying to protect everyone, including you."

She snorted. "By treating me like I'm incompetent? Or a monster?"

His jaw worked. "I *said* you're not a monster. But this is dangerously close to—"

She cut him off with a furious glare, stepping nose to nose with him. "You talk like you have all the answers, but you can't see beyond your fear. Maybe you should trust me for once."

Silence hung, thick and charged. Their breaths mingled, hearts pounding. Something snapped. In one fluid motion, he grabbed her by the shoulders, pressing her back against the barn's wooden wall. She gasped, anger flaring into something hotter. Their eyes locked, the distance crackling with unspoken longing and rage.

Becca's back thumped against the barn boards, sending a small cloud of dust drifting down. Her heart hammered so hard she thought it might burst. Declan's hand remained on her shoulder, his grip strong but not painful. She stared up at him, fury and desire churning in her gut.

He hesitated—just a heartbeat—like he was giving her a chance to shove him away or cuss him out. Instead, she lunged, seizing the collar of his shirt and yanking him down. Their mouths collided in a frantic, heated kiss that tasted of anger and pent-up longing.

She moaned into the kiss, feeling his breath hitch. His free hand slid to her waist, pulling her closer, pinning her firmly against the rough barn wall. The kiss was fierce, all teeth and muffled groans, as if both were exorcising weeks of unresolved tension.

Her fingers dug into his shoulders, nails scraping fabric. He responded with a low growl, lips moving hungrily against hers. The barn boards pressed into her back, but she barely noticed. She parted her lips, letting his tongue slide against hers, the heat between them spiking to near unbearable levels.

He broke away just enough to mutter, "Damn it, Becca…" before crushing his mouth to hers again. She clutched him tighter, a swarm of sensations flooding her—his stubble rasping her cheek, his chest solid against her body, the taste of salt and need.

She let out a strangled laugh, breathless. "You… you piss me off… so much," she gasped between kisses.

His response was a bruising press of his lips to hers, one hand sliding up to tangle in her hair. "Feeling's… mutual," he growled, voice husky. She arched against him, toes curling in the dirt, devouring him as if the world might end any second. (Well, it *had* ended, but that only fueled their desperation.)

Seconds stretched into a blur of hot, open-mouthed kisses, ragged breathing, and the creak of the barn. At some point, he moved to her neck, leaving a trail of heated pecks along her jawline, exhaling roughly. She groaned, letting her head tip back. Electricity jolted through her veins, each touch igniting sparks beneath her skin.

Eventually, logic forced its way in. They were in broad daylight, near a barn that others could pass by. She placed a palm on his chest, gently pushing. "Hold on," she murmured, breath shaky, heart hammering.

He stilled, panting. The frustration and desire in his eyes mirrored her own. Slowly, they separated, though neither stepped far. He kept one hand on her hip, and she gripped his shirt collar. Their lips were swollen, breath ragged.

They stared at each other, reeling. For a moment, the entire farm, the undead, the new survivors—they all faded away, leaving just this crackling intimacy.

Becca swallowed. "That was… something."

He let out a breathless half-laugh, still bristling with tension. "Yeah." Another beat passed, and he loosened his grip, though he didn't back up more than a few inches.

She blinked, her mind racing. *We just made out like wild animals, pinned to the barn.* "Uh, so, I guess… we should get back to chores?" she finally managed, voice unsteady.

He released a shaky breath. "Probably." But he didn't move.

She bit her lip, meeting his gaze. The anger had dulled, replaced by a confused swirl of longing. She pushed down her own confusion, forcing a grin. "We can talk about this later? Or maybe never?"

He gave a mirthless chuckle. "We'll see." Then, with visible reluctance, he stepped back, letting the space between them fill with warm afternoon air. The tension remained, a thrumming undercurrent that threatened to pull them back into each other's arms. Instead, she turned, adjusting her shirt, cheeks blazing.

They both caught sight of Jace standing a few yards away, arms folded, wearing the biggest smirk in the apocalypse. *Oh, shit.* Had he witnessed the entire meltdown?

Jace sidled closer, glancing between them with a mischievous gleam. "Well, well, well," he drawled, "look who's got barn makeout privileges. This was so worth checking fences for."

Becca's mortification soared. Declan stiffened, adopting his usual scowl, though a faint flush stained his cheeks. "Mind your own business," he growled, pushing past Jace.

Jace shot a finger-gun gesture at Becca, wiggling his brows. "Girl, I see you. Finally hooking up with Officer Grumpypants?"

She rubbed her face. "Jace, oh my God, shut up." Her cheeks burned. She half-expected him to cackle. Instead, he just patted her shoulder, snickering.

"Relax, Monty. I'm happy for you, truly. Tension was thick enough to cut with a machete. Surprised it took this long." He paused, eyeing the barn's scuffed boards, then shot her a grin. "Just be careful not to cause structural damage next time, okay?"

She groaned, pushing him away. "I hate you sometimes."

He laughed, stepping back. "Sure, sure. Now, come on, we got newly arrived survivors milling about, asking for your blessing or something. Let's not keep the cult waiting." He sashayed off, humming, leaving her wishing the ground would swallow her whole.

Trying to shake off the lingering taste of Declan's lips, Becca emerged from behind the barn to find a small crowd of new arrivals and older residents gathered in a loose circle near the orchard. They parted as she approached, revealing a scrawny teen who stepped forward with a timid expression.

"Um, hi," the teen stammered. "We heard you can command zombies. And—and that they do what you say. Is that, like, real?"

Becca forced a friendly smile, ignoring the leftover adrenaline from her barn fiasco. "Yeah, sort of. They don't exactly worship me, but they listen to me. We can use them for chores or defense."

A middle-aged woman in tattered cargo pants chimed in, "We're grateful you took us in. We, uh, wanted to give you this." She offered a small cloth bundle. Inside was a half-faded patch embroidered with some weird symbol. "We made it for your… group. Like an emblem. For your leadership."

Becca nearly choked. *An emblem?* She stifled a laugh, glancing at Jace, who stood behind the crowd, pantomiming *jackets*. She suppressed an eyeroll. "That's… thoughtful," she said carefully. "Thank you. But this isn't a monarchy or anything. We're all in this together."

A gaunt man with haunted eyes shook his head. "No, you're more than that. You keep the undead under control. You keep us safe. We'll do whatever you say. Just… don't cast us out or let them attack us."

Her stomach twisted. *This is exactly what Declan was worried about.* "Look, you can stay if you follow the rules—pull your weight, don't harm each other, or the zombies. That's all. I'm not a goddess or queen. I'm just… me, okay?"

They nodded, but she saw it in their eyes: a strange worshipful gleam. *Damn.* She felt a hand on her shoulder—Lisa, who murmured, "Maybe we can integrate them better if we set schedules, chores, routines. That might curb the cult vibe."

Becca nodded. "Yeah. Good idea." She faced the survivors with what she hoped was a confident stance. "All right, folks, let's talk about how we do things around here. We'll start with daily tasks: orchard picks, barn cleaning, farmland expansions… and so on." She tried not to notice how some gazed at her like she was the messiah.

Later that afternoon, after delegating chores and calming the new arrivals, Becca retreated to a quiet spot by the barn. She caught sight of Zane approaching, hands shoved in his pockets. He wore that earnest, slightly shy expression that made her heart ache with guilt.

"You okay?" he asked softly. "I, uh, sensed… something earlier. Emotions running high? Are you and Declan… fighting more?"

She flushed, remembering the *opposite* of fighting that took place. "We're... working it out, sort of. How are you?"

He offered a wry smile. "Confused. Seems we have a mini-cult forming. And I keep hearing them call you the 'Chosen One' or something." He shook his head, worry clouding his eyes. "Doesn't that freak you out?"

She sighed, running a hand through her hair. "It does. But I can't turn them away. They're survivors, like us. And if I can keep them alive with my... powers, maybe that's not so bad."

He nodded, though anxiety lingered in his gaze. "Just be careful. People can be unpredictable when they think you have godlike power. And you do, in a way."

She forced a smile, patting his shoulder. "I'll watch my back. Don't worry."

By dusk, the farm bustled with new communal routines: survivors cooperatively cooking a big pot of stew, Tasha and Leslie distributing rations, Jace leading a group in zombie-related orientation. Meanwhile, Eli holed up in his lab, analyzing data from the day's new arrivals and trying to see if any other partial immunities existed.

Becca wandered near the barn, drawn by the memory of that fiery makeout session. A swirl of emotions churned—part excitement, part dread. *Where do I go from here with Declan?* She saw him in the distance, patrolling the fence with two or three zombies in tow, as if trying to distract himself. She didn't dare approach, not after that meltdown. Not yet.

Jace sauntered by, carrying a homemade sign that read "Welcome, Don't Annoy the Zombies." He winked at Becca. "Sign's going up near the orchard. Thought I'd lighten the mood."

She snorted. "You're incorrigible." Then she paused, face serious. "Thanks for, you know, not teasing me too hard about… you-know-what."

He grinned. "Oh, I'm definitely teasing you, just in smaller doses. But hey, I want you happy." He ruffled her hair like a bratty older brother. She smacked his hand away, smiling despite herself.

After dinner, a group of new arrivals approached, timidly asking if they could "hear the queen speak." Becca nearly spat out her stew. "I'm not giving a sermon," she tried to protest, but they insisted. They'd even gathered flowers from the roadside, offering them to her like tributes.

Lisa found it half-hilarious, half-disturbing. "You might have to stand on a crate and say something like 'We're all in this together!' Or they won't sleep at night."

Becca groaned. "Fine. A quick pep talk. That's it."

So under the flicker of lanterns, she climbed onto a wooden crate near the orchard. A dozen or so new survivors, plus some curious older ones, circled around. The zombies patrolled in the backdrop, like silent guardians. She cleared her throat awkwardly.

"Um, hi, everyone. I'm Becca," she began lamely. "I'm, uh, not your queen or goddess or whatever you've heard. I just… can communicate with zombies and keep them from eating us. So welcome to the farm. If you pull your weight, we share resources. We do chores, we watch each other's backs, and we don't kill or harm each other. That's basically it."

A moment of silence, then polite applause. Some parted to let her step down. She forced a grin, trying not to cringe. *At least they didn't ask me to bless them.* Then a wiry man with hollow cheeks stepped forward, tears in his eyes. "Thank you for saving us," he whispered. "We owe you everything."

She patted his shoulder, feeling uncomfortable. "Just keep the orchard weeded, and we're even, yeah?" She tried a light joke. It earned her some hesitant laughs. *All right, maybe this cult vibe can be softened with humor*

Eventually, the crowd dispersed. Some survivors set up small tents in the orchard, others bunked in corners of the farmhouse. The zombies continued their watch, moaning softly under the star-littered sky. Becca found herself alone again by the barn, leaning on the same spot where she and Declan had shared that scorching kiss.

Her mind replayed the heated press of his lips, the taste of his frustration, the near-furious desire that had left them both breathless. A swirl of guilt tugged at her. She was the so-called "zombie queen," now also grappling with a complicated love… geometry—Declan, Jace, Zane, and even sparks with Eli. But that raw moment with Declan was beyond anything she'd experienced so far. *We can't ignore it forever.*

She sensed movement behind her. Turning, she saw Declan stepping out of the shadows, arms still folded. Her pulse kicked up. Did he want a round two? She swallowed.

He rubbed the back of his neck, not meeting her eyes. "I, uh… wanted to say I didn't mean to—" He paused, frustration evident.

She let out a slow breath. "I know. We… it just happened."

He nodded curtly, jaw tight. Then quietly, "Doesn't change the fact that I still think this cult nonsense is insane. More people means more vulnerability."

She forced a small smile. "I know. You're right, partially. But this is the world now—people cling to hope, and if that hope is me or these undead, so be it. We adapt."

A flicker of respect crossed his face. "Fine," he allowed. "But don't expect me to hold your hand if this backfires."

She snorted softly. "I wasn't planning on it, though you seemed pretty willing to hold more than my hand earlier." She raised a brow suggestively, ignoring the blush creeping up her neck.

He tensed, color flooding his cheeks. "That was… a moment of weakness."

She couldn't help a half-laugh. "Sure, Graves. A 'moment of weakness.' Good to know." She turned away, biting her lip to hide a smirk. The tension sizzled again, but they both let it lie, for now. He gave her a final nod and strode off into the night, leaving her with the memory of his breath against her mouth, the hot press of his body.

Late that night, Jace found Becca outside near the orchard, gazing at the fence line. He sidled up, hands in his pockets. "So, Monty, you realize we officially started a cult, right?"

She groaned, head tilting back. "Don't remind me. I didn't plan this."

He grinned, patting her shoulder. "Relax, it's not so bad. We can pass out membership badges, get a catchy chant. Maybe Tasha can handle PR. This might be the start of something big." He wiggled his brows dramatically.

She shoved him lightly, rolling her eyes. "You're impossible."

He chuckled, stepping away. "Get some rest, oh fearless queen. Tomorrow, we can teach the new folks how to feed the zombies without losing fingers." He tipped an imaginary hat and strolled off.

Becca exhaled, scanning the quiet farm. Survivors bunked down in corners, the undead stood watch, the orchard rustled with night breezes. The cult had begun, apparently—her cult, to everyone else's confusion. She'd have to figure out how to lead these people without letting the worship get out of control, while also juggling complicated feelings for multiple men in her orbit. Good times indeed.

A wry smile tugged her lips. She had no illusions that it'd be easy. But hey, if an ex-grocery clerk turned zombie queen couldn't handle a ragtag cult in the apocalypse, who could?

CHAPTER FOURTEEN

Becca awoke to the morning sun filtering through cracks in the old farmhouse roof, sending thin beams of light across her makeshift cot. She lay there for a moment, willing her mind to stay blank, but of course it didn't cooperate.

How could it, when every day brought new arrivals to "Zombie Acres," half of whom called her their *queen*? How could it, when she'd recently pinned Declan Graves to the side of a barn in a furious, heart-thundering kiss? Or, for that matter, when her brain kept pinging her with memories of Dr. Hawthorne's strong forearms, Jace's constant flirtations, and Zane's puppy-like devotion?

She groaned into her pillow, as if burying her face could stave off the swirling confusion and the unrelenting feeling that she was juggling more guys than any sane apocalypse survivor should.

She eventually threw off the thin blanket, shivering a bit in the early morning chill. The farmhouse still didn't have proper heating, and the nights sometimes got cold enough that she had to cuddle under layers of mismatched quilts.

Now, though, the fresh dawn air beckoned her outside. She might as well check on the undead workforce, see if any more strangers had shown up to worship her or squat on her land, and maybe—just *maybe*—find Zane for the chat she'd been putting off.

Stepping into her worn jeans and a loose T-shirt, she shoved her feet into battered boots and ran a hand through her messy hair. The ground floor of the house was already bustling with some of the new arrivals rummaging for breakfast. They called out cheerful greetings like, "Morning, your majesty!" or "Hello, Zombie Queen!" which made her cringe, though she tried to be polite. She forced a friendly wave, refusing to correct them yet again.

If she was honest with herself, part of her was too tired to keep telling them not to call her that. And maybe, just maybe, she enjoyed a smidge of the adoration.

Once outside, the sunlight warmed her face. Across the yard, a few of her more loyal undead were shuffling around with buckets and tools. There were a dozen or so new arrivals who had arrived in the past week, and a half-dozen older folks who'd been around for a while. The orchard stood to the south, apple trees swaying gently in the breeze, while the barn—scene of her and Declan's scandalous moment—loomed large and rustic to the east. She spotted Jace near the barn entrance, tossing feed to the poor, confused cow named Latte. She almost chuckled at the bizarre normalcy of it all: an ex-con feeding a cow in a place where zombies roamed and people half-worshipped her.

"Hey, Monty," Jace called, noticing her with a grin. "Cow says moo, orchard's quiet, and the new cultists are hoping for a sermon after lunch. You want me to sign you up for a 2 p.m. preaching slot?"

She wrinkled her nose, trudging over. "Please, no. Don't they have chores to do? If they think I'm giving them daily sermons about undead synergy, they'll be disappointed."

He laughed, setting the feed bucket down. "You sure? I can pass around a donation plate. Maybe we'll score more coffee."

His snark made her roll her eyes, though she let a smile slip. It was comforting that no matter how insane things got, Jace remained unflappably comedic. "Very funny," she said. "But honestly, I'll probably skip the big talk. Let them worship in peace."

He gave a mock salute. "As you command, Your Royal Zombieness." She flicked him in the arm, hissing in mock indignation. He just smirked, running a hand through his hair. "Anyway, you see Declan yet? He's stalking around here somewhere, super extra sour this morning. Probably worried about the horde."

Her heart did a nervous little skip at the mention of Declan. She schooled her features into a neutral expression. "No, haven't seen him. I'll keep an eye out. You know how he gets if I let too many strangers roam around without hearing his lecture about security."

Jace's grin turned sly. "Might also be that you two nearly banged against the barn last time you were alone. That'll put a guy in a mood."

She groaned, cheeks flushing despite herself. "Shut up, ex-con. Weren't you supposed to be training some new people on how to feed the zombies without losing fingers?"

He patted Latte's flank, ignoring her attempt to deflect. "On my to-do list. Don't worry, Monty, I'll let you get back to your smoochy apocalypse harem." He wiggled his eyebrows, dodging her halfhearted swat with a laugh. "But seriously, watch out. I hear Dr. Hawthorne's rummaging around for you, too. Must be tough being so popular."

Her heart flipped again, this time at the mention of the doc. "He's just doing research," she muttered, forcing a casual shrug. "It's not… I mean, we're not hooking up or anything. Right?"

Jace looked on the verge of cracking a joke, but an older woman from the new arrivals shouted his name, needing help with water. He offered a salute to Becca. "Time to play helpful farmhand. We'll pick this up later. Don't do anything *too* scandalous before lunch, yeah?" And off he went, leaving her alone with Latte the cow, who mooed plaintively.

She exhaled, patting Latte's flank. The poor bovine had no clue about the complicated soap opera swirling around this farm. "You've got it easy," she murmured. "All you want is grass and an occasional pat on the head."

As if summoned by her mood, she heard footsteps on the gravel behind her. She turned, half-expecting Declan's scowl or Jace's grin. Instead, she found Zane—the sweet, half-zombie-turned-nearly-human who'd quietly claimed a corner of her heart. His dark hair flopped over his forehead, and color had fully returned to his once-pale cheeks. If not for a faint scar on his arm, no one would suspect he'd been half-undead a month ago.

"Hey," he said softly, hands in his pockets. "You, uh, have a minute?"

She nodded, feeling a pang of guilt that she'd been avoiding a real talk with him. She liked him, truly, and he'd always been so supportive. But between the new arrivals, the insane "cult" scenario, and her sizzling moment with Declan, her emotional bandwidth had been maxed out. "Of course," she replied. "Everything okay?"

He shrugged. "Just wanted to check in, see how you're holding up with all these new people worshipping you. And... talk about us, I guess."

Her heart squeezed. "Us?"

He offered a small, hesitant smile. "Well, yeah, we haven't had a real conversation in days. Thought we might… you know, figure out where we stand."

She glanced around, noticing a few zombies wandering near the orchard gate. The morning crowd was busy with chores, so it might be safe to slip away for a private chat. "Want to walk?" she suggested. "It's too busy around here."

"Sure," he said, relief evident in his eyes. They headed toward the orchard, meandering between rows of apple trees that swayed in the light breeze. A few undead strolled lazily among the branches, occasionally plucking a rotting apple and moaning in disappointment. She guided them away with a soft command to "go patrol," and they shuffled off obediently.

Zane walked beside her, silent at first. The orchard smelled of earth and overripe fruit. Birds fluttered overhead, a fleeting reminder that nature went on, apocalypse or not. She tried to still her pounding heart, bracing for the talk that was coming.

Finally, near a quiet clearing with a half-fallen apple tree trunk, she stopped. "Okay," she said, turning to face him. "You wanted to talk, so… talk away."

He inhaled, running a hand through his dark hair. "It's just… I've been feeling so much better physically. Nearly human, thanks to you. But emotionally, I'm… a mess. I see how you are with Declan, or Jace, or even Dr. Hawthorne, and it's like I'm stuck in limbo."

Her stomach twisted. She softened her tone. "I never meant to lead you on, Zane. I like you— really. You've been nothing but sweet and loyal. But, if I'm honest, I have feelings for multiple guys right now. It's the apocalypse. It's weird. I'm weird."

He let out a breath, shoulders slumping. "I get it. I do. The world ended, normal dating rules went out the window, and… you're the center of everything. It's natural you'd be close to a few people. I just—sometimes I worry I'll revert to that half-zombie state, or I'll lose your attention."

She placed a hand on his arm, meeting his gaze. "You're not going anywhere, Zane. You're stuck with me, if you want to be. I promise I'm not going to toss you aside like old rations." She attempted a small laugh, which he returned, albeit quietly. "But I can't promise monogamous romance right now. I have no clue what I'm doing. Honestly, it's like I'm juggling chainsaws while riding a unicycle."

He laughed for real this time, the tension in his posture loosening. "That's an image. Are the zombies your safety net?"

"Pretty much," she said, smiling. Then her expression turned earnest. "Look, I want you to stay here, keep healing, keep doing your thing. If we figure out more between us, great. If we stay… close friends with occasional orchard walks, that's good too. I'm open to what this becomes. No expectations."

He studied her face, and for a moment, she thought he might tear up. Instead, he just nodded, placing his hand gently over hers. "You're amazing, you know that? Even if you're juggling chainsaws. I... I do want more. I can't deny it. But I'm willing to go slow, especially if you— if it helps your stress levels."

A pang of affection swelled in her chest. She realized how safe she felt around him. How tender he was, how considerate. "Slow is good," she murmured, sliding her fingers through his. "But... maybe not *too* slow. Because who knows how long we have in this messed-up world?"

He breathed a soft laugh. "Right, apocalypse time is short." He ducked his head, eyes flicking to her lips. "Can I... kiss you?"

Her heart skipped. She remembered the furious, fiery makeout with Declan, but this was different. Gentle, sweet, like a slow warm dawn. She found herself nodding, her voice a whisper. "Yeah, you can."

He leaned in carefully, almost shyly, pressing his lips to hers. It was tender, a soft brush that sent a gentle ripple of warmth through her. She kissed him back, letting her other hand rest on his shoulder. The orchard around them blurred into a haze of rustling leaves and distant moans from patrolling zombies.

Zane's mouth was soft and tentative, so unlike the aggressive hunger she'd felt with Declan. She melted into it, savoring the delicate exploration, her pulse beating steadily. It was almost comforting, a soothing contrast to the chaotic swirl of her life. She felt his arms slip around her waist, drawing her closer, and she parted her lips slightly, deepening the kiss with a slow, sensual slide.

He let out a muffled groan, responding with more confidence. Their mouths fit together in a lingering warmth, tongues meeting in gentle, hesitant strokes. She looped her arms around his neck, fingers tangling in his dark hair. He tasted faintly of the apples they'd been harvesting earlier. *So different from… well, from everything else.* The orchard breeze played with her hair as they kissed, and in the distance, a few zombies meandered. She could sense their presence but didn't feel any alarm. They were just watchers in the background, mindless guardians to her orchard rendezvous.

Zane's hand drifted lower, resting on the small of her back, and she shivered at the intimate contact. A hot flush spread across her skin, a sweet ache building in her belly. He angled his head, kissing her more firmly, and she let out a small sigh of pleasure. For a moment, she forgot the complicated reality outside. She forgot about Declan's scorching kiss, Jace's teasing, Hawthorne's research. Right now, there was just Zane, all gentle devotion.

They pulled back eventually, breath mingling. His eyes flickered with uncertainty, searching hers. "Was that okay?" he asked softly, cheeks pink.

A tender smile curved her lips. "That was more than okay. You're… a good kisser," she teased. He blushed deeper, managing a quiet laugh. She brushed a thumb along his jaw. "I'm glad we talked."

He leaned his forehead against hers, closing his eyes. "Me too. If this is what living feels like, I want more."

She kissed his forehead gently, feeling a swell of affection. But at the edge of her mind, a trickle of guilt surfaced. She had a swirling attraction to so many men here—Zane, Declan, Jace, maybe even the doc. *This is going to explode eventually.* Still, she embraced the moment for what it was: a sweet, honest connection that gave her battered heart some solace.

They remained in each other's arms for a minute longer, the orchard rustling around them. Then a low moan startled them both—one of the zombies had wandered closer, tilting its head in confusion at the hugging humans. She and Zane broke into soft giggles.

"I guess we have an audience," she murmured, patting the zombie's shoulder lightly. "Hey, buddy, give us some privacy, huh?"

The zombie moaned, shuffling off as if it understood. Zane turned back to her, reticence flitting across his features. "We should probably get back before someone notices we're missing. Or thinks you're, you know, conjuring a love potion or something."

She snorted, stepping away with a playful grin. "We definitely don't need more cult rumors about orchard orgies." He let out a startled laugh, and they walked back toward the farm together, hands briefly linked until they neared the house, where prying eyes might see.

As they approached the main yard, they spotted a few new arrivals carting supplies, a cluster of undead carrying garden tools, and Tasha organizing rations. The orchard scene they left behind felt like a tiny bubble of intimacy in an otherwise chaotic community. But stepping onto the farm's dirt path, Becca squared her shoulders, bracing for reality. Her cheeks still felt warm from the orchard makeout, and she had no doubt she'd be teased mercilessly if anyone caught wind of it—especially Jace.

Sure enough, as soon as they reached the yard, Jace strolled by, eyeing them both with a wicked gleam. "Did I see you two wandering off alone, hmm?" he asked in a singsong voice, bouncing on his heels. "Should I set aside a wedding chapel in the orchard, Monty?"

She shot him a glare, face flaming. "You hush, or I'll let the zombies play fetch with you."

He cackled in glee, but Zane simply gave a polite half-smile and slipped away to help another survivor stack crates, leaving Becca to face Jace's amused gaze alone. She folded her arms. "Seriously, do you have to comment on everything?"

"I do if it's entertaining," he countered, winking. "But hey, no judgment. Zane's a sweet kid. I'm kinda rooting for him. Also rooting for you and Declan, and maybe you and Hawthorne, too. I'm basically shipping you with everyone, Monty."

She groaned. "You're the worst." Yet she couldn't hide a reluctant grin. His playful acceptance was oddly comforting. Maybe the farm's ragtag "cult" could handle multiple suitors in a single apocalypse. Stranger things had happened.

Feeling a bit lighter, she left Jace to his wisecracks and made her way into the farmhouse. She needed water, maybe a breather, and a moment to process the swirl of her emotions. Her mind replayed the orchard kiss, the gentle press of Zane's lips, the warmth of his chest. Meanwhile, echoes of the barn kiss with Declan flickered in her thoughts, sending a different kind of heat coursing through her. *Multiple guys. Everyone knows. Nobody knows what to do with it. This is my life now.*

Inside, she found an unoccupied corner of the living room, sinking onto a rickety chair. The house smelled of cooking stew and stale coffee. A few new arrivals bustled by, nodding respectfully. She nodded back, a halfhearted smile. *They worship me, but they also see me making out with different men. Must be confusing,* she mused wryly. Then again, no one was about to question her, the "zombie queen." Right?

She closed her eyes, letting a real emotional wave wash over her. *How did I become the anchor for so many people?* She thought of the orchard, the sudden cultlike worship, the near-violent synergy with which the zombies defended her. It was a lot. A year ago, she'd been a nobody stacking shelves at a grocery store, dreaming of a pay raise, worrying about which brand of cereal was on sale. Now, she commanded hordes of the undead, had a farm full of survivors looking to her for leadership, and wrestled with complicated romantic entanglements. She felt her eyes burn with tears that she refused to shed in front of everyone.

A gentle voice broke her reverie. "Becca?" It was Lisa, the once-store-manager who'd become a voice of reason. She knelt by the chair, concern etched on her face. "You okay?"

Becca swallowed, giving a shaky laugh. "I'm fine. Just… everything's so big. People worship me, I have a weird hormone-laden love life, the apocalypse rages on. I can't pretend it's all sunshine."

Lisa set a comforting hand on her knee. "It's okay not to be okay, you know. You do so much. You can take a break, or… cry if you need to. We won't think less of you."

Becca's throat tightened. She gave a watery smile. "Thanks. I might… cry later, in private. Right now, I guess I'll keep it together so the cult doesn't freak out." She let out a small, humorless laugh. "Cult. Ugh, that word gives me hives."

Lisa gently squeezed her knee, then stood, offering a hand. "Well, remember I'm here to help. We can figure out how to transition from random worship to an actual working community, one step at a time. If we do this right, maybe it won't be so culty."

Becca accepted Lisa's hand, rising to her feet. "Let's hope so." She steadied her breath. "Thanks. I'll be out soon. Just… needed a breather."

Lisa nodded, shooting her a supportive smile before heading off to handle ration distribution or a new crisis—whatever the day required.

After a beat, Becca exhaled, letting the swirl of feelings settle. She thought of Zane, sweet and gentle, offering her a soft place to land in the orchard. Thought of Declan, all anger and scorching desire pinned to the barn. Thought of Jace's teasing, Hawthorne's shy forearms, the new arrivals' wide-eyed devotion. *Yes, it's complicated. But it's my life, and I'll handle it.*

She mustered the energy to step outside once more, blinking at the bright afternoon sunshine. A handful of zombies ambled near the porch, moaning softly in greeting. She patted one on the shoulder, a half-smile curving her lips. Even with everything, she was grateful for them—for the bizarre bond that let her keep people alive, for the weird sense of companionship they offered in a world gone mad.

Spying a cluster of new arrivals gathered for orchard work, she strode over to them, determined to keep the day's momentum going. "Okay, folks," she called, voice echoing with more confidence than she felt. "Let's check the orchard for fallen branches, gather ripe apples, and store them in the barn. And try not to get smacked by any zombies who think fruit picking is a group activity, yeah?"

A few chuckles rose from the group. They grabbed baskets, heading orchard-ward. She joined them, mind drifting yet again to that secret orchard clearing, where Zane's kisses still lingered on her lips. *This is real, too,* she reminded herself. She might be flustered, emotional, even borderline heartbroken by her own confusion, but she was also alive. Alive enough to juggle multiple affections and handle a half-crazed "cult" while commanding an undead workforce.

As the day wore on, she helped newcomers with orchard chores, sorted supplies, and intervened whenever the zombies got overzealous in their tasks. Jace could be heard jokingly reciting a "Cult of Monty" pledge whenever he passed by, making her roll her eyes and grin in equal measure. Declan lurked on the outskirts, quiet tension in his stance, while Zane slipped in and out of tasks, sending her gentle smiles that made her heart flutter. Dr. Hawthorne popped in occasionally to request a vital reading or ask if she felt any mental strain commanding the horde.

By evening, she was exhausted physically, but emotionally she felt a strange calm. She'd had a tearful near-breakdown that morning, a sweet orchard makeout with Zane, and had confronted some real feelings. It was progress. Messy progress, but progress nonetheless.

After dinner—a communal stew that everyone contributed to—she lingered in the orchard, helping a pair of newly arrived teens gather leftover apples. The sun sank below the horizon, bathing the orchard in lavender twilight. Eventually, the teens headed back to the farmhouse, leaving her alone under the trees, surrounded by the quiet hum of nighttime insects and the soft moans of a few patrolling zombies.

She strolled deeper between the rows, inhaling the earthy scents of fallen fruit and dew. Her thoughts spun with the day's events, the swirl of men in her life, the unstoppable tide of new worshippers. She felt a little surge of longing, wanting comfort but unsure which direction to find it in.

This orchard's become my private solace, she mused, letting a gentle breeze rustle her hair. Despite the chaos, she felt weirdly hopeful, a sense that she might just figure it all out eventually, one day at a time.

Above her, the stars emerged in a deepening sky, pinpricks of light scattered across the darkness. A pair of zombies meandered nearby, moaning softly, watchful in their own dopey, protective way. She approached them, offering a gentle command to keep the orchard perimeter secure. They groaned in acquiescence and shuffled off, leaving her with a pocket of solitude. She closed her eyes, exhaling.

Yes, it was complicated. But for now, with the orchard's hush, Zane's kiss still tingling on her lips, and the memory of everyone else's presence warming her heart, she felt a rare sense of peace. The cult might be growing, the romances might be tangling, but she could handle it. She was Becca, ex-grocery clerk, now accidental queen of the undead, with a big messy heart and no shortage of suitors. Maybe that was reason enough to keep moving forward, day after day, orchard walk after orchard walk, kiss after chaotic kiss.

She smiled, letting the orchard darkness envelop her. Somewhere out there, Declan was prowling with unresolved desire, Jace was probably cracking jokes about "Team Monty," Dr. Hawthorne was analyzing her blood, and Zane was no doubt cherishing the memory of their orchard embrace. Everyone knew about her multiple attachments, and no one quite knew how to proceed. But that was all right. The apocalypse had shattered normalcy; maybe it was time to build a new normal, one silly orchard kiss at a time.

Eventually, she turned, heading back toward the farmhouse lights. The soft moans of patrolling zombies accompanied her, an odd lullaby in the night. Let tomorrow bring whatever it wanted—she would meet it with a grin, a stubborn spirit, and a heart big enough to love more than one person if fate allowed. Because in the end, *this* was her world now, and she wasn't afraid of its complications. She was ready to live it, regrets be damned.

CHAPTER FIFTEEN

Becca sometimes wondered if the apocalypse was one gigantic cosmic prank, orchestrated by some bored higher power who found it hilarious to watch her juggle zombie minions, new survivors with worshipful gazes, and an ever-expanding tangle of romantic drama.

In the pre-apocalypse days, her biggest problem had been paying rent on time and avoiding annoying co-workers. Now, she fielded requests from a borderline cult that insisted on calling her "Queen," broke up scuffles among half-decayed corpses, and tried to manage a swirling mess of feelings for at least four men in her orbit—all while fighting off rival gangs who wanted her head.

It was enough to make her want to bury herself in orchard compost for a week.

She did not, however, bury herself. Instead, she trudged through each day, handing out chores to gawking newcomers, patrolling the farm fence with her undead workforce, and balancing heartbreak, lust, and the occasional adrenaline-fueled kisses with men who couldn't decide if they wanted to kill her or date her.

And apparently, this day would be no different—only more chaotic. Because rumors of the rival gang's return were swirling, the new arrivals were clamoring for more "blessings" from their "zombie queen," and Becca was starting to suspect she wasn't going to get a moment's peace. Not even to sort out her complicated romantic entanglements.

She woke up in the farmhouse, the morning sun leaking through the battered windows. The living room was jammed with new survivors slumbering in makeshift beds, and Dr. Eli Hawthorne was already up, perched at the dining table-turned-lab station, taking notes on Becca's "community" (though sometimes he jokingly referred to it as "the cult phenomenon").

She gave him a crooked half-smile, ignoring the flutter in her belly when he glanced up and caught her eye. He returned the smile, and she quickly ducked out to the porch, heart pounding with a swirl of embarrassment and attraction. So it began.

Outside, her loyal zombies—some with half-rotted faces, others missing arms or eyes—patrolled the perimeter, moaning in what she'd come to interpret as "happy diligence." The orchard behind the barn was alive with the rustle of wind and the chatter of a few early-bird survivors picking apples.

She spotted the big barn in the distance, remembering with a hot flash how she and Declan had recently pinned each other to those boards in a fiery, teeth-clacking kiss. Now, she could hardly look at the barn without feeling breathless. She scolded herself: *Focus, Monty. You have chores. Possibly an entire war to prepare for.*

A few minutes into surveying the morning routine—checking which zombies needed new tasks and which newcomers needed guidance—she felt a presence behind her. Turning, she was greeted by Jace's trademark smirk. The ex-con wore that sleeveless shirt that showed off his tattoos, and he had a mischievous glint in his eye that boded no good.

"Morning, Monty," he drawled, leaning against a fence post. "How's the cult worship? They sacrificing goats to you yet? Or maybe they're printing T-shirts?"

She swatted his arm, cheeks warming. "Stop calling it a cult, for the hundredth time. And no T-shirts. Unless you want to pay for them."

He snickered. "If they do, I'm definitely wearing one that says, 'Property of the Zombie Queen.' Unless you want me to get *that* one tattooed." He wiggled his eyebrows.

She rolled her eyes, though a grin slipped free. "You're incorrigible." But inside, she was secretly thankful for his unbreakable sense of humor. He steadied her in a weird way—like a comedic anchor in a sea of weirdness. "Anyway, help me check the orchard? I'd prefer if the new arrivals don't get brained by an overzealous zombie who mistakes them for intruders."

He gave a mock salute. "Yes, ma'am." Together, they strolled across the yard, weaving around a trio of zombies hauling buckets of feed. She and Jace bantered about random nonsense: the new recruits who insisted on calling her "Your Majesty," the dog Chewie's sudden habit of chasing any zombie that smelled too rotten, and how Tasha was organizing a "Farmhouse Talent Show" next week to keep morale up.

Typical apocalypse small talk, basically.

Reaching the orchard's edge, they found a handful of survivors plucking apples from low branches, dropping them into wooden crates. A couple zombies stood by, moaning uncertainly, unsure if they should help or just stare.

Becca nodded at them, giving a soft command to "gather fallen branches," and they shuffled off in compliance. She turned to Jace. "Hey, want to help me drag some crates deeper into the orchard? That big tree in the middle has a ton of apples that nobody's touched yet."

He wiggled his eyebrows. "Alone time with you in the orchard? I'd love to." But there was a sincere note beneath his teasing.

"Alone time for chores," she emphasized, ignoring the swoop in her belly. She started lugging a wooden crate, and Jace took another, trailing behind. They tramped down a winding orchard path until the chatter of other survivors faded behind thick clusters of apple trees.

The warm sunshine filtered through the leaves, creating dappled light across the ground. A breeze ruffled Becca's hair, carrying the scent of ripe fruit and earth. One or two zombies meandered in the background, obeying her last command to pick up fallen branches.

When they reached the big old apple tree at the orchard's center, Jace set down his crate. "This place is kind of pretty, huh? For a zombie apocalypse orchard." He glanced around, eyes lingering on the half-gnarled trunk and the sunlight dancing on leaves. Then his gaze drifted to Becca, a playful grin tugging his lips. "We're alone now, you realize."

She arched a brow, placing her crate next to his. "We're here to get apples, wiseass." Even as she said it, her pulse throbbed. There'd always been a crackling chemistry with Jace— a blend of danger, humor, and raw confidence.

He stepped closer, brushing a stray apple off a low branch, then letting his gaze slide to her mouth. "Sure, we can pick apples. Or we can… do a different orchard activity. I recall you and I have some orchard-based history with tag. And you're quite the orchard runner." He smirked. "Wouldn't mind a re-match."

She flushed, remembering that day's chase and the adrenaline spike, and the accidentle kiss they had when they first arrived at the farm. But also recalling Declan's barn fiasco, Zane's orchard kisses—*this orchard is too symbolic.* She forced a laugh. "And you would bring that up now? I have a million things to handle."

He shrugged, stepping into her personal space. "Just offering my services if you need to blow off steam." His voice dipped low, a husky note creeping in. Her pulse fluttered. *Well, you do have a lot of tension to blow off, Monty.*

It was so easy to yield to that sly grin. She found herself letting out a shaky breath. "You're ridiculous, you know that?"

He grinned wider. "I do. And you love it." Then he dipped his head, pressing his mouth to hers in a sudden, firm kiss. She let out a muffled sound of surprise, only half-resisting before melting into it.

His lips tasted sweet, probably from the fresh apple he'd snagged. Or maybe her own breath was sweet from orchard air. Either way, it didn't matter. She parted her lips with a soft moan, letting him deepen the kiss.

She slid her arms around his neck, the crates and orchard chores forgotten. He hauled her closer, a low chuckle vibrating against her lips. "Been wanting to do this again," he murmured against her mouth.

She responded by tangling her fingers in his hair, feeling that familiar rush of heat swirl in her belly. Everything about him was playful yet intense, the ex-con who'd joked about being her "bodyguard" and "arm candy." But in moments like this, he was also undeniably skilled at making her head spin.

The orchard around them seemed to hush. A few zombies lurked at a distance, moaning softly, but they posed no threat—just silent watchers for the orchard's repeated romantic fiasco. She angled her head, giving Jace better access, and let him slip his tongue into her mouth in a teasing brush.

She tasted his laughter, his adrenaline. He pressed her back gently against the tree trunk, careful not to smash her with the rough bark. She arched against him, hooking a leg around his calf.

His hand roamed up under her shirt, brushing along her spine with feather-light touches. She inhaled sharply, hips canting forward, electric sparks shooting through her nerves. "You sure you want orchard scraps in your hair?" he joked mid-kiss, nipping her lower lip.

She half-laughed, half-gasped. "Shut up, or I'll feed you to the undead." But her threat was empty as she kissed him again, deeply, letting that thick wave of desire crash over her. She felt a throbbing heat low in her abdomen, that familiar ache of wanting more.

They were teetering on the edge of something definitely Rated R for orchard standards, and her mind flicked to the many times she'd told herself to keep a handle on the swirl of attractions.

But Jace's hands were so sure, his kisses so confident, that for a moment, it was all she could do not to drag him to the ground right there in a bed of fallen apples. She moaned softly, lost in the hungry press of his lips.

Then, a startled cough broke the moment. "Um… sorry to interrupt," came Dr. Eli Hawthorne's mortified voice. "I just— someone said you two were out here, and we need help with— oh God, I'll come back— or— I just — oh wow, sorry!"

Becca wrenched her mouth free from Jace's, heart hammering, breath ragged. She saw Eli standing a few yards away, holding a clipboard and looking like he wanted to vanish. She stumbled away from Jace's embrace, cheeks scorching. "Eli! Uh— I— sorry, we were just— orchard stuff." She wanted to die of embarrassment.

Jace gave a lazy grin, wiping the corner of his mouth with a thumb. "Doc, you pick the best times, man. We were in the middle of some, uh, crucial orchard research."

Eli cleared his throat, face flushing pink. "I see that." He fiddled with his clipboard, eyes darting away. "I —I came to ask Becca if she could help me re-check the new arrivals for infection markers. But if you're… busy—"

She let out a shaky exhale, dragging a hand through her mussed hair. "No, it's fine. We can do that. S-sorry, Jace." She turned to him, half sheepish, half frustrated. "Another time, maybe."

He winked at her, stepping away with a mock salute. "I'll just gather apples by my lonely self. But I'll remember where we left off, Monty." Then he scooped up a random apple from the ground and swaggered away, leaving her to face the doc's mortified expression.

She cleared her throat. "So, you need me for… something?"

Eli exhaled, running a hand over his face. "Yes— sorry. Didn't mean to ruin your, um, orchard date. The new arrivals keep complaining about headaches, dizziness. I wanted to see if it's related to the virus or if they're just dehydrated. You know, standard checks. But I'd like your input— you seem to pick up on infection signs quickly. And, uh, I also have a few results on your latest blood sample."

Her cheeks cooled a bit, curiosity piqued. "Blood sample results? Sure. Let's go." She tried to pretend she wasn't one second away from an orchard meltdown. Maybe focusing on science would calm her hormones.

Eli nodded, relief washing over his features. He turned to lead the way back toward the farmhouse, but halfway there, he paused, rubbing the back of his neck. "Sorry again. For, you know, interrupting. I wasn't expecting—"

She forced a half-laugh. "It's apocalypse dating, doc. We're all a mess. Don't worry about it." Then a traitorous thought rose up: *Wait, do I want to kiss him, too? Because I've definitely been noticing those arms.* She shoved the thought aside. *Focus on the new arrivals, not more orchard smooches, Becca.*

But fate, it seemed, had other plans. They reached a relatively quiet corner near the farmhouse side door, away from the bustle of newcomers rummaging for supplies. Eli paused again, turning to face her, a flicker of something in his gaze. She frowned. "Everything okay?"

He hesitated, nibbling his lower lip. "Yeah, just… you said apocalypse dating is messy, and I realize you probably have enough complications. But sometimes, I can't help noticing, uh, you. And feeling… well, drawn to you." He cleared his throat, cheeks coloring. "It's probably unethical. I'm your— your weird doc friend. But… yeah."

Her heart jerked. *Oh no, not again.* Or maybe *oh yes.* She realized, with a sudden flush, she was indeed attracted to him, too. She remembered that day measuring vitals, how his forearms had looked so good. Her brain short-circuited momentarily. "Eli, I— you're not unethical. You've saved my life with your tests. You're an integral part of the farm. And you're… well, you're sweet. Also, I might have the hots for you." She wanted to sink into the ground after that final admission, but the adrenaline-fueled honesty spurred her on. "I'm just juggling a lot. And me, apparently. With guys, I mean. Or— oh God, kill me now."

He huffed a shaky laugh, eyes bright with nerves. "Kill you is ironically the last thing I want. If we're being honest, I can't deny I've, uh, thought about kissing you more than once. Possibly more than a hundred times." His face was bright red, but he was all in.

She parted her lips, heart thudding. *This is insane. Jace literally just had his tongue in my mouth, and now I'm two seconds from letting the doc do the same.* Yet the swirl of tension beckoned, and she reasoned, *It's the apocalypse. Why not?*

She stepped closer, letting her gaze flick to his mouth. He inhaled shakily. "Becca— if we do this, it's probably a bad idea. People might talk. Or—"

She cut him off by brushing her lips against his. It started gentle, almost tentative, a slow press of mouths. He made a soft sound of surprise, but then responded, placing a hand on her waist. She exhaled, parting her lips slightly, letting him deepen it.

It was a different vibe from Jace's playful heat or Declan's furious passion. Eli's kiss felt almost reverent, brimming with intellectual curiosity and a sweet yearning. She let her hands slide up his arms, definitely noticing the toned muscles. *Science is hot, apparently,* her mind teased.

He angled his head, kissing her more firmly, and she melted into it, tension spiraling. A low moan escaped her as he pressed forward, and she realized with a jolt that they were definitely crossing into rated R territory, right here in the yard. She let out a quiet gasp when his tongue brushed hers, exploring with a sweet urgency. Her body hummed, craving more closeness. She half-laughed between kisses, thinking, *I can't believe I'm hooking up with the doc right after hooking up with Jace. My life is insane.*

But it felt good, so good. She let out a soft whimper, her hands sliding around his neck. He moaned softly into her mouth. The orchard breeze rustled behind them, carrying faint moans of zombies in the distance. Time blurred. She was vaguely aware that if anyone wandered past, they'd get an eyeful.

But the apocalypse had effectively nuked her sense of shame. Right now, all that mattered was the gentle, hungry pressure of his lips, the warmth of his chest, the way he smelled of old books and fresh soap.

Then, an all-too-familiar pattern repeated: an abrupt interruption. This time, the interruption was not a cough or a grin. It was Zane, sprinting across the yard, eyes wide with alarm, half-shouting her name. "Becca! We need you— now!"

She jerked away from Eli, breath ragged, heart hammering. She turned to see Zane racing up, skidding to a stop with panic in his face. "Zane, what's—" she started, trying to steady her voice. Then she noticed the fear in his eyes and realized he wasn't just interrupting for a casual chat. Something serious was happening.

"It's the rival group," Zane gasped, hands on his knees. "They came back. And they're armed to the teeth.

They shot at a couple zombies near the main road. They've got bigger guns this time. They're marching this way."

Her stomach dropped. *Oh, crap.* She mentally pivoted from orchard kisses to crisis mode. "Where are they?"

Zane pointed beyond the fence. "Probably half a mile out, but they're on foot, coming in from the south. They must want revenge for last time."

Eli swore softly, stepping away from Becca. She tasted the last hint of his lips on hers before her adrenaline spiked. "We gotta mobilize," she said, scanning the yard. "Sound the alarm. Get everyone inside, except the ones who can fight. And get me my zombies."

Zane nodded, sprinting off. She exchanged a wide-eyed glance with Eli. There was no time to talk about the kiss, about how insane it was that she'd locked lips with him just now. *Later.* She shot him a tense smile. "We'll finish that conversation. If we live," she joked darkly.

He nodded, already collecting himself. "I'll check if anyone's wounded. I have basic triage supplies." Then he took off at a run, leaving her standing alone, flushed and reeling. She inhaled, forced composure, and rushed to the orchard fence to gather her undead. Showdown time.

She summoned a group of zombies with a series of sharp commands, voice echoing across the orchard. They moaned in response, lurching toward her. She motioned them to the south fence, giving them orders to defend the farm if threatened.

The new arrivals, many of whom worshipped her, stared in awe as the undead lined up like an unholy battalion. She tried not to think about the morality or the potential gore. She just needed them to keep everyone safe.

Moments later, the rival group arrived in the distance, brandishing assault rifles and shotguns. There must have been at least a dozen. Declan barked for survivors to get behind cover, while Jace stood near the barn, knives at the ready, grinning like a maniac. "Oh, I've been waiting for a good fight."

Zane sprinted up behind Becca, chest heaving. "They're close, maybe fifty yards. Are we sure about this? We might—"

Too late. A gunshot rang out, striking a zombie near the fence. The undead reeled, half its face blown off, yet it kept shambling forward, undeterred. The farm exploded into chaos. The rival gang advanced, firing indiscriminately. Bullets whizzed overhead, smacking into barn walls or orchard trees. Two or three zombies collapsed, their heads splattering. But more surged in a frenzy, fueled by Becca's mental link and the group's protective rage.

"Y'all, can we NOT do this now?" Becca shouted to the world at large, half-laughing in hysterical frustration. She ducked behind a fence post as a bullet ricocheted off a nearby plank.

Her undead minions roared a collective moan, surging forward. Meanwhile, survivors hunkered behind crates or inside the farmhouse, some with scavenged guns, returning fire in a sporadic attempt at defense.

Declan emerged from behind the barn, shouting, "Becca, get down!" as a hail of bullets raked across the yard. She yelped, dropping to her knees behind a half-broken crate. She spotted him sprinting across open ground, crowbar in one hand, a pistol in the other.

He fired off a shot, grazing a rival attacker. "I might have feelings for you—" he began, voice tight, "— but we can talk about it later— oh shit!" He cut off as a zombie lunged at him, tackling him inadvertently, sending them both crashing to the ground. She stifled a hysterical giggle. *Fantastic timing, Declan.*

Elsewhere, Jace let out a wild laugh, ducking behind a bale of hay, then leaping up to fling a knife at a gang member who'd crept too close. The knife embedded in the man's shoulder with a sickening *thunk.* The guy screamed, dropping his weapon. Jace winked at Becca from across the yard, as if to say, *This is fun.* She almost rolled her eyes, but a bullet zipped past, refocusing her on the chaos.

The undead workforce lunged at the rival group, a few managing to clamp jaws around arms or torsos. Gory, disgusting carnage followed. The orchard grasses soaked in blood. One attacker's screams cut off abruptly as a zombie tore out his throat.

Another survivor tried to flee but was tackled by two moaning corpses. The attacking gang realized too late that while guns could drop a zombie or two, they couldn't outshoot a coordinated horde of enraged undead.

Somewhere amid the frenzy, she saw Zane let out a guttural roar. He'd picked up a scavenged shotgun, but his eyes glowed with that old half-zombie rage. For a moment, it looked like he was having some kind of metamorphosis.

He full-on *hulked out,* ignoring bullet grazes. Then he body-slammed a rival attacker, flinging him into a cluster of zombies, who swarmed the poor bastard. Another attacker shot at Zane, but Zane roared, tackled the shooter, and slammed him to the ground with superhuman strength. She'd never seen him so feral and unstoppable. A twinge of fear and awe churned in her gut.

Becca scrambled for better cover behind a broken cart, seeing Dr. Hawthorne crouched near the farmhouse steps, frantically checking a wounded survivor's leg. She tried to mentally direct the zombies to press forward, but half the undead were too busy mauling aggressors to listen. *At least they're on our side,* she mused, though the carnage was unbelievably gross. Limbs flew, blood spattered across orchard grass. She had to choke back a wave of nausea.

"This is insane," she muttered, peeking over the cart. Another bullet flew overhead, clipping the cart's edge. She ducked again, cursing. "Okay, time to end this." She inhaled, then shouted with all her might, "ZOMBIES, GET THEM!" pouring as much mental force as she could into the command. The moaning swelled into a unified roar. The undead scrambled to converge, overwhelming the last pockets of the rival gang.

 In a matter of brutal minutes, it was done. The few surviving attackers realized they were outmatched, dropping their weapons and bolting into the orchard, screaming. One or two managed to hobble away, possibly to spread the rumor that tangling with the "zombie queen" was suicidal. The rest were either torn apart or pinned under undead bodies, battered and bleeding. The orchard smelled like coppery blood and rancid flesh, the ground littered with corpses, both living and undead.

 Becca slumped behind the cart, shoulders trembling. She had to remind herself to breathe. Another fight, another gruesome victory. She emerged carefully, scanning for injuries among her group. Jace was standing near the barn, wiping a bloody knife on his pant leg, grinning like he'd just had the best time. "I stabbed a guy," he shouted to Becca, chest heaving. "He tried to shoot me, and I was like—" He mimed a stabbing motion, then gave her a thumbs-up. *Absolute psycho,* she thought, exhaling a semi-hysterical laugh.

 Declan stumbled into view, crowbar clutched, half his shirt torn. A random zombie had tackled him mid-sentence, but he looked okay, aside from a fresh bruise on his jaw. Their eyes met across the gore-strewn yard. She read relief in his gaze, along with that conflicting swirl of emotion. He gave a curt nod. She nodded back, equally speechless. *We'll talk about the "I might have feelings" thing later. Jesus, this is too much.*

Zane stumbled up next, covered in grime and blood splatter, panting. He seemed rattled, like he'd tapped into that half-zombie power he hated. "I… I lost control," he mumbled, eyes wide. She reached for him, but he shook his head, stepping back, guilt flooding his face.

"It's okay," she said softly, but her voice was drowned out by the moans of the undead milling around. He clenched his fists, eyes flaring with confusion, then turned and stalked away, presumably to calm down. Her heart twisted for him. She'd have to find him later, reassure him.

Meanwhile, survivors emerged from the farmhouse, eyes wide at the carnage. Some cheered, others looked sick. Dr. Hawthorne rushed around, checking for wounded. She rubbed her temples, feeling a pounding headache from the mental link to her zombies. "Y'all, can we NOT do this now?" she murmured in exasperation to the universe, though ironically, the battle was already over.

She moved through the orchard, giving the final command for the undead to "stand down." The moaning receded into a calmer drone. Some zombies had lost limbs or chunks of flesh, but they didn't seem to notice. The orchard grass was a churned-up mess of gore and bullet casings. She steeled herself, forcibly ignoring the reek of blood. *At least we're alive. At least they won't come back easily.* She tried to find a silver lining.

In the distance, Jace was still cackling, crowing about how one of the gang members "ran screaming like a baby" after Jace stuck him with a thrown knife. Declan was corralling the last of the undead away from the wounded attackers, presumably ensuring no more or partial kills. Zane had disappeared, presumably in emotional turmoil. Dr. Hawthorne knelt near a fallen newcomer who'd taken a bullet to the shoulder. And Becca, queen of the undead, found herself weirdly calm in the aftermath.

As calm as one can be while standing in a field of fresh corpses, that is.

She inhaled a shaky breath, heading to help the doc with triage. *We'll need to bury bodies again.* The orchard was fast becoming a graveyard. She dreaded the next wave of attacks or rumors. But for now, they'd survived. The farm held, the "cult" or community was safe, and her men—if she dared call them that—still lived, albeit battered and complicated as hell.

She was exhausted, sticky with sweat and gore, and definitely in need of a shower or at least a wet rag. She pictured the orchard scene from earlier, kissing Jace, then making out with Eli, only to have Zane rush in announcing doomsday. *My entire life is a chaotic comedic tragedy, basically,* she mused.

But she had no regrets. Because this was the apocalypse, and love triangles—or squares, or pentagons—plus full-on zombie armies, plus rival gangs with vendettas, was the new normal. She'd handle it with humor, a bit of heartbreak, and a loyal legion of undead.

And if she needed a pick-me-up, well, there were plenty of orchard kisses to be had, apparently. She allowed herself a grim little smile, mentally scheduling more orchard nonsense *after* the cleanup. Because in the apocalypse, you took your pockets of happiness whenever you could—especially if they involved scandalous orchard sessions. And that was enough to keep her going, one insane day at a time.

CHAPTER SIXTEEN

Becca could hardly believe she'd made it this far: her farm teeming with new survivors, an entire legion of undead under her beck and call, and about four different guys she'd kissed in the past week. Frankly, the apocalypse was the least of her problems.

One might think the end of the world would be the toughest hurdle. But no. Juggling a love quadrangle and a horde of zombies—now *that* was top-tier stress.

She stood on her farmhouse's battered porch, leaning against the railing while a light breeze rustled her hair. Below, the yard bustled with activity. A dozen or more of her loyal undead were bustling around in a bizarre display of domestic service—carrying crates of supplies, sweeping up debris, and even carefully watering some potted herbs that Tasha had insisted on salvaging.

Yes, they had become her zombie butlers. She didn't know whether to laugh or cry sometimes, so she usually settled on laughter.

In the distance, the orchard was calm, the leaves fluttering in a gentle hush. Hard to believe that orchard had served as a backdrop to so many comedic fiascos—and more than a few stolen kisses with at least three men. Four, if one counted the doc's shy brand of flirting as an actual date. She shook her head at the insanity of it all. If anyone had told her pre-apocalypse that she'd be heading a "zombie farm" of sorts—where the undead wore aprons and newbies worshipped her as a queen—she'd have smacked them with a mop. Now, well… it was Tuesday. Just another day in her unbelievably strange life.

"Morning, Monty," came a teasing voice from below. She peered over the porch railing to see Jace leaning against a post, that perpetual smirk plastered on his face. He wore a sleeveless shirt that showed off his extensive ink, and he winked when she caught his eye. "The newly trained zombies are ready for your inspection. They even folded laundry, I think."

She couldn't help a snort of laughter. "Good. They can handle my underwear while they're at it. Are we sure they're not creeped out by it, though?"

He shrugged, stepping closer until he was nearly under her vantage point. "Hard to tell with half-rotted expressions. But they moaned happily enough. I guess they don't mind. Maybe your underwear is revered now." He broke into a wide grin at her eye-roll. "Anyway, no new 'worshippers' at the gates, if that's what you're worried about."

She let out a feigned sigh of relief. "Thank God. One more person calls me 'Your Highness' and I might teach the zombies a new command: *Bite that one.*"

He chuckled, hooking his thumbs into his belt loops. "I'd pay to watch that. But hey, the day's still young." With a two-finger salute, he strolled off to oversee more undead chores or possibly flirt with a newcomer. Hard to say with Jace. He thrived in chaos.

Becca shook her head, turning to gaze over the orchard. Quiet, indeed. If not for the occasional moan from patrolling zombies, one might think they were in a peaceful countryside. Except, you know, the world had ended, and she'd just recently fought off that rival group for the final time, apparently. They'd come at her farm with an arsenal, only to be met with her well-trained undead army and the combined might of her human allies. The battle had been bloody, disgusting, and rife with comedic banter. And in the end, she'd officially emerged victorious, wearing that accidental crown as the "Zombie Queen."

She sighed, letting the memories wash over her: the final confrontation had taken place just days ago, with the rival gang returning to settle the score. They'd had bigger guns, bigger grudges, and a thirst for revenge after her zombies had mauled them the last time. She still recalled the adrenaline spike as they'd crossed the orchard perimeter, taking potshots at the fence. Her entire horde had roared to life, launching a savage counterattack—like well-trained bodyguards. Meanwhile, her friends had jumped into the fray: Jace stabbing someone while cackling, Zane hulking out as if channeling some half-zombie super-strength, Declan dramatically confessing feelings mere seconds before a zombie tackled him, and Dr. Hawthorne scribbling notes even as bullets whizzed by. The memory almost made her laugh out loud. *She'd literally shouted, "Y'all, can we NOT do this now?" as the orchard turned into a gorefest.* Typical day in her insane kingdom.

But hey, final battle won, apparently. The rival group had fled or died, leaving the farm at relative peace. The orchard got a fresh coating of blood that fertilized the apples (morbid, yes), and she got a new wave of perplexed survivors who'd heard about her unstoppable undead legion. The net result? She was more cemented than ever as the so-called Zombie Queen, and the world was still ending outside their fences. Yet she was weirdly… happy. The threat was gone, at least for now, the farm was thriving, and she had an entire horde of zombie butlers who answered her beck and call. *Silly? Absolutely. But I'll take it.*

She hopped off the porch, wandering across the yard toward the barn. The half-dozen zombies near the entrance paused in their tasks—sweeping, carrying crates, reorganizing some leftover scraps. When they sensed her approach, they gave soft moans of greeting, as if saying "Good morning, oh queen!" She stifled a giggle, noticing how one zombie straightened the collar of a filthy apron like it was trying to impress her. Zombie butlers indeed. She gave them each a pat on the shoulder or a friendly "Thanks, guys," which earned her a chorus of appreciative moans. If she wasn't living it, she'd never believe it.

"Hey," came a familiar low voice. She turned to see Zane emerging from the barn's side door, carrying a box of supplies. He looked calmer, more assured, his once-ghastly pallor replaced by the near-perfect color in his cheeks. A faint scar on his forearm remained the only testament to his half-zombie days. He still had that sweet, earnest gaze that always tugged at her heart.

"Morning," she greeted, stepping closer. She noticed the quick flash of relief in his eyes. They'd come a long way since he'd freaked out after unleashing his monstrous side in the final battle. She'd spent hours after that, reassuring him that his half-zombie transformation or "hulking out" was heroic, not monstrous. And, of course, she might've shared a few orchard kisses with him to soothe his worries. Just a few. Because that was what one did in the apocalypse.

He offered a small smile, leaning the box on his hip. "Everything looks so normal here, which is weird. I sometimes expect more raiders or random undead attacks. But your horde's scaring everyone off."

She shrugged, glancing at the yard. "Guess we reached a point where rumor alone keeps trouble away. Anyone who tries messing with 'the Zombie Queen' ends up feeding the orchard's topsoil, apparently." She gave a mock wry grin, though a flicker of guilt nagged her. She didn't want to be a monster, but hey, self-defense was self-defense.

Zane nodded, stepping a bit closer, a quiet fondness in his expression. She knew that look—like he wanted to hug her or kiss her, but was too shy to do it in plain view of the entire farm. She offered a reassuring pat on his arm, ignoring the swirl of warmth in her belly. He had that effect on her, a gentle comfort that made her heart sigh. "You sure you're okay?" she asked softly. "No more nightmares?"

He shook his head. "No, I'm good. I've, uh, actually been sleeping well. Helps that the orchard's quiet at night. And, well, being near you always helps." He gave a tiny self-conscious laugh, color blooming in his cheeks. She resisted the urge to lean in and give him a quick peck, worried about the onlookers—like, for instance, Jace or Declan or even Dr. Hawthorne. The entire love quadrangle (or pentagon, or whatever) was still unresolved, and everyone knew it. She was not about to start more rumors by kissing Zane next to the barn in full view.

She squeezed his hand instead, letting a soft smile show him she cared. "Glad you're resting. We'll talk more later, yeah?" He nodded, returning the smile. Then a low moan from a zombie hauling feed interrupted them, and they parted ways, each returning to the day's chores. She swallowed a lump of mixed emotions, forging ahead.

Moving through the farm, she spotted a group of newcomers who waved cheerfully at her, calling out "Good morning, Queen!" She mustered a grin, ignoring the way her skin crawled at the formal address. At least they were happy, right? No one was trying to dethrone her or burn her at the stake. That was an improvement over the last few weeks.

She reached the orchard's edge, scanning for potential trouble. Instead, she found Declan—the ex-cop who'd once threatened to shoot her if she turned zombie, who'd also pinned her to a barn wall for a scorching makeout session. He was standing near a tree, arms crossed, radiating tension. She sighed internally. Another complicated conversation loomed.

She approached carefully, noticing how he tensed when she drew near. "Morning," she greeted, voice cautious. He grunted in response, glancing sideways at her. She studied him, trying to read his expression. He looked as broody as ever, though there was a flicker of something else. Possibly longing. Possibly annoyance. Possibly both. *We definitely haven't talked about that barn kiss. We probably should.* She found her heart thudding.

"You out here taking a break?" she asked, nodding to the orchard around them.

He exhaled, dropping his arms to his sides. "Just checking the perimeter. Making sure no more raiders come sniffing around."

She ventured a small smile. "That's good. We want to keep it quiet for a while." Then, gathering courage, she stepped a bit closer, voice soft. "About... the other day, after the big fight. You kinda said you might have feelings for me. And we haven't... you know, talked about that."

A muscle jumped in his jaw. He stared at the apple-littered ground. "I did say that," he admitted. "Maybe I do. I just... you've got multiple guys swirling around, and you're leading a zombie army, and I'm not good at… any of this."

Her heart squeezed. *He's adorable in a grumpy way.* "Me neither," she confessed, letting out a shaky laugh. "Look, I can't promise a tidy romance. I have Jace flirting, Zane being sweet, Dr. Hawthorne eyeing me from behind test tubes. It's complicated." She paused, meeting his gaze. "But I'm not dismissing you, either. If you want to… see where it goes."

He swallowed, stepping nearer. "I'm not the sharing type," he muttered, eyes flicking to her mouth. She felt a jolt of heat. If he kissed her again, would they end up tangling in orchard grass? Possibly. Instead, he clenched his fists, holding back. "But I can't deny… I do want you. More than I should."

Her breath caught. The orchard seemed to hush around them. She parted her lips, half hoping for a kiss, half terrified. Then, as if on cue, a moan from a nearby zombie startled them both. She huffed a laugh, stepping back. "Saved by the moan, I guess. Or not. We can talk more later. We have, you know, a farm to run."

He sighed, nodding. "Yeah. Later." She gave him a last, lingering look before turning away, heart pounding. One more piece of the puzzle left incomplete, one more chunk of tension to weigh on her. She might spontaneously combust if she had to keep juggling these feelings without resolution. But apparently, that was her life now.

And the day wasn't done messing with her. Barely had she left Declan's orbit when she bumped into Dr. Hawthorne near the barn, fussing with medical supplies. He nearly dropped a box of bandages at the sight of her. "Oh, Becca. Good timing," he blurted, setting the box down carefully. "I wanted to show you some data. I've been monitoring your heart rate and brain waves— as best as I can with the salvaged equipment— during your, er, interactions with the zombies. The results are fascinating."

She forced a grin. "Let me guess: I'm a freak of nature?"

He shook his head, eyes lighting with that earnest curiosity that tugged at her heart. "Not a freak. More like... a miracle? The virus in your bloodstream seems stable, but it adapts whenever you exert mental control. I suspect it's bonded with your neurons in a truly unique way." He paused, then added softly, "And for what it's worth, you're definitely not just a science project to me."

Her stomach flipped. *Right. You made that clear with your orchard kiss.* The memory made her cheeks burn. She swallowed, nodding. "I appreciate that, doc. I— I know we got, you know, carried away that day. I'm not regretting it, but... I'm just saying, it's complicated. We both have roles to fill."

He gave a shy smile, dropping his gaze. "Agreed. But I'd be lying if I said I haven't thought about it. A lot. Despite everything, I— well, I... enjoy your company." His hand hovered near hers, as if longing to hold it, but he refrained. The tension thrummed again, that spark of attraction pulling them together.

Before the moment could escalate, a piercing shriek sounded from the orchard path. "Oh God, what now?" Becca muttered. She and Hawthorne rushed toward the sound, finding Tasha standing near a zombie who'd apparently gotten tangled in some netting. Tasha had stumbled onto it and freaked out. They quickly freed the undead from the net, rolling their eyes at each other in relief. The doc gave her a half-apologetic shrug, then slipped away to help.

Becca sighed heavily. *Always an interruption, always chaos.* Was she doomed to half-finished romantic entanglements forever?

Still, the hours marched on. The farm hummed with activity. She found herself distributing tasks to the newly minted zombie butlers—some assigned to watch the front gate, others to handle orchard chores. Another group was trained to deliver messages around the property, which gave them a postman-like flair, albeit drooling and stumbling. She tried not to laugh at the comedic absurdity whenever an undead "messenger" arrived, moaning softly and handing over a scrap of paper with childlike care.

Late afternoon brought a lull in the frenzy, letting her wander near the orchard again. She paused by the familiar cluster of apple trees where she'd once shared orchard kisses with multiple men. A wave of exhaustion and amusement washed over her. She'd basically made out with Jace, Eli, and Zane in this orchard, and nearly had an orchard meltdown with Declan. *If the orchard had a mouth, it'd gossip me to death.* She smirked at the mental image.

Meanwhile, the final battle's aftermath still echoed in her mind. The rival group was gone for good, their weapons scattered or reclaimed. She had, unbelievably, emerged victorious with minimal losses among her people. Her undead had proven unstoppable, and the farm was safer than ever. The survivors—some borderline worshippers—were settling into farm life, training with the zombies, and basically praising her name. She was the official Zombie Queen, and the world was still ending, but… she was having fun, in a twisted sense. It was almost *too* easy.

"Hey, Monty!" called a teasing voice from behind. She turned to see Jace again, strolling up with a grin. "You look like you're daydreaming about orchard smooches. Looking to continue from earlier?"

She felt heat surge in her cheeks. "Gosh, you never stop, do you?" She half-laughed, though a spark of desire flitted in her belly. Maybe she was too worn out from the day's crazy, or maybe she wanted one last fling before dinner.

He stepped closer, brushing a stray leaf from her shoulder. "I find it hard to stop, especially when I see how you keep collecting guys like baseball cards. Is that your superpower, Monty?"

She snorted. "It's not my fault you're all conveniently hot, okay?" She poked him in the chest. "Now hush before I let a zombie deliver your underwear to the orchard for public display."

He laughed, sliding an arm around her waist. "Careful, or I might enjoy that." Then, with a deliberate slowness, he leaned in, pressing his mouth to hers in a playful, heated kiss. She let out a surprised squeak, but quickly melted into it, hooking her arms around his neck.

The orchard breeze rustled leaves overhead, as if it were an audience to their rated-R orchard escapades. She parted her lips, letting him deepen the kiss, ignoring the swirl of guilt that always flared at each new orchard smooch. The apocalypse had no rules, right?

And in typical orchard tradition, they barely got more than a minute of steamy lip-locking before footsteps crunched on the grass behind them. They broke apart, panting lightly, to see Dr. Hawthorne standing there with a wide-eyed expression. *Again? Seriously?*

"Uh—" the doc stammered, adjusting his glasses. "I was just— wanted to, um, see if— oh dear." His face turned pink as he realized *he'd* walked in on them, yet again. She raked a hand over her face. *Is this orchard cursed or something?*

Jace, of course, found it hilarious. "Doc, you gotta time these orchard visits better," he teased, wiping his mouth with the back of his hand. "You keep interrupting important orchard business."

Hawthorne spluttered, shifting his clipboard as if it would hide him. "I— I'm sorry. I didn't realize you two were... busy. But I, I wanted to say dinner's nearly ready, and also some new data on the last sample. But— never mind, I can come back— or— oh dear." He turned as if to flee, but paused. "Actually, while we're all here, I might as well... oh God, this is awkward."

Becca rubbed her temples, stepping away from Jace. "Right, yes, we're heading in. Sorry, doc. Let's talk over dinner, okay? Some official meltdown of your findings or something." She offered a conciliatory smile.

Eli nodded, forcing a polite grin, but a flicker of disappointment or jealousy lingered in his eyes. "Sure. I'll meet you inside." He hurried off, nearly tripping over a half-buried tree root. She stifled a groan, shoulders sagging. *Orchard kisses. Why do I keep doing orchard kisses if they always get interrupted by a different love interest?*

Jace gave her a mischievous grin, leaning in to whisper, "We'll finish that some other time, yeah?" She couldn't help a small, exasperated laugh.

They parted ways, heading back to the farmhouse. The yard was calm again, zombies finishing up chores, survivors milling about. The horde was officially trained enough that it felt like she had an entire staff. One undead carried water jugs to the new garden plot, another undead followed Tasha around, picking up trash. The final battle was over, the threat presumably gone, and she was free to run a weirdly domestic settlement with a comedic undead twist. Even the orchard fiascos and random love triangles felt oddly normal now.

Dinner was a communal affair. The stew was half beans, half vegetables from the orchard, seasoned with random spices. Survivors sat on crates or stools, chatting amicably about the day's chores. Some gave Becca respectful nods or shy smiles. She was definitely the recognized leader, or "queen," though she pretended otherwise. The tension from the morning orchard kisses simmered beneath everything. She caught glimpses of Jace winking at her from across the table, Zane watching her with a gentle longing, Dr. Hawthorne fiddling with his spoon, and Declan sitting on the far end, arms folded, occasionally glancing her way. *Yes, folks, I kissed them all,* she thought ironically. *This is my life. Everyone knows, no one knows what to do about it, and the apocalypse is still happening outside these fences. Great times.*

Despite the swirl of unresolved tension, dinner was surprisingly fun. People cracked jokes about how they'd gone from a ragtag group of strangers to a functioning settlement with zombie butlers. One newcomer said she'd seen a zombie in the orchard wearing a top hat someone must've found in a trunk. Another newcomer asked if the orchard was haunted by a kissing ghost since she'd found footprints and half-eaten apples near a certain tree. Becca choked on her stew at that. *Yes, orchard is haunted by my chaotic romantic life,* she thought, stifling a laugh.

When dinner wrapped up, the group dispersed, some heading to night chores, others to bed. The orchard's dark silhouette loomed in the distance, calling to her like a comedic siren. *No more orchard kisses tonight,* she resolved, ignoring the hum of possibility. She ended up in the living room with a handful of loyal survivors discussing next-day tasks. With the final battle won, the farm actually felt… safe. The world was still ending outside, but here, she'd carved out a slice of silly serenity. Another day, another comedic, disgusting, endearing fiasco survived.

Finally, with the night pressing in, she strolled outside one last time to check on the undead. A few patrolled near the porch, moaning softly in greeting. She gave them a gentle smile, patting a decaying shoulder or two. "Thanks for everything, guys," she said softly. The horde had come so far—no longer just random shambling corpses, but a trained force that responded to her commands. *Zombie butlers, indeed.* She decided she could get used to that. If the apocalypse had to be insane, might as well have well-trained undead friends.

She thought of the final battle, how they'd triumphed with minimal casualties, how she'd felt that rush of power and relief seeing her horde stand victorious. She was "officially" the Zombie Queen now— unstoppable, unstoppable enough that no one dared challenge her. The love quadrangle, on the other hand, was far from unstoppable. It was more like unstoppable chaos. She definitely wasn't choosing anytime soon. Why should she, when the apocalypse had torn the rulebook to shreds? Let them all stew in comedic limbo while she sorted out her feelings. She wasn't monogamous and that was that, or maybe she was poly, or maybe she was just too scattered to pick. So be it.

Glancing at the silent orchard, she let out a low chuckle. "World's ending, but I'm having fun," she murmured to no one. Because in truth, she was. Sure, it was messy—zombie battles, orchard kisses, a community that borderline worshipped her, a brood of possible suitors, and an entire farm to manage. But it was also thrilling, comedic, and full of stolen moments of joy she never would have imagined back when her life revolved around stocking Doritos.

Yawning, she made her way back inside, leaving the zombie butlers to finish their nightly tasks. She slipped into her small room upstairs, which used to be some kid's bedroom, judging by faded cartoon wallpaper. Collapsing onto her makeshift bed, she let out a satisfied sigh. The final big conflict was over, the orchard was secure, her horde was well-trained, and the rival gang had been chased off or destroyed.

Life, in a bizarre sense, was good. If complicated. *But I thrive in complicated, apparently.* She closed her eyes, letting herself drift. Tomorrow, new comedic nonsense would undoubtedly strike, maybe more orchard smooches or stabbings or worship ceremonies. She found herself almost looking forward to the next fiasco. Because, ironically, in the apocalypse, she felt more alive than ever.

Downstairs, she heard the faint moans of zombies carrying out final chores. She heard a few survivors chatting, possibly about how they'd never have believed they'd follow a "zombie queen." She heard Jace's laughter from the back porch, Declan's low murmur as he planned watch rotations, Zane's soft voice comforting someone, and Dr. Hawthorne's scribbling. All her men, all her complicated feelings, all the comedic glory of being an ex-grocery clerk turned unstoppable necromancer. She let out one last snort of amusement, letting sleep tug her under.

SNEAK PEEK

The farm might be peaceful now—sort of—but Becca's life is never *that* simple. Sure, she's got a zombie army at her beck and call, a gaggle of worshipful survivors, and four guys she can't stop smooching when orchard opportunities arise. But she can't shake the nagging feeling something bigger (and badder) is looming on the horizon. Call it intuition, call it the subtle pulses from her virus-tainted blood, or call it plain old apocalypse paranoia—she knows the calm won't last forever.

And maybe—just *maybe*—it's because of that quiet little deal she struck with the zombie virus itself. An accident, really, but the virus didn't see it that way. Now it's in her head, forging a connection deeper than any she's had with living or undead. She's not sure what it wants, but each day, she senses its presence, whispering dark promises and half-formed demands. She might have made a devil's bargain, and she's only scratched the surface of what that means—for her, for her horde, and for the entire post-apocalyptic world.

Meanwhile, rumors swirl of another faction hell-bent on controlling or eradicating her. Whispers say they're the remnants of a high-tech paramilitary group who blame her for the unstoppable plague of well-trained zombies. If they find her, they won't bother with negotiations. They want her blood on a microscope slide, her mind pried open for the virus's secrets, and her body six feet under. Possibly re-dead. If that's even a thing.

And then there's the matter of her complicated love geometry. Because as if commanding undead minions and fending off rival gangs wasn't enough, she's also juggling four men who each stir a different blend of desire, comfort, and maddening confusion. So of course, more kissing is on the horizon. Maybe orchard makeouts, maybe barn-wall collisions, maybe stolen moments behind a hay bale in the warm glow of sunset. Definitely more awkward interruptions, because this is Becca's life.

So if you thought the final battle was the grand finale, think again. The story's far from over. With the zombie virus whispering in her ear, a new threat marching her way, and a tangle of hearts she's unwilling to unravel just yet, Becca's next chapter promises more chaos, more laughter, more terrifying revelations—and yes, more mouth-on-mouth action than any apocalypse should logically allow.

Stay tuned. Because the next time the world picks a fight with Becca Montgomery and her horde of undead butlers, it might just discover that messing with a self-made Zombie Queen—who might or might not be half-allied with the virus itself—is the worst idea in the entire end times. And with every faction, every lover, and every rotting minion under the sun in play, one thing's for sure: the apocalypse has *never* been this fun.

Made in the USA
Coppell, TX
29 March 2025